By the same author

_____

God and Man at Yale
McCarthy and His Enemies (with L. Brent Bozell)
Up from Liberalism
Rumbles Left and Right
The Unmaking of a Mayor
The Jeweler's Eye
The Governor Listeth
Cruising Speed
Inveighing We Will Go
Four Reforms
United Nations Journal: A Delegate's Odyssey
Execution Eve
Saving the Queen
Airborne
Stained Glass
A Hymnal: The Controversial Arts
Who's on First
Marco Polo, If You Can
Atlantic High: A Celebration
Overdrive: A Personal Documentary
The Story of Henri Tod
See You Later Alligator
Right Reason
The Temptation of Wilfred Malachey
High Jinx
Mongoose, R.I.P.
Racing Through Paradise
On the Firing Line: The Public Life of Our Public Figures
Gratitude: Reflections on What We Owe to Our Country
Tucker's Last Stand
In Search of Anti-Semitism
WindFall
Happy Days Were Here Again
A Very Private Plot

EDITOR

The Committee and Its Critics
Odyssey of a Friend: Whittaker Chambers' Letters to William F. Buckley, Jr.
W.F.B.: An Appreciation
Did You Ever See a Dream Walking?
American Conservative Thought in the Twentieth Century

William F. Buckley Jr.

THE

Blackford Oakes

READER

ANDREWS AND McMEEL

A Universal Press Syndicate Company

KANSAS CITY

3 6 9 0 7 4 0 0

Designed by Cameron Poulter

Library of Congress Cataloging-in-Publication Data

Buckley, William F. (William Frank), 1925–
    The Blackford Oakes reader.
        p.   cm.
    ISBN 0-8362-8098-9
    1. Oakes, Blackford (Fictitious character)—Fiction.
    2. Intelligence service—United States—Fiction.   3. Spy stories, American.   I. Title.
PS3552.U344A6   1994
813'.54—dc20   94-47235
                                                                                    CIP

For Henry and Eleanor

ACKNOWLEDGMENTS

My thanks to the proprietors of Random House and William Morrow for permission to use that material to which they have the copyright. The portraits in *The Blackford Oakes Reader* are taken from *Saving the Queen; Stained Glass; Who's on First; Marco Polo, If You Can; The Story of Henri Tod; See You Later Alligator; High Jinx; Mongoose, R.I.P.; Tucker's Last Stand;* and *A Very Private Plot,* the Blackford Oakes novels by William F. Buckley Jr., 1976–1994.

Contents

Introduction

I TAKE THE OPPORTUNITY to answer some of the questions most often put to me as the author of the ten novels featuring Blackford Oakes. A question that continues to intrigue is: What is it that, at age fifty, beckoned me to write fiction?

It's a brief story, rather mundane, but it has its charm. I had for many years been in touch with Samuel Vaughan, then of Doubleday, a gentle, bright, shrewd man of letters who suggested we lunch and said he'd bring along two friends. It developed that they two were associates of Doubleday. The agenda for the lunch never materialized formally, though at some point, Sam asked if I had recently read any action thriller I thought especially well of and I said, Yes, I read *Day of the Jackal* last week and thought it tremendous. "Why don't you try writing a novel?" he said. I answered, as I remember, "Sam, why don't you play a trumpet concerto?" The conversation proceeded, pleasantly and aimlessly, and the next morning I found on my desk a proposed contract to write a novel for Doubleday.

I was titillated by the entrepreneurial initiative of my friend Sam, but it happened that that very day, the newspapers carried the story of William Safire. It was this, that

he had turned in, to Morrow, his volume on Richard Nixon, for which an advance commitment had been made to pay him $250,000. What the news story told us was that William Morrow had rejected his manuscript on the grounds that it was not "satisfactory."

Now what everybody who knows anything knew, indeed knows, is that Bill Safire does not submit "unsatisfactory" manuscripts. What was "unsatisfactory," in the summer of 1975, was Richard Nixon. He had a year before left office, the first American president to be run out of town so to speak with wet towels. The publishing company was taking an unseemly advantage of that little phrase in the publisher's contract that specifies that the writer's manuscript has to be "satisfactory" and that the publisher is the sole judge of whether that criterion has been met.

Accordingly I wrote to Sam Vaughan and said, Well sure, I'll try to write a novel, but how about this: You pay me up front one third of the advance and I write one hundred pages. I send these to you, and you then say after reading them: "Go ahead"—in which case you are committed to paying me the balance of the advance. Or else you say, "It was a fun idea, but kindly abort immediately"—in which case I'll have become an ex-novelist before ever becoming a novelist. . . . As it turned out, it was all very good news. *Saving the Queen* appeared on the best-seller list one week before its official publication date, and stayed there for thirteen weeks.

What was the novel about? Well, it featured one Blackford Oakes.

I am occasionally asked about the genesis of Blackford Oakes, the protagonist of my novels.

He was a kind of distillate. I arrived in Switzerland

(which is where I do my book writing) with only a single idea in mind, and that idea was to commit literary iconoclasm: I would write a book in which the good guys and the bad guys were actually distinguishable from one another. I took a deep breath and further resolved that the good guys would be—the Americans!

I had recently seen a movie called *Three Days of the Condor.* Perhaps you will remember that Robert Redford, a CIA agent of Restless Intelligence, working in a CIA front in New York City called the American Literary Historical Society, goes out one day to buy a hamburger, and returns to the CIA brownstone to find all nine of his colleagues quite dead. Murdered. By pistols firing ice pellets. In due course we discover that the Mr. Big who ordered the killings isn't a robber or a member of the Mafia or of the KGB. He is very high up in the government of the United States. Indeed, if the movie had endured another half hour, by the law of compound interest the viewer would have been satisfied only on discovering that the evil spirit behind the killing of Robert Redford's CIA colleagues was the president of the United States; or, to be really dramatic and reach all the way up to the highest vault in the national pantheon, maybe Ralph Nader.

Thus the movie went, deep in suspense. Mr. Big, who had ordered the mass killings, might have been exposed, finally, as a conventional double agent: posing as an American patriot, but actually a spy working for the Soviet Union. It transpired, however, that the man who ordered the slaughter was a 100 percent American, period. And there was nothing at all unusual about him in the movie. His decision to eliminate all those nice people at the American Literary Historical Society was entirely routine. He did so

because they were about to stumble on a secret, contingent CIA operation—by following a lead turned up by Robert Redford's Restless Intelligence.

So finally, in a dramatic sidewalk confrontation, Mr. Big's deputy—on instructions from Mr. Big—explains to Redford that the unfortunate killings were motivated by high patriotism: they were a necessary safeguard against the discovery of a top secret plan to protect America against a contingent shortage of oil. Stressing the importance of keeping Redford's knowledge secret, the deputy invites Redford to come back into the Agency, no hard feelings, and simply accept the imperatives of real life . . . of an intelligence agent in the modern world.

But Redford, taking off his glasses in anticipation of heady thought, says, "No, *never*. This very day, I have disclosed everything to . . ." The camera slithers up to a marquee above the two men and you see the logo of . . . *The New York Times*. The director of *Three Days of the Condor* neglected only to emblazon on it, "Daniel Ellsberg Slept Here."

The deputy reacts like the witch come in contact with water. He snarls and shivers and slinks away after muttering half-desperately: *"Maybe they won't print it!"* But Redford has by now seeded the audience with his Restless Intelligence, and we all know that *The New York Times will* print it, and thus we shall all be free.

The film's production notes stated, "Over a year ago, Stanley Schneider, Robert Redford, Sidney Pollack, and Dino de Laurentiis decided to create a film that would reflect the climate of America in the aftermath of the Watergate crisis."

"The climate of America" is a pretty broad term. They really meant, "the climate of America" as seen by Jane

Fonda, the Institute for Policy Studies, and *The Nation* magazine. One recalls Will Rogers returning, in 1927, from the Soviet Union, where he had witnessed a communal bath at which the bathers were nude.

"Did you see all of Russia?" a reporter asked.

"No," Rogers said, weighing his answer carefully. "But I saw all of parts of Russia."

Redford–Pollack–de Laurentiis had shown us the climate in all of parts of America. It was very cold out there.

And so I thought to attempt to write a book in which it was never left in doubt that the CIA, for all the complaints about its performance, is, when all is said and done, not persuasively likened to the KGB.

I was myself an agent of the CIA, for nine months beginning in 1951 when I left college. I do not confuse my admiration for the mission of the CIA with its overall effectiveness. A few years after leaving the CIA I published in *National Review* an editorial paragraph that read, "The attempted assassination of Sukarno in Jakarta last week had all the earmarks of a CIA operation. Everyone in the room was killed except Sukarno."

The point I sought to make, and continued to do so in subsequent novels, is that the CIA, whatever its failures, sought, during those long years in the struggle for the world, to advance the honorable alternative. When I wrote, it wasn't only Robert Redford who was however obliquely traducing the work of our central intelligence agency. He had starred in a movie the point of which was that the CIA is a corrupt and bloody-minded secret instrument of an amoral government, and that it routinely embarks on stratagems that beggar moral justification. Many others were

making similar points in every branch of the media: in novels of the recent past, novels by Graham Greene, and John Le Carré, and Len Deighton, for instance. The point, really, was that there wasn't all that much to choose from in a contest between the KGB and the CIA. Both organizations, it was fashionable to believe, were defined by their practices. I said to Johnny Carson, when on his program he raised just that question, that to say that the CIA and the KGB engage in similar practices is the equivalent of saying that the man who pushes an old lady into the path of a hurtling bus is not to be distinguished from the man who pushes an old lady out of the way of a hurtling bus, on the grounds that, after all, in both cases someone is pushing an old lady around.

The novelistic urge of the great ideological egalitarians who wrote books under such titles as *The Ugly American* had been to invest in their Western protagonists appropriately disfiguring personal characteristics. So that the American (or British) spy had become, conglomerately, a paunchy, alcoholic, late-middle-aged cuckold—moreover, an agent who late at night, well along in booze, ruminates to the effect that, when all is said and done, who really was to judge so indecipherable a question as whether the United States was all that much better than the Soviet Union? The KGB and the CIA really engage in the same kind of thing, and what they do defines them, not why they do it, right?

When I sat down, a yellow sheet of paper in my typewriter, to begin writing that first novel, it suddenly occurred to me that it would need a protagonist. By the end of the afternoon I had created Blackford Oakes, the principal character in *Saving the Queen*.

A year later, the editor of *Vogue* magazine wrote to me to

say that many reviewers had denominated Blackford Oakes as being "quintessentially" American. She invited me to explain, explicitly, what was the "American look." I thought to reject the invitation, because I resist the very notion of quintessentiality, as here invoked. It seems to me an image that runs into its inherent incredibility. You will remember that F.P. Adams once said that the average American is a little above average.

The reason you cannot have the quintessential American is the very same reason you cannot have a quintessential apple pie, or indeed a quintessential anything that is composed of so many ingredients. In all composites there has got to be an arrangement of attributes, and no such arrangement can project one quality to the point of distorting others. This is true even in the matter of physical beauty. An absolutely perfect nose has the effect of satellizing the other features of a human face; a beautiful face is a comprehensive achievement.

So anyway, Blackford Oakes is not the quintessential American, but I fancy he is *distinctively* American, and the first feature of the distinctively American male is, I think, spontaneity, a freshness of sorts born of curiosity and enterprise and native wit.

Would you believe that three days after meeting her, Blackford Oakes was in bed with the queen of England? (Not, I hasten to elucidate, the incumbent queen. Blackford Oakes, as the distinctive American, is a young man of taste, who sleeps only with fictitious queens, thereby avoiding international incidents.) There was something yes, distinctively, wonderfully American, it struck me, about bedding down a British queen: a kind of arrant yet lovable presumption. But always on the understanding that it were done decorously, and that there was no aftertaste of the

gigolo in the encounter. Moreover, in my novel the queen was the seducer, Blackford the seduced.

I remember with some trepidation—even now, almost twenty years later—the day that my novel came out in London. The first questioner at the televised exchange was, no less, the editor of *The Economist*, Andrew Knight, and he asked me a question I thought quite un-English in its lack of circumspection: "Mr. Buckley, would you like to sleep with the queen?"

Now such a question poses quite awful responsibilities. Just to begin with, I am a married man. And then, there being a most conspicuous incumbent queen, one could hardly wrinkle up one's nose as if the question evoked the vision of an evening with Queen Victoria on her diamond jubilee. The American with taste has to guard against any lack of gallantry, so that the first order of business became the assertion of an emancipating perspective, which would escort Queen Elizabeth II gently out of the room, lest she be embarrassed. This I hoped to accomplish by saying, just a little sleepily, as Blackford Oakes might have done, "*Which queen?*"—and then quickly, before the interrogator could lug his incumbent monarch back into the smoker—"Judging from historical experience, I would need to consult my lawyer before risking an affair with *any* British queen."

The American male must be tactful, and tact is most generally accomplished by changing the subject without its appearing that you have done so as a rebuke. It worked, and another aspect of my novel came before the house, the character of Blackford Oakes.

He appears on the scene at age twenty-two, a veteran of the war. So I stuck him in Yale, which gave me the advantage of being able to write about a familiar few acres. It has

been observed by several critics that Blackford Oakes emerged with characteristics associated, in the literature, with Yale men.

Like what?

Principally, I suppose, self-confidence; a certain worldliness that is neither bookish nor in any sense of the word anti-intellectual. Blackford Oakes is an engineer by training, the kind of engineer who learns how to build bridges, and his nonroyal girlfriend is studying for her Ph.D. and doing her doctorate on Jane Austen. *She* is not expected to dwell in conversation on her own specialty, let alone show any curiosity about how to build bridges. The American look wears quite offhandedly its special proficiencies: If one is a lawyer, one does not go about talking like Oliver Wendell Holmes, any more than Charles Lindbergh went about sounding like Charles Lindbergh. Though Blackford quite rightly shows a qualified, if not extensive, curiosity about Jane Austen, and probably has read (actually, reread: one never reads Jane Austen, one only *rereads* her) *Pride and Prejudice* and his girlfriend has no objection to the profession of engineering.

Now Blackford Oakes is physically handsome, in a sense a metaphor for his ideals. Here I took something of a chance. I decided not only to make him routinely good looking, but to make him startlingly so. I don't mean startling in the sense that, let us say, Elizabeth Taylor is startlingly beautiful. It is hard to imagine a male counterpart for what we understand as pulchritude. An extremely handsome man is not the *equivalent* of an extremely beautiful woman, he is her complement, and that is very important to bear in mind in probing the American look—which is not, for example, the same thing as the Italian look. When

Schopenhauer exclaimed that a sixteen-year-old girl is the "smash triumph of nature," he made a cosmic statement that could only have been made about the female sex.

So that when I decided that Blackford Oakes should be startlingly handsome, it was required that he be that in a distinctively American way, and what does *that* mean? Well it doesn't mean you look like Mickey Rooney, obviously. But it doesn't mean you have to look like Tyrone Power, either. I think the startlingly handsome American male is not made so by the regularity of his features, however necessary that regularity may be, but by the special quality of his expression. It has to be for this reason that, flipping past the male models exhibited in the advertising sections of the local newspaper or of *Esquire* magazine, one seldom finds oneself pausing to think: That man is startlingly handsome. But such an impression *is* taken away, from time to time, from a personal encounter, or even from a candid photograph. Because the American look, in the startlingly handsome man, requires animation, but tempered by a certain shyness; a reserve.

I thought of Billy Budd. I have long since forgotten just how Melville actually described him, but Melville communicated that Billy Budd was startlingly handsome. But looks aside, his distinctiveness was not that of Blackford Oakes. Billy Budd is practically an eponym for innocence, purity. Oakes, though far removed from jadedness, is worldly. And then, and then . . .

Billy Budd, alas, is humorless. Correction: not *alas.* "Do not go about as a demagogue, urging a triangle to break out of the prison of its three sides," G.K. Chesterton warned us, "because if you succeed, its life will come to a lamentable end." Give Billy Budd a sense of humor and he shatters

in front of you into thousands of little pieces, which you can never reconstruct. Blackford Oakes doesn't go about like Wilfrid Sheed's protagonist in *Transatlantic Blues,* or John Gregory Dunne's in *True Confessions,* being hilariously mordant. The American look here is a leavened sarcasm. But careful, now: Escalate sarcasm and you break through the clouds into the ice-cold of nihilism. The American must *believe.* However discreetly or understatedly. Blackford Oakes believed. He tended to divulge his beliefs in a kind of slouchy, oblique way. But at the margin he was, well—an American, with Judeo-Christian predilections; and he knew, as with the clothes he wore so casually, that he was snug as such; that, like his easygoing sweater and trousers, they—fitted him. As did the ideals, and even most of the practices, of his country.

I remember with delight reading a review of that first novel, published in *The Kansas City Star,* written by a professor of English from the University of Missouri, I think it was. I had never heard of the gentleman, but he made it quite clear that he had spent a considerable part of his adult life abominating me and my works and my opinions. He was manifestly distressed at not quite disliking my first novel, which he proceeded to describe. He salved his conscience by concluding, "The hero of *Saving the Queen,* Mr. Blackford Oakes, is tall, handsome, witty, agreeable, compassionate and likeable, from which at least we can take comfort in knowing that the book is not autobiographical."

There arose, as a practical matter, the responsibility of recreating in fiction men who have been very much alive in recent history, and investing in them conspicuous attributes for which they were well known.

Consider, for instance, the proud, patrician, sarcastic Dean Acheson, secretary of state under Harry Truman. He is an adamant critic of the Republican party, the party of his old friend Allen Dulles, the director of the Central Intelligence Agency who, one afternoon in 1953, soon after Truman was replaced by President Eisenhower, comes to call on him to confer about a looming crisis in West Germany:

Allen Dulles had missed the day-to-day analysis of international events—mordant, clairvoyant—of this infuriating man, with whom he had been officially associated, until the last election, in the administration of President Truman. Now Mr. Acheson had just published a book, called *A Democrat Looks at His Party,* in which he had calmly announced that the principal distinction between a Republican and a Democrat is that Democrats tend to be bright, and Republicans tend to be stupid.

"It's just that easy," he now teased his guest while tea was being poured. "You mustn't be offended by this, Allen. Besides, you must find it consoling that your people will stay in power a good long time."

There was a special tone of mock resignation in Acheson's observation.

"In some discursive reading the other day I found interesting corroboration for this thesis. It is from a speech by John Stuart Mill delivered, I believe, in the British parliament."

With his left hand, Acheson extends his teacup to the maid who refilled it as he adjusted his glasses with his right hand.

"Mill said"—Acheson reads now from a book—"'I never meant to say that the Conservatives are generally stupid. I meant to say that stupid people are generally Conservative. I believe that is so obviously and universally admitted a principle'"—the Secretary raised his eyebrows in tribute to the majesty of First Principles—"'that I hardly think any gentleman will deny it. Suppose any

party, in addition to whatever share it may possess of the ability of the community, had nearly the whole of its stupidity, that party must'—take heart, Allen—'by the laws of its constitution be the stupidest party; and I do not see why honorable gentlemen should see that position as at all offensive to them, for it ensures their being always an extremely powerful party.'" Dean Acheson smiled with great satisfaction, and looked up again, as if to acknowledge, reverently, yet another providential insight.

Here, then, was an attempt to recreate theoretically, if you like, a dominant impulse in a dominating American character of the fifties. I would write a dozen such vignettes in the novels that lay ahead. I needed, for instance, to cope with John Fitzgerald Kennedy. How to do so? I elected the device of the soliloquy. Talking to himself. He is all alone in the Oval Office, at the end of a day, a few minutes before he is summoned upstairs to prepare for a state dinner. Listen. . . .

I've got just one hour before I need to go upstairs to dress for the state dinner for what's-his-name, the little hypocrite. Allen Dulles told me he's stolen maybe forty, maybe fifty million bucks, and he is always poor-mouthing about his people. Damn right they're poor. He stays in power another ten years, what's-his-name (I must make it a serious point to get his name straight before the state dinner—why aren't they all called Gonzalez? I mean, most of them are as it is)—ten more years and his "people" will have nothing at all left.

Ah, but if only the worst problems were Latin American. Latin America. Chiquita Banana, da-da-da da-da. How does it go?

. . . But I'm putting off what I need to concentrate on. More hard thought on Khrushchev, the bastard, and Berlin. I can't remember whether Dad told me that all Communist chiefs of state, like all American businessmen, were s.o.b.'s. Maybe he thought I'd simply take that for granted.

Two weeks from now I'll have met with Khrushchev . . . Is it

possible to count the number of hours I've spent studying Khrushchev? With Dean Acheson, for instance? Good old Dean, he wants just one little world war before he dies . . . What do they say about Khrushchev? Pretty much the same thing. I've studied the minutes of: God! Geneva summit, 1955. Camp David summit, 1959. And Paris summit, 1960. Khrushchev aborted the damned thing on account of our U2 flight! That was vintage Khrushchev, right? Complaining about espionage! Especially the press conference he gave when he stopped over in Vienna. Said maybe Ike was just a little cuckoo . . .

Brings up an interesting point. One of the things I have to ask myself is: How far do I let him go? I mean, if he starts to scream and yell, what do I do in the cause of Peace with Honor? God, I wish that phrase had never been coined. Fact is, you don't often get both at the same time.

Okay, so what's he up to? Seriously, what is he up to? Jack old boy, I mean, Mr. President old boy, let's start that at the other end. What's he *not* up to?

Well, he's not up to beginning a nuclear war. Among other things, Poppa Marx wouldn't like that. A nuclear war with maybe only Patagonians left over isn't going to do much to validate the Marxist theory of class struggle. Okay, at what point do we start dropping nuclear bombs? A hell of a question to ask, but I'm the one who's going to decide.

Khrushchev is sort of unique, they all say. But so are all Soviet chiefs of state. That's the way they talk, the way they behave.

Well by God, that's not the way they're going to talk to me! Screw summit conferences.

No, that's the wrong word. Don't want to say anything unfriendly about screwing.

To hell with summit conferences.

If Khrushchev is just being Khrushchev, then the boys have got to weigh whether just being Khrushchev is the best way to advance their cause. And the only means they have to measure that is me. How do I react? That's the question. How does John Fitzgerald Kennedy, president of the United States, maximum leader of the imperialist powers, react? And what will I come up

with, in my search for something we can give them, that we can do without?

The special telephone on his desk rang, to which, at the other end, only one person had access.

"I'm coming, dear."

There is JFK. The second book confronted a dilemma. What to do about the inspiring young West German nobleman who in 1953 was emerging as the probable victor of impending national elections on a platform of reuniting Germany at any cost? Stalin had communicated to Eisenhower: Get rid of that man, or—prepare for a Russian invasion of Germany.

What to do?

Stained Glass, I happily recall, went on to win the American Book Award as the best mystery story of the year. I like to think it was not the narrative suspense that overwhelmed the judges. What the book did was to pose the central question of counterintelligence and espionage as conducted by a free society.

The decision had finally been reached, in Washington, to accede to the demands of the Kremlin and to assassinate my fictional West German, Count Axel Wintergrin, whose startling rise to power threatened a world war.

And so the execution—rigged as an electrical accident, at the count's old Gothic castle—was arranged. Blackford Oakes supervised the plan (even though, at the end, he refused to take a personal hand in its consummation). And so the gallant and idealistic young German politician, who might seriously have challenged the Russian hegemony, was dead. And a devoted legend about him was born, so that every year, around the reconstructed thirteenth-century family chapel, larger and larger crowds gathered to commemorate the anniversary of his death. On the tenth anni-

versary, Blackford Oakes, the count's executioner, was discreetly present in the chapel and he spotted, traveling incognito, the man who, by coded telegraph ten years ago had given him that awful, terminal command to proceed with the execution: It was retired CIA chief Allen Dulles.

By now—ten years later—it was retrospectively clear that Stalin would not have reacted to a political victory by Wintergrin by moving into Europe. So that the execution, in hindsight, had been a most gruesome mistake strategically, its moral hideousness quite apart.

Walking back to his car in the parking lot, after the memorial services, Blackford Oakes suddenly espied the man, the head of the agency for which he worked, but a man he had never laid eyes on before today. Inflamed by the memories evoked during the ceremony mourning the young man he had put to death, Oakes suddenly—impulsively—approaches the car of Allen Dulles. The text reads . . .

He waited until the old man had unlocked the door at the driver's side and entered. He knocked on the window opposite. Surprised, but without hesitation the old man reached over and tripped open the door handle. Blackford opened the door, got in, and closed it. Sitting with his hands on the steering wheel, Dulles turned his head. Blackford did not extend his hand. He said simply,

"I am Blackford Oakes."

"I see." Allen Dulles did not go through the formality of introducing himself.

There was a pause.

"Well, Mr. Dulles, did we do the right thing in 1952?"

"Mr. Oakes, the question you asked, I do not permit myself to explore, not under any circumstances."

"Why not?"

"Because in this world, if you let them, the ambiguists will kill you."

"The ambiguists, as you call them, were dead right about Count Wintergrin."

"You are asking me to break my rule."

Blackford replied: "Excuse me, sir, but is your goddamn rule more important than Wintergrin and his cause?"

"Actually," said Dulles, "it is. Or, if you prefer, put it this way, Oakes: I have no alternative than to believe it is more important. And I hope you will understand, because if you do it will be easier. If you do not, you are still too inexperienced to discuss these matters with me."

"I don't want it to be easier for me." Oakes turned now to look directly at the man whose will had governed Blackford's own for ten years. He found himself raising his voice, something he never did. "Wintergrin was the great hope for the west. The great opportunity. The incarnation of western idealism. You made me . . ."

He stopped. Already ashamed of a formulation that stripped him of his manhood. Nobody had forced Blackford to lead Axel Wintergrin to the execution chamber.

He changed, as quickly as possible, the arrangement of his thought. "You lost a great chance."

Dulles was now aroused. He lit his pipe with jagged movements of his hands.

"I believe you are right. I believe Wintergrin was right. The Russians, I believe, would not in fact have moved. But do you want to know something I don't believe?" His voice was strained.

Blackford was silent.

"I don't believe the lesson to draw is that we must not act because, in acting, we may prove to be wrong. And I know,"—his eyes turned to meet Blackford's—"that you know that Axel Wintergrin thought so too."

There was nothing more to say. Impulsively, Blackford extended his hand, and Dulles took it.

When I finished that book, and before I had given it a title, I wrote to an old friend—we had met in 1954—to say, "Henry, I have written a book, the narrative of which is set

forth in the accompanying blurb written by the publisher. I should like to dedicate it to you, and perhaps to call the book *Detente.* But I would not want to do this if it would cause you any embarrassment."

Henry Kissinger wrote back, "Dear Bill: Many thanks, but I think the book, which I look forward to reading, would best be inscribed to someone else while I am Secretary of State. If you wish to dedicate your next novel to me, I would be very grateful. Provided it isn't on the subject of Cyprus."

Well, Blackford Oakes has not visited Cyprus. After his terrible mission in Germany he was in Paris, in *Who's on First,* where he faced a moral dilemma—that got him fired.

He was next seen *(Marco Polo, If You Can)* in the Lubyanka Prison in Moscow, condemned to death after his U-2 plane was shot down over southwest Asia, a constituent episode in a great master plot designed to accelerate crystallizing differences between Khrushchev's Soviet Union and Mao's China.

He went then, in *The Story of Henri Tod,* to Berlin, where he immobilized himself—rather than abort a patriotic attempt by West German patriots to frustrate the Soviet creation of the Berlin Wall.

In *See You Later Alligator,* Blackford Oakes was in Cuba, negotiating, at the direction of President Kennedy, with Che Gueverra a possible detente. At one point in the story he declines to obey abrupt orders from Washington to abort his mission and return home.

In *High Jinx* he was in London, on assignment to penetrate the leak of highly secret documents which foretold the slaughter of the men sent out to liberate Albania.

In *Mongoose, R.I.P.,* we learned that the Russians, retreating from Cuba after the missile crisis, had left one missile secretly

in place, that it was programmed to land in Dallas. Fidel Castro had ordered the missile to be fired at Dallas—on November 22, 1963, when President Kennedy would be there.

In *Tucker's Last Stand,* the protagonist—yes, an American intelligence officer—turns over our critical plans on how to block the Ho Chi Minh trail to his girlfriend, even after he learns that she is an agent, working for the enemy. Blackford Oakes finds himself powerless to intervene.

And in *A Very Private Plot,* Blackford Oakes has to report to President Reagan that there is an entirely native plot afoot in Moscow to assassinate Gorbachev. And how does Reagan react? With excruciating difficulty.

In the first novel I guess it is correct to say that I intuitively got the idea that the novel should frame a single person (primarily). That person's character and experiences should illuminate the story. In *Saving the Queen* it was Blackford himself, at school in England, developing a character and a knowledge of Britain and its institutions that he would come to lean on only six years later.

In *Stained Glass* I sought to portray a young, aristocratic German idealist, to tell what he did when Hitler took Germany to war, how he comported himself during the war years and immediately after, as the dream consolidated in his mind: that his mission would be to deliver his country from the post-Hitler tyranny.

In *Who's on First* I felt the need to convey something of the feeling of life in Gulag. I had read Solzhenitsyn and sought to explore what life was like for two dissenting scientists during the last few years of Stalin, and what it was like to emerge from Gulag and confront the challenge of servitude to the new Soviet masters.

In *The Story of Henri Tod* I focused on a young Jewish boy, in hiding with his family from Hitler, spirited away to Great Britain, cut off from a younger sister with whom he had been inseparable, and the hardening of a resolve, like that of the aristocratic young count in Stained Glass, to lift the iron curtain that divided Berlin.

In the two Cuban-set novels I focused on a young Spaniard, lured to the Communists after the civil war. He was the object of a quixotic effort to rob a bank which resulted in years' imprisonment, followed by a devoted apprenticeship to the Party—which dispatched him to Mexico to take part in the assassination of Leon Trotsky. He found himself a party to the (historically correct) assassination of Soviet ambassador Oumansky—and his own wife.

And *A Very Private Plot* gives us a portrait of a young Ukrainian growing up under the Communist lash, a prodigy at school, sent to Afghanistan front where, viewing the carnage, a slow resolve within him consolidates. He decides, quietly, that he will assassinate Gorbachev.

Some of the portraits lean directly on history. They are the kernel of the ten novels, and are here set down for the first time, unencumbered.

Well, the Cold War ended. Blackford Oakes, in a few flash-forward scenes in *Plot,* is seventy years old. The time had come to pack it in. The novels will, it is my judgment, survive, for reasons I leave it to others to indite. The purpose of this volume is to extract from each one of them one portrait, perhaps memorable.

I have taken care to isolate the portraits in this volume so that they stand on their own two legs. No reader need know anything that happened before in that novel or, for that

matter, anything that happened subsequently. We meet young Count Wintergrin at age nineteen when the Nazis invade and he flees to Poland, and from there to Sweden where he works with the Resistance, returning to his widowed mother's ancient castle after the war, on to Oxford, then back to begin a movement to liberate his country. Platov and Kapitsa become friends on the train taking them to Vorkuta, the great prison camp in Gulag where they spend eight years and live to see the day when Josef Stalin dies. And on with the succeeding seven novels.

I pray that the reader will enjoy even languorously the animations here collected. I can guarantee the reader will not be bored, because there is too much movement, too much color, too much life, sufficient to keep my own engine at much better than cruising speed, the speed where in my judgment the novelist should work, solicitous for the reader's time.

Entertainment and distraction are the objective. The educational objective in the novels has been to make the point, so difficult for so many Westerners to comprehend, that counterintelligence and espionage, conducted under Western auspices, weren't exercises in conventional political geometry. They were—they are—a moral art.

Consider one hypothetical dilemma and reason backward, from the particular to the generality. I give you a question and ask that you wrestle with it, confining yourself, if you can, within the maxims of the conventional morality.

Is it wrong to effect the execution of a chief of a state with which you are not at war?

Yes, it is wrong to do so.

Is it wrong to countenance a destructive event of such magnitude as conceivably to trigger a world war?

Yes, it is wrong.

What then do you call it when it appears to rational men that the second injunction cannot be observed save by defying the first?

Scene: Uganda. Colonel Idi Amin has got possession of a nuclear bomb and plans at midnight to dispatch a low-flying plane to drop that bomb on Jerusalem. A CIA agent, in the field, communicates to Washington that Idi Amin will lie between the cross hairs of the agent's rifle at the airport before the bomber is dispatched. Should he squeeze the trigger?

There are those, and Blackford Oakes was one of them, who would address that morally wrenching point by saying two things: (1) As to the particular question, yes, authorize the agent to shoot, in order to abort the destruction of Jerusalem, and all that might then follow. But (2), do not then require as a condition of this decision that laws or rules be set down that embody the distinction. It isn't possible to write such judgments into law, no more than to specify to the artist the exact arrangement of circumstances that call for a daub of Prussian blue or, to the composer, the exact harmonic situation that benefits from rules that admit the striking of an A-augmented eleventh chord.

Blackford Oakes lived in an age when what mattered most was the survival of one of two systems. Us and Them—that was the difference that mattered. The failure by beneficiaries of life in the free world to recognize what it was that we had here, over against what it would have been had our lives been transformed so that we too might live under totalitarianism, amounted to moral and intellectual nihilism. This was far more incriminating of our culture than any transgression against eristic scruples of the kind

that preoccupied so many of our moralists who inveighed against the protocols of the CIA and MI-6.

Blackford Oakes had weaknesses spiritual and corporal. But a basic assumption guided him. It was that the survival of everything we cherish depended on the survival of the culture of liberty; and that this hung on our willingness to defend this extraordinary country of ours, so awfully mixed up so much of the time, so schizophrenic in our understanding of ourselves and our purposes, so crazily indulgent in our legion of wildly ungovernable miscreants. Yet, without ever saying so in so many words, Oakes thought this country the finest bloom of nationhood in all recorded time, worth the risk, which he so often took, of life and limb.

He did all that, but he recognized also that a vital part of America's singularity is its capacity to give pleasure, which it is the primary aim of the Oakes novels to do.

W.F.B.
Stamford, Connecticut
July 15, 1994

Blackford Oakes

WHEN THE LETTER from his mother arrived Blackford was at Camp Blakey, in Maine. He opened it eagerly, in the presence of his tent mates, and read. His eyes blurred so that he couldn't see, not even his two silent companions, but when his vision returned, he streaked out—by the Old Schoolhouse, along the shore of the lake, past the dozen tidy canoes, into the forest, whose shadows slightly slowed him down, but never to a walk—the whole two miles to the main highway where, breathless, he stopped, sticking up his thumb with that supernal confidence of the young that he would not, by that Providence he had grown up with on such companionable terms, be kept waiting, which he wasn't. The farmer who picked him up took him as far as Bath. Then, in minutes, he was on a truck headed for Boston. The driver stopped for gas and food and asked Black if he was going to eat anything, and Black said no, he wasn't hungry. He was very hungry, and he had no money in his pocket, only the letter, lodged permanently in his memory, word for word, after that one reading. The driver returned with two sandwiches, ate one slowly as he drove, and told the boy to toss the second one out at the next garbage can, because one had satisfied him after all. Black

said that although he wasn't hungry, maybe he would eat it himself rather than waste it, and the driver said suit yourself. The driver asked Black no questions about himself, but volunteered copious details about his own humdrum life, confessing that he rather hoped the United States would get into the war, since he was still just young enough to join the army or preferably the navy in the event of a general draft, and would like to see something of the world besides the run from Portland to Boston before he got any older, and, frankly, he didn't think his wife would mind it all that much if he went away for a while. Black woke from his trance at this and sternly discoursed on the illogic and immorality of the United States getting involved in a European war, recapitulating with considerable skill, analytical and mimetic, the phrases and paragraphs he had so often heard his father so earnestly intone. The driver retreated, leaving the impression that his desire for war was at most a velleity and turned to other matters. Black listened, and commented as necessary, dozed off, wondering, detachedly, how he would get from Boston to New York—to his aunt's house—before dying of hunger.

He arrived in the late afternoon, the beneficiary of random highway philanthropies including a plate of french-fried potatoes from the Howard Johnson waitress who, when he had sat down after his driver dropped him to go north to Hartford, and asked, at the counter, for a glass of water, said he was cute, which, suddenly, he realized self-consciously, he probably was, wearing trim white shorts, and a T-shirt marked CAMP BLAKEY, and white socks and tennis shoes, a rope belt and a watch with an Indian bead band he had sewn himself. At 5'7" and 120 pounds he was growing fast, but not in those mutant leaps and bounds that

leave the mid-adolescent looking like a gazelle. His hair was a dark blond, with the same yellow-white strains that even now came out on the least touch of the sun. Though his lips were normally set, he was quick to smile, a charming and precocious smile, somehow wise and amused, and he smiled when the waitress, varying very little from the basic gambit of the truck driver, said there were excess potatoes, that a dumb cook had prepared too many. But after eating only a few, suddenly his stomach was narcotized by his mind's return to the letter, and he walked quickly to the men's room and wept silently in the toilet compartment, wedging his weight against the door because there was no lock. When he regained control, he left through the back way, and resumed hitchhiking, out of sight of the waitress, whose generous impulse he could not trust himself to acknowledge without betraying himself, or embarrassing her.

He flagged a taxi at 125th Street and Lexington—awful extravagance—but he did not feel strong enough to walk to 69th Street, and he knew of no other vehicle that would deliver him collect. He said nothing to the driver, and on arriving asked him to wait. Georgianna opened the door, black and dour as ever, but instantly docile when he said, "Georgy, lend me a dollar quickly."

He came back from the cab: "Is Aunt Alice here?"

No, but she would be back for dinner.

He went upstairs, not needing Georgianna's guidance, nor soliciting her permission, and took a bath in his cousin's room, lay down and slept until Alice Gonzalez prodded him awake. He reached to the chair and pulled the letter out from his shorts and gave it to her. She went to the end of the room to catch the light and read it.

"Did you know, Aunt Alice?"

"No," she said. "But I'm not surprised. At least, not by the first part."

The first part was his mother's information that she had secured a divorce from his father in England, where his father's work had taken them in May. "Darling, there's no reason to tell you *why*, and I don't want to say *anything* that would injure your father, or *you*, or your *relations* with your father. You'll just have to take *my* word for it that I *couldn't* go on."

The second part was her announcement that she had remarried.

"His name is Alec Sharkey. He is, in fact, Sir Alec Sharkey. His first wife died in a car crash a year ago, with their daughter. He is an architect, and a very kind man, and I pray that you will grow to love him. I know that you will like him—I promise you—and he knows already that he will like you."

There followed what he could only take to be instructions. He inferred that his mother was in charge of him. He knew, generally, that that was how it worked after divorces. Besides, he had had no communication from his father—which didn't surprise him because he was always bad about writing—and anyway, his father had set out in June for a trip to the Far East to look into the possibility of brokering some airplanes to the beleaguered Chinese, and the mail from the Orient was problematic.

Blackford's instructions were to take the S.S. *Wakefield,* sailing from New York on September 9. "Your stepfather has enrolled you in Greyburn College, his alma mater. It is very old, and very famous; you will get a fine education there before going to college, either here in England or in America."

"Frankly," said Black at dinner, to his aunt and her phleg-matic, ever-silent husband, "the idea of going to school in England gives me the creeps. Don't you have to dress like an ambassador? And don't they beat you?" His aunt soothed him and told him he would have a great experience, which was correct.

His mother was waiting for him at Waterloo Station, and they hugged like lovers. The schedule provided for three days at home, and his stepfather had tactfully left London for the first of these to permit the reunion between mother and son without the restraint of an alien presence. Black realized quickly that his mother was not going to talk about his father, and indeed she never brought up his name again, though on the infrequent occasions when Blacky gave her news about him, she was affectionately attentive. Black stopped mentioning his father. During the war years, he saw him less than once a year. On those occasions, and while Blackford was at college, there was a strained man-to-manness, a lot of bluff advice, which grew progressively vinous as the evening wore along. Yet however desultorily, his father always kept in touch with him, and the more easily as his son grew older, and the two, though apart, did not grow apart.

Mother and son went by taxi to 50 Portland Place, a comfortable house in a fashionable area by Regent's Park, a block or so from Queen's Hall. A cook, a butler, and a maid were in attendance, but the butler had given notice—the War Office required him to take a war-related job. It was expected that the same would happen soon to the maid. The cook, old and devoted to Sir Alec, would stay.

Black was struck by the signs, paraphernalia, and scars of

modern war. The streets were filled with martial posters, cluttered with soldiers and sailors. Half the air raid wardens were women. The next morning, he had been advised at Southampton, he would be required to be fitted for a gas mask. He passed several areas of recent devastation—from fire bombs, mostly; and he noticed how dim the lights were, how dark the central city as they drove through it.

He bathed and went down to dinner, and his mother, who looked younger than in the spring when he had last seen her—more beautiful than he ever remembered her—gazing adoringly on her beautiful son, said that they must be practical for a moment.

The next morning would be given over to outfitting him for Greyburn. He would need three pairs of gray flannel pants, two vests, two school blazers, a cap, sports shoes, gray woolen shirts, two school ties, socks and underwear, all of it available at Harrods.

"They have a quite extensive store of sorts at the school and you can buy there, or order, anything else you need. Your stepfather drove up there a week ago after he got your school records from Scarsdale. The headmaster went over them very carefully. You would be going into your sophomore year at Scarsdale. The equivalent at Greyburn is the fourth form. Dr. Chase thinks you'd be better off, and happier, entering the third form. Later, in a year or two, you might be able to skip a form. But right now, you haven't had as advanced work as the English boys of your age in Latin and French. And, of course, they've done a lot of English history and you've had none. Your stepfather decided we should take the headmaster's advice."

"Was there any choice?" asked Black, rueful at repeating an entire year.

"No, darling. There really wasn't. Greyburn made a huge exception in taking you. Everything is very tight with the war, and in any case Greyburn has a very long line of boys waiting to get in." Black wondered whether in Greyburn there was a very long line of boys waiting to get out; but he said nothing. The whole thought of the place—he had never been to boarding school—depressed him; he supposed he would get used to it, and his naturally high spirits, since his flight from Camp Blakey, were restored, though he was nervous at the prospect of meeting his stepfather.

This happened at lunch; and this time, his mother slipped away.

Sir Alec was, Black guessed, forty-five years old. What was most conspicuous at first was the formality of his dress. He could have walked directly into Westminster Abbey with that costume, Black thought, and married a princess at high noon. Even the carnation was there, and on coming into the hall, he had put aside an umbrella and a derby. He was middle-sized, and balding, with heavy glasses, a beefy face, and a trim red mustache. Black had studied, the night before in his stepfather's study, pictures of him as a boy: on the rugger team at Greyburn, crewing at Cambridge. He had then a profusion of what must have been red hair, and he always looked solemn, as though no other pose was suitable for a gentleman to strike before a photographer. There was a picture, in a black frame, of his wife, who looked austere and rather helpless as she held, self-consciously, the hand of their ten-year-old daughter, only a few months, he deduced from the date of the inscription, before the fatal accident.

"This is rather awkward, isn't it?" he heard his stepfather saying. "Sit down. I have given it a lot of thought, and it

occurs to me we should handle some of the practical problems first, such as how you are to address me. I expect you do not want to call me 'Father,' and of course I shan't ask you to. There is, in England, a surviving tradition which permits calling one's stepfather 'Stepfather.' But it is shaky, even as the bourgeois tradition of calling one's cook 'Cook.' If I hadn't been knighted, we might have experimented with your calling me 'Mr. Sharkey.' But 'Sir Alec' is, I think you would agree, uncomfortable.

"Thus I have been driven by the process of elimination, which, incidentally, Blackford, is the secret behind most successful architecture, never mind the popular superstition that all those beautiful contrivances are born of poetic inspiration or theoretical sunbursts, to conclude that you will have to address me—brace yourself—as *Alec.*"

He pronounced the syllables distastefully.

"I never thought before now that there were uses in being christened something more formal, like 'Algernon' or 'Auberon.' Now, *I* have the same objection to this that *you* may be thinking. In the first place, I dislike precipitate informality. In the second place, I dislike it *in particular* when it is otherwise fitting to emphasize a relationship, one of the parties to which is subordinate—as you, necessarily, will be subordinate to me over the next few years. It is useful that terms of address should suggest such authority. And, finally, there *is* a hint of modernism in the arrangement, and *I resist modernism in all its forms,* with conviction, and indeed *implacability.* At the same time, if there are no alternatives, there are no alternatives. Under the circumstances, I am: Alec. Good afternoon, Blackford."

Black was breathless. Still, as Sir Alec sat down, he caught a trace of a smile in the studiedly dour countenance,

and his whole frame—as when, tensing up again for another painful shaft of the dentist's drill, one is told that it is all over—relaxed. Black didn't feel he could let down his guard. Nor could he predict he would ever feel affection for his stepfather. But he felt, already, a certain . . . security in his presence. And no feeling at all that doing so implied any infidelity to his father.

Sir Alec rang a bell, and a tray of sandwiches and hot soup was brought in, with a glass of milk and a half bottle of claret. He spoke at a rapid rate about war developments and asked Blackford if he had any views of his own on the matter.

Black took a deep breath and said he did not believe the United States should intervene.

"Well," Sir Alec said, casting a cautious glance at Blackford, "Churchill has said to you Americans: 'Give us the tools and we will do the job.' That seems fair, doesn't it?"

"I guess so," said Black, electing not to recapitulate the ardent analyses of his father, that U.S. aid would necessarily lead to full U.S. participation in the war.

"Well," said Sir Alec after a pause, "we will have to see. Meanwhile it is not to be overruled that that madman will, in his triumphant exuberance, portage his army across the Channel, and it is by no means certain that if he tries it he won't succeed. But that kind of talk we reserve for *indoors. Outdoors* we use only defiant rhetoric. *Grrr!!*" Black looked up at his stepfather making a most hideous face. He laughed. So did Sir Alec: long laughter, waves of relief, submerging, slowly, and forever, a web of nerves exposed.

That afternoon they walked together, through the Tower of London, and Madame Tussaud's, and into Westminster Abbey, and past Buckingham Palace, taking tea—Black's

first—at a Lyons, with cookies and fancy pastries of assorted kinds. Sir Alec asked for chocolates and the waitress said, "Sir, you know there aren't any chocolates these days." Black suspected that Sir Alec did know this, but that he had asked for them anyway, to show his American stepson how grave was the situation. Black understood, but thought that, really, he *should* be given credit for being almost sixteen. After all, he didn't think a shortage of chocolates was the surest sign of a collapsed order. Though he did wonder, idly, whether Aunt Alice could be got to send him some Milky Ways to Greyburn, as she had to Camp Blakey.

School! The day after tomorrow.

He looked up at his stepfather—he had not yet brought himself to refer to him as "Alec," was looking for the opportunity, and meanwhile he called him—nothing at all—

"How big is Greyburn?" he asked suddenly.

"Greyburn has six hundred and twenty-five boys and thirteen forms. The top four forms—the Upper School—have seventy-five boys in each form, approximately. The school was founded in the eighteenth century, under the special protection of the Duke of Caulfield, on whose estate it was built. The present Duke, who is all of twenty-three years old, is ex officio the chairman of the board of trustees. It has supplied as high a percentage of graduates to Oxford and Cambridge in the past century as any school in the kingdom. I finished in 1914, just in time to fight in a very long war, from which, for reasons I cannot understand, I emerged not only intact, but positively roaring with health, which made me hugely conspicuous alongside my emaciated and mutilated classmates who went up with me to Cambridge in 1919.

"Greyburn is a rigid school, insists on the highest stan-

dards, academic and other, and has means, mostly painful, of forcing the boys to meet these standards. I don't know the present chap, Dr. Chase, at all—met him for the first time when I went over there to discuss you. He was headmaster of a grammar school before going to Greyburn, and wrote a research study on medieval pedagogy, for which he received an advanced degree. Cold fish. But the trustees think highly of him, and now that the whole bloody country is regimented, the regimentation at Greyburn doesn't strike one as all *that* unusual. It will take you time to get used to it. But if you are like most of the others, you will find it an exhilarating experience. I did, though of course I had my unhappy moments. You get one weekend a term to come home, and we are permitted, after you have been there for ten weeks, to take you out three Saturday afternoons, provided you have not been 'confined'; and we may attend—again, after your initial ten weeks—any school game and have tea later on the grounds. You look fit for the junior teams, but first you'll have to do something to bring order to your rather chaotic academic background."

"Why 'chaotic'? Scarsdale High School has a very good reputation," Blackford said defensively.

"Nothing personal. All other educational systems appear chaotic alongside one's own. No doubt Scarsdale High School would find a matriculant from Greyburn dreadfully in need of adjustments. By the way, you will find an almost uniform ignorance, at Greyburn, of the causes, and ideals, of the American War of Independence."

That night all three had dinner, and Sir Alec announced, just before the soup was served, that they must hurry, because he had three tickets to a film being shown down Oxford Street, within walking distance. It was a thriller, in

which Walter Pidgeon very nearly shot Hitler at Berchtesgaden, and the anguished disappointment felt by Black's fellow viewers at Walter Pidgeon's failure to squeeze the trigger when the hairline neatly and lethally bisected the Führer's head was emotionally overwhelming in the packed theater. To think of it! That one man, with one rifle, might have spared England the ordeal into which she was entered. After the movie ended, Black, seated by the aisle, rose and stepped automatically out. His mother grabbed him by the arm. The audience was risen and motionless, while the loudspeakers gave out the majestic chords of "God Save the King."

As Blackford cheered on the team, he suddenly realized that what had been, up until only a week or so ago—at last Saturday's game—purely perfunctory cheers for the home team were now genuine. He really did want his school to win the game against Harrow, and he wondered why. He wondered, to begin with, how he had survived the first week, and the nights, when in his solitary cubicle, his pillow over his head so that he would not be heard by his neighbors through the flimsy plyboard partitions, he wept, longing for his mother, his friends at Scarsdale, and above all for the easygoing liberties that had been taken from him as abruptly as if he had been clapped into prison.

He could not *believe* the supervision. The detailed concern. When, on the first morning, while still brushing his teeth in his dressing gown, he saw his classmates, similarly dressed, leaving the communal lavatory with its forty washbasins, queuing by a master before whom they opened their mouths wide and exhibited both sides of their hands, Blackford thought he must there and then laugh, cry, or

flee. He did none of these, but in showing his hands and opening his mouth, he inaugurated that cultivated air of discreet defiance which had made him now, after only eight weeks, something of a celebrity.

He found, for instance, the cloying repetition of the word "sir" obsequious to the point of debasement. "You know, Aunt Alice," he had written from the depths of despair on the fourth day, "around here you are supposed to say *sir* every other word, practically. I'll give you an example. You want the butter, and it's sitting in front of the master. You're supposed to say, *Sir? Please, sir. Would you pass the butter, sir?* Well, as they say here, I'm bloody well not going to do that c-r-a-p."

He wondered, worriedly, whether, at this safe distance, he wasn't taking cowardly liberties—using an obscenity in a letter to his aunt. He reckoned correctly that in her absorbing concern for him she would not pause to reproach him on this count. She wrote: "My darling Blacky: You mustn't be defiant, dear. The English are after all a different people from us, and they have their own customs. Remember, dear, they didn't ask you to go to their school, you asked (through your stepfather) to go, and they let you in, so it's only fair to do it their way. Besides, you will be a lot happier."

But Blackford found himself happiest when skating breezily along the edges of defiance. ("Would you pass the butter? . . . sir?") After the first week his reliable spirits began, after measured decompressions, to revive. He was, in any case, desperately busy, from 6:45 A.M., when the bell in the cold-cold antiseptic dormitory clanged and the boys in dressing gowns rushed down to the lavatory, until 9 P.M., when a master at one end of the dormitory recited the psalm De Profundis, and the boys gave the responses in

Latin, read out in the dim light of their cubicles, from a printed card permanently tacked to the inside of the door of the dresser which opened so that, lying on their beds, they could discern the ten-point print; whereupon all the lights went, implacably, out.

Blackford's first concern was his academic work. He had no trouble in English or in history—it was as easy to learn about the Plantagenet kings as about the Founding Fathers; in fact, he found the kings, on casual acquaintance, less confusing and (he did not divulge this) rather more exciting. In beginning French he found he could easily stay abreast of his class, and in mathematics he showed the flair that later would put him at the top percentile in his college aptitude tests. Geography was a bore—simply another subject—and his quick memory was wonderfully useful to him.

His trouble was with Latin. Although he had had a year of it at Scarsdale and was only in second-year Latin at Greyburn, here the boys were already reading Caesar, and Blackford found Caesar *utterly impenetrable*. The master, Mr. Simon, was a veteran of generations of ineptitude in teaching Latin and reacted to student mystification with a blend of scorn and tyranny. A grizzled man in his late fifties, with sideburns and spectacles, Mr. Simon—one of the boys told Blackford—had many years ago proposed to a lady in Latin and, on finding her response ungrammatical, resolved upon celibacy. Latin was his wife, and mistress, and catamite. He wooed his muse with seductive little mannerisms he had over the years satisfied himself were endearing to young boys, and marvelous instruments of a successful pedagogy.

Blackford began on the wrong side of Mr. Simon by suggesting that, as an American, he should, by all rights, be permitted to continue to inflect Latin nouns according to

the American sequence rather than the English sequence— on the grounds that to change now from nominative, genitive, dative, accusative, and ablative to the English sequence would terribly and prejudicially confuse him.

The other twenty boys in the class were awed into silence. Only the older boy in the back row, a fifth-former and prefect who, because he too was behind, was required to take third-form Latin with his juniors, dared to speak out.

"Sir, that's a pretty good point."

The boys all laughed, because he was the *other* American at Greyburn.

Mr. Simon replied: "You will have harder adjustments to make, Oakes, than slightly to rearrange the order of noun inflections. I *suggest* you resolve to learn it the right way, or, I suppose, I had better say"—and he smiled, lifting his hands to tug on the lapels of his academic robe, the characteristic posture when he thought himself about to say something withering or amusing—"the English way."

"Hear, hear!" the boys said, at once docile and chauvinistic.

"Do you also conjugate the *verbs* differently in America, Oakes? Another habit acquired from the Indians?"

The boys roared. Oakes flushed, doodling on his pad, conscious that everyone was looking at him, unlearned in the artifices of appearing indifferent. Mr. Simon then delivered what Blackford came to recognize as his favorite homily: the necessity of learning Latin nouns and their declensions, and Latin verbs and their conjugations, particularly the irregular verbs, by repeating them to oneself *in every circumstance.*

"Don't put the subject *out of your mind* when you leave the classroom. *Think* about a *difficult* verb when you are walking along the corridors between classes. When you are

having your *tea*. When you are *running out to the playing field*. Remember: *Qui cogitat quod debet facere, solet conficere quod debet facere*." Mr. Simon beamed as he attempted to dittify his maxim in English: "Those who think about their duty / Are those who end by doing their duty!"

At tea that afternoon—the sole, blissful repast at which the boys were unsupervised, and their banter unheard by a presiding master—Blackford remarked to the boy opposite, who was also in the class, that Simon was a pompous ass, and the boy replied in the public school drawl (one Blackford was determined would never be allowed to creep into his own speech) that how else could he have achieved such high standing at Greyburn? The veteran Greyburnian remarked: "Simon's been here practically since he left his blubbing mother's arms. He used to recite an original poem in Latin at Class Day exercises, until five years ago when he just plain overdid it—he recited thirty-two verses. When Dr. Chase came in, he changed the ceremony, moving Mr. Simon back to the 'Academic Reminiscences' hour scheduled the day before, which is voluntary. . . . He's always in a bad humor now, because he really thinks that, though he is tops in Latin, he really ought to be a *general!*"

The boys laughed. "He was a lieutenant in the last war. He'll tell you about it."

"He'll tell you about it for three hours, if you don't watch yourself," another boy chimed in, reaching over Blackford for the jam.

"*I'm* surprised," a third boy said, munching a piece of bread piled high with butter and marmalade, "he doesn't begin his classes with 'God Save the King.' He tunes in to the BBC five times a day to get the war news. The man he hates most in the world, after Hitler, is Charles Lindbergh."

Blackford said nothing. He was paralyzed with indignation. The great hero of world aviation! Charles Lindbergh, the scientist and patriot! Charles Lindbergh, the great advocate of American peace! Charles Lindbergh, his father's *earliest and best friend!*

Blackford had had experience in America, as the divisions over there hardened between the interventionists and the isolationists, with boys who, usually echoing their parents' views, disparaged Lindbergh, the leader of the America First movement. Blackford had a fistfight with a Lindbergh iconoclast at Scarsdale. But here, three thousand miles away from America, he found it a corporate affront that a sacrosanct master should feel free to belittle so great a man (who, when Blackford was ten years old, had taken him up in his own airplane for a joyride that unforgettable afternoon when his family visited the Lindberghs in Rhode Island).

Dear Aunt Alice:

This is very important. Please, even if you forget to send me the Milky Ways, don't forget this. I want you to send me right away two buttons (the kind you stick into your lapels), one button that just says on it *America First,* another button that has Lindbergh's face on it, with his name under it. If you don't have these buttons around, please go, or send Billy, to the America First Headquarters, where they will give them to you for nothing. It is on 44th Street, Lexington Avenue. DON'T FORGET!!!

Much love,
Blacky

At the end of the second week at Greyburn, he attended the third, and final, compulsory lecture about school life given for the new boys, of whom there were thirty in the

Upper School, twenty of them third-formers. The first two lectures had touched on school practices, holidays, vacations, sports, academic schedules, regulations involving health, writing home. This one concerned discipline.

The speaker was a tall, spare, youngish man whose title was School Secretary and Assistant to the Headmaster. He taught one class in ancient history and was otherwise occupied helping the headmaster with his administrative chores, interviewing prospective students, collating the grades that went out to the parents, and occasionally representing the headmaster at official functions. His face was pallid, and without expression, except for what seemed like a running, permanent, ineradicable leer (his name, as if to rub it in, was Mr. *Leary!*). His accent was the most exaggeratedly British Blackford had ever heard. It was a strain even to understand him.

What Mr. Leary said was that the standards of Greyburn had always been high, but that in time of war they would be set higher than ever before, that this was a time of great national tribulation, that the sons of England's most privileged families in particular should recognize their special obligation to grow quickly, to do their work well, and to obey their superiors.

"Now," he continued, "as some of you no doubt have heard, Dr. Chase, on becoming headmaster, withdrew from the school's prefects the privilege, or rather the *duty*—a much better way to put it—of administering the rod. It was widely suggested among some Old Boys that Dr. Chase was 'modernizing' the school and permitting its standards to deteriorate. *That*"—Mr. Leary . . . leered—"*any* boy who has been at Greyburn during the past five years would now know better than to believe. Although the use of the rod is

now reserved to housemasters and to the headmaster, its use is not for that reason any the more . . . disdained. There is no reason for anybody sitting in this room," said Mr. Leary, "to experience the birch before graduating from Greyburn. But," he warned, with a tight smile, "the statistics are heavily against such a probability—that boys *will be* boys is *more* than a *mere* truism—but after all, the *purpose* of punishment is to *advance* a boy's understanding of his obligations, and therefore the use of the rod is, really, *designed* to bring boys to the stage where they *do not need the rod* to behave like civilized human beings."

Friday, he said, is the day in which the headmaster interviews miscreants and administers punishment, after weighing reports on the behavior of individual boys. At tea time, any boy who is to report to the headmaster's office will find a blue slip on his plate with his name on it.

"As for the housemasters, they attend to their own corrections in their own way at their own time."

Were there questions?

There were none. The room was as silent as any Blackford had ever been in. He could hear only his heart beating, and he noticed that even after Mr. Leary had left the platform, the boys stayed briefly in their chairs, before getting up and, silently, filing out.

Another month went by, and now instead of cheering the team, Blackford was on it—the junior team to be sure—being cheered. He had quickly adjusted to rugger, and his fleet-footedness and natural sense of tactical guile were of great advantage—to be preferred, he reluctantly concluded, to the hulking Maginot Line of football at Scarsdale, where the huge shoulder and hip pads always made him feel a little

creaky, and the quarterbacks thought in terms of feet and even inches gained, as against tens of yards. He made dazzling runs on three successive Saturdays, and there was even talk that he might be put on the senior team, though he was a little light for the senior scrum, and it was said that Mr. Long thought it advisable to wait until the next season. Meanwhile, Oakes would be tried out in cricket.

He was popular with the boys quite apart from his athletic prowess. They liked his natural manners, his frankness of expression, his ingenuous American informality, especially in tight situations involving the masters and the prefects. Mr. Manning, his housemaster, observed him with something like fascination and desisted from pulling him up short, which he had several concrete provocations for doing, most concretely after *twice* discovering Oakes calmly reading in bed with a flashlight—strictly forbidden in the rules. He excused his indulgence on the grounds that Blackford was after all American, and needed time to make the sharp adjustment to English ways. At a faculty tea, Mr. Manning defended his permissiveness toward Oakes in a casual comment that suddenly engrossed the entire company in a general discussion about the extraordinarily self-assured young American who was lightheartedly making his way through Greyburn with an indefinable cultural insouciance, the most palpable feature of which was a total absence of that docility which was universally accepted as something on the order of a genetic attribute in Greyburn Boys.

"I tell him to fetch the atlas," the geography teacher, lowering his teacup, remarked, "and he pauses—for *just a moment*—as if he is *considering* whether he will *grant* my request! And then, just one second short of refractoriness,

he will say, with an incandescent smile, 'Sure!' Somehow *I can't make myself* say to him: 'Say, "Yes, *sir!*"' It would leave me feeling not only the martinet, but as if I had earned his absolutely predictable condescension . . . the strangest, most independent boy I have ever known, and frankly, one of the most attractive."

Mr. Long, the athletic coach, saw an opening and moved in heavily—as an outspoken defender of Oakes. "I have never found him insolent, and he is every bit the team player. With his legs and lungs he could hang on to the ball and play only for the gallery. He works with the team, though, and they like and admire him even though he is . . . different."

Dr. Chase, in an infrequent appearance at the weekly faculty tea, said nothing.

Nor did Mr. Simon, for fear he would betray his very strong feelings about Oakes.

Mr. Long—under fire from Oakes's history teacher—did admit that Oakes's outspoken advocacy of the cause of American isolation *was* galling.

"You would think," the history teacher said, "he would keep his views to himself for so long as he is a student at a British school."

At this Mr. Simon could not keep silent. "You would think he would take the trouble to learn something about Hitler's global ambitions before urging the position that only the British should shed blood in defense of the English-speaking world."

"Actually," Mr. Long persisted, "I overheard him yesterday arguing with two of the boys at lunch, and his arguments are remarkably well marshaled. He made it a point of saying that *he* doesn't bring up the subject except when one

of the English boys does, and that far from being presumptuous in speaking out on the subject, he is presumptively—that wasn't the word he used—better entitled to express himself on what America should do than Englishmen."

Dr. Chase spoke up, lifting an eyebrow customarily set in concrete. "He said that?"

"Yes, Head; exactly that."

Dr. Chase was silent; then he rose, and without looking to right or left, intoned quietly, "Come along, Leary," and they filed out of the faculty lounge, the headmaster and the assistant to the headmaster.

"Good afternoon, gentlemen," he said on reaching the door, again without looking aside.

"Good afternoon, Head," was the chorused response.

By early December, it was somehow palpable that the crisis of Blackford Oakes must come. It had to happen was the consensus, and even the strongest partisans of Blackford sensed inevitability—the institutional integrity of Greyburn required the formal subjugation of this coltish alien. Last week he had shown up at Mr. Simon's class, a serene expression on his handsome boyish features, flaunting, on his lapels, an *America First* button and a *Lindbergh* button. Mr. Simon had looked down on him—Blackford sat, as a new boy, in the front row—very nearly speechless (indeed he had to clear his throat the better part of a full minute before proceeding), and then delivered, defensively and to gain the time necessary to settle his emotions, his standard lecture on the need to Think Latin outside the classroom. Blackford pocketed the buttons on leaving Mr. Simon's classroom; but every day, at ten in the morning, which was the Latin III hour, he would reach into his

pocket, fasten the two buttons on his lapels, and stride jauntily into the room, sometimes whistling a tune. At this he was not competent, since he could not carry a melody, but those who listened hard could discern an effort at "Yankee Doodle Dandy."

The end came early in December. The French teacher announced that he would have to leave his class at a quarter before the hour because he had to catch the eleven-fifteen train to London. So, finding ten minutes of leisure, the six boys from the French class who would also meet together for Latin III at ten strolled down the hallway, passing a half-dozen classrooms in session, reaching Mr. Simon's ten minutes early. It was empty. Blackford, giving way to a pent-up fancy, found himself at the blackboard, chalk in hand, sketching furiously. From the swift and authoritative strokes there emerged a most recognizable caricature of Mr. Simon, bushy sideburns and all, academic cape flowing in the wind. His legs, however, were awkwardly separated, his member exposed, the stream issuing from it arcing splashily to the ground. A dotted line from the lips of the master led to a balloon, within which Blackford, imitating the holographic style of his teacher, who a few days earlier had explained the English evolution ("micturate") of Caesar's word to describe his soldiers' careless habits when emptying their bladder, indited the words: "Mingo, Mingere, Minxi, Mictum." Triumphantly, Blackford autographed the sketch: "B. Oakes, discipulus."

The boys howled with laughter and glee, overcome with pleasure at the artistic feat of retaliation. One of them in due course said, "Oakes, you had better rub it off. It's five minutes to ten."

But Mr. Simon was always *exactly* on time, and Black-

ford wanted to share his creation with more of his classmates, who already were dribbling in and, alerted to the
cause of the excitement, looked instantly at the cynosure
on the blackboard and exploded in squeals of delight and
ribaldry.

It was those yells, issuing from his own classroom, that
prompted Mr. Simon to snuff out his cigarette, rather than
finish it outdoors, so as to time his entry, as was his habit, to
ten o'clock exactly, and stride into the Caulfield Center
building. As senior master, he had title to the first classroom
on the right. Thus he entered the room two and one-half
minutes before the hour. There was sudden, stunned silence. He followed the boys' eyes to the blackboard. He
lifted his head slightly to study the sketch through the
appropriate lenses of his bifocals. He then shut the classroom door and walked deliberately down the passage to the
teacher's platform, up the single step, sat down at his desk,
hinged open the cover, and drew out stationery and, from
his vest pocket, a fountain pen.

"Jennings," he said, without even looking in the direction of the boy who that week was in charge of wiping the
blackboard before, during, and after Latin III, "wipe the
board."

Quickly, nervously, Jennings, plump and bespectacled,
slid in the continuing silence to the board and with a few
vigorous strokes, beginning furtively with one that erased
Blackford's signature, eliminated the lapidary caricature of
the Latin master, shown constructively engaged in following his own advice of Thinking Latin on every occasion.

You could hear in the room only the stroking of Mr.
Simon's pen on his note pad.

"Dr. Chase, FOR IMMEDIATE ATTENTION," he wrote.

Sir:

B. Oakes, who is in my division Latin III, has committed
an offense, gross, insolent, and obscene—a drawing on the
blackboard seen by all the other students—more disgusting
than anything I have seen in my thirty-three years' experience as a teacher. I request—nay, I require—that he receive
the most vigorous punishment, or else that he be expelled
from Greyburn. No alternative treatment of him would
make it possible for me to continue to discharge my responsibilities.

Yours truly,
A. Simon.

He folded the note into an envelope, scratched out "Dr.
Chase, For Immediate Attention," and called out, "Prefect."

"Yes, sir." The other American stood at the rear of the
room.

"You will take this message to the headmaster at his study
and conduct Oakes there—immediately."

Anthony Trust waited at the door as Blackford, turned
faintly white, rose, walked across the classroom, and came
back along the length of it to where the prefect stood waiting. Trust closed the classroom door quietly behind them
and led the way to the front door.

The headmaster's office was diagonally across the huge
campus, a ten-minute walk.

"What will he do?" Oakes found himself asking, as he
walked alongside Trust. The morning's frost lingered on
the pathway in the cold winter gray of Berkshire.

"What will he do? He'll beat you."

"When?"

"Probably this afternoon, after tea. I doubt he'll put it off a whole week till the usual time on Friday, if I can guess what's sizzling inside this letter. Maybe he'll even do it right now."

"Has it ever happened to you?"

"Sure. Twice, last year—once in the fall, once in the winter."

"Is it pretty . . . bad?"

"It's bad. It is indescribably bad. But really, Oakes, you *were*, as the guys here say, an awful *ass*."

They passed by his dormitory, and Oakes's housemaster, walking in the opposite direction, gave him a cheerful greeting, which Oakes returned, with effort.

"How do they do it?"

"How?"

Trust groaned at the ignorance of his compatriot. "Well, you get a lecture first. Then Leary-deary will pull over the library step—what you use to reach for a book on a high shelf—and drag it over until the back is up against the arm of Dr. Chase's big black leather sofa. Then you kneel on the block—that's what they call it—over the arm of the chair. But before, they make you take off your coat and loosen your suspenders—they call them braces here, in case you don't yet know that. Then Leary slides up your shirt and pulls down your shorts."

"Pulls down my shorts!" Oakes stopped in mid campus, his mouth open, eyes flashing. "You're *kidding!*"

"I am not *'kidding.'* They've been doing it that way for three hundred years, and the Old Boys wouldn't want any detail to change, no siree. After all, they went through it, and look how *marvelous* they are—that's the argument."

Oakes was silent again as they resumed their walk toward Execution Hall.

"How many strokes will I get?" he suddenly asked.

"It's usually six maximum. You'll get the maximum, all right."

"What does a birch rod look like?"

"Like a lot of long twigs, maybe a dozen, tied together at the bottom by string. They're made up by Johnson." Oakes liked Johnson, Greyburn's kindly man of all trades who only last week had fixed Blackford's bicycle chain. "After two weeks, Leary will tell you with great pride, *all* Dr. Chase's rods are automatically replaced. He doesn't like them to get stale. Less sting. Only the best of *everything* at Greyburn."

"Will I . . . cry?"

"If you're normal."

"Is it only Leary and Dr. Chase in the room?"

"No. There's a prefect. I hope to *God* he does it after tea, or next week, because then some other prefect will be there. If he does it now, it will be me, sure as shooting. How do you like that! Come all the way from Toledo, Ohio, to Berks., England, to hold down a kid from New York being spanked on his ass—that's great!"

They arrived at the stone building, the Elizabeth Caulfield Memorial Building, the first floor of which was occupied by the record and bill keepers, the second reserved for the headmaster. Trust led the way, going up the steep stone staircase. He knocked on the door of the headmaster's antechamber. Mr. Leary's voice sounded through the thick oak door.

"Come in."

Mr. Leary sat at his desk, opposite a sofa. At the far end of the long room, eight or ten chairs were spread about and a few old magazines on a small table. On the walls, a half-

dozen etchings and photographs of Greyburn, four of them, dating back to the eighteenth century, faded into a sepia brown.

"What is it?" asked Leary, looking up at the two boys.

"I have been instructed by Mr. Simon to bring Dr. Chase this, sir," Trust said, handing the letter to him.

Leary seized it. Though it was addressed directly to Chase, he broke the seal without a moment's hesitation, passing his eyes, unhurriedly, over the enclosure.

He looked up.

"Sit down, both of you." And to Oakes, softly, with a hint of the hangman's humor: ". . . while you can."

He opened the door on the left end of the room by his desk, closed it, and strode down the length of the dark library, past the single window, opening, without knocking, a door at the left, at the far corner.

Dr. Chase was on the telephone.

The inner sanctum of Greyburn College was not large. When Dr. Chase had more than two visitors, he would elect to sit with them in the roomy library next door. Here it was just the two chairs opposite his authoritative desk, a few shelves of books, one or two pictures, a door to a private lavatory, and, through a bay window, a fine view of the college quadrangle. But the light, in the winter, was weak, so that the lamp on Dr. Chase's desk was lit, X-raying his long thin hand, outstretched, now, to receive the envelope his automated servant Leary had wordlessly extended to him.

Whoever was on the line was doing most of the talking. By the time Dr. Chase had got around to saying, "Very well, then, we'll meet in London rather than here, Your Grace," he had read the missive Mr. Simon had handed him. He

hung up the telephone and eased his chair forward into the light's territory, no longer a penumbral figure with a disembodied hand reaching like a tentacle from under the rock into the lit spaces of the world to transact necessary business. His rhythm through it all was unbroken, from the shadow of his telephone to the operating-table brilliance of the appointments calendar on his desk.

"Well, I suppose we shall have to have him come in after tea. No, dash it, I see I shan't be here—a council meeting in the town . . . tomorrow seems too far away. Sunday is bad for this kind of thing. And anyway, it's no way to placate old Simon. He is very riled, and"—Dr. Chase exposed for the first time his extra-perfunctory interest in Blackford Oakes— "I wouldn't say I'd blame him, dealing with that cheeky American brat."

"May I make a suggestion, sir?" Leary was valuable not only for making helpful suggestions but for making suggestions of particular, though not obvious, appeal to Dr. Chase. "Why not do it now? Your appointment with Dr. Keith isn't until eleven, and it's only ten-twenty. You wouldn't have to leave here for fifteen or twenty minutes in any case."

Dr. Chase reflected, primarily for the sake of appearing deliberate. He made decisions quickly.

"Very well. But is there a prefect about?"

"Mr. Simon thinks of everything," Mr. Leary smiled. "He sent Anthony Trust along as an escort."

"Very well." Dr. Chase was now the man of action. "Never mind bringing the boy in here first. We'll omit that. Put him straight down. I'll talk to him when he's ready."

Mr. Leary walked back to his office, saying nothing to the boys as he opened the door of the antechamber and posted,

on the permanent hook outside, the frayed cardboard notice, "PLEASE DO NOT DISTURB," normally reserved for late Friday afternoons and for faculty meetings. Then he turned to the boys, who had risen respectfully on his entrance. "Follow me."

They went into the library. Sitting in a chair and leafing through a black-bound register, Leary addressed Anthony without looking up at him, standing across the way, self-consciously, in the gray light, Oakes at his side. "Trust, it hasn't been all that long since you were here on . . . official business. You do remember what is expected of a prefect?" Trust said nothing, from which Leary assumed he had the answer he wanted.

To Oakes:

"Take off your coat, put it on the chair over there"—he pointed to an upright chair all but hidden behind the window light—"and loosen your braces. It's quite *simple*, Oakes, merely unbutton the buttons forward and back; or, if you prefer, take off your vest and slide the braces off your shoulders."

Leary went off to the corner of the room and lifted the two-tiered block from under the bookcases, depositing it up against the sofa. It reposed now directly under the window, the shaft of light sharply but severely illuminating the block, isolating it altogether from the shadowed arm of the sofa to which it was now conjoined.

Oakes stood, coatless, not knowing, exactly, what to do. His trousers did not need the braces to keep them up, so his arms hung limp by his sides.

"Come here," Leary motioned.

Oakes approached him.

"Unbutton your fly buttons." He waited.

"Now, kneel on the *lower* step, and bring your arms over the arm of the sofa."

Blackford did so. He felt, then, the cold hands of Mr. Leary taking up his shirttail and tucking it, tidily under his vest. And then, with a snapping motion, Leary yanked down the shorts, leaving Oakes with naked posteriors, cold, and— he thought in his fright and amazement—trembling, as they jutted up at a forty-five-degree angle, as exquisitely postured as any guillotine block to oblige the executioner.

"Ready, Head," Mr. Leary sang out without actually approaching the headmaster's door.

Dr. Chase did not materialize instantly. There was a long minute's wait before Blackford could hear the steps approaching. He looked up as best he could at the tall and silent face of this man who ruled thus conclusively over the bodies and minds of 625 boys. Dr. Chase moved to a long cupboard directly opposite from that part of the sofa over which Black's head was suspended, took a key chain from his pocket, located the right key, and opened the cupboard. At that moment, back in the study, the telephone rang. Leaving the door open, Dr. Chase walked resolutely, unhurriedly, back into his study, and though the sounds of the brief conversation reached the library, the words did not. Meanwhile Black, bent over, stared at the contents of the open closet. Two or three bundles of birch rods, several bamboo canes, and what appeared to be a collection of slippers, sitting at the bottom. Dr. Chase returned, selected, after some deliberation, a particular birch rod, withdrew it, laid it on a table by the far end of the sofa, sat down opposite Oakes, and took the black leather register handed to him by Mr. Leary, opened at the right page. Dr. Chase spoke for the first time.

"Oakes. O-a-k-e-s. I have a good many complaints here about you, Oakes, though I have not previously acted on any of them. My mistake, I can see now. Tell me, sir, have you ever been beaten?"

Blackford was hot now not only with fear but with rage. But he knew that nothing—no threat, no punishment— would deprive him of the imperative satisfaction of answering curtly. "No," he said.

Dr. Chase seemed to grow whiter, but then the same chalk-white shaft of light that shone on Oakes's rear end now flooded Dr. Chase's face as he bent over his register, scribbling on the page reserved for *O-a-k-e-s, B.,* a record of the forthcoming ministration.

"Perhaps, sir," Dr. Chase said icily, "that accounts for your bad manners?"

Oakes said nothing.

"We have a great deal to accomplish, here in Britain, during the next period. But we are not unwilling to take time for a little foreign aid. Perhaps America is not prepared to help Britain. But here at Greyburn, Britain is prepared to help America"—he stood up, handed the book to Mr. Leary, and walked over toward the rod—"even if our aid is administered to only one American at a time."

The moment had come, and suddenly Oakes found Trust's hands grabbing him at the armpits, forcing his head down. Now, his face on the leather cushion, he could see the bottom half of Dr. Chase, walking over toward the executioner's position.

"You will receive nine strokes."

Black could hear Anthony gasp.

Again there was a pause, and the whistling sound of the rod as Dr. Chase limbered his arm. After that, a moment

such as, Oakes thought—in the furious state of his mind, recalling the war stories he had read so avidly that summer— the soldiers experience just before beginning their charge: the whole body and mind frozen in anticipation. What happened then he could not have anticipated. The rod, the instrument of all Dr. Chase's strength, wrath, and resentment, descended, and the pain was indescribable, outrageous, unforgettable. Oakes shouted as if he had been hosed down by a flamethrower. His legs shot out from the block. *"Hold him tight,"* Dr. Chase hissed at Trust, who applied his whole body's strength to holding Blackford down. The rod descended again, and Oakes's lower body writhed in spastic reaction, but could not avoid the descending birch, which came down, again; and again; and again. There was a slight, endless interval between the strokes—five, ten seconds—during which Dr. Chase, grim satisfaction written on his face, studied Oakes's movements like a hunter the movements of a bird dog, the better to anticipate, and connect the rod to, the buttocks with maximum effect. Oakes's screams were continuous, uncontrollable, an amalgam of pain, fear, mortification. But when the ninth stroke was given he suddenly fell silent, as Trust's grip relaxed. The room was noiseless. Dr. Chase, breathing heavily and drawing back his rod, red with Blackford's blood, said raspily:

"Courtesy of Great Britain, sir."

He handed the rod to Leary, disdaining to return it himself to the closet, walked rhythmically to his office, and closed the door. Oakes did not change his position for a minute or two during which he was convulsed with a silent sobbing. Leary busied himself for a moment with unimportant details, shutting the closet door, replacing the register

in the drawer; and then, finally, left to go to his own office, leaving the library to Trust and Oakes.

"You'd better try to come along now, Oakes." Trust discreetly pulled up the shorts, and gently prodded him by the shoulder, first to lean back, and, finally, to stand up.

"Now, try raising your pants. Easy."

Blackford's blond face was ashen, but his eyes had dried. He struggled to lift up his pants. Without bothering to fasten his suspenders, he reached for his coat, and Trust helped him put it on. He groped his way to Mr. Leary's back door, opened it, and passed through the antechamber without comment to the assistant to the headmaster, walking, as best he could, down the staircase. As he passed through the front door, held open for him by Trust, he detected the gaze of the two ladies in the administrative office, who no doubt had stopped their work to pity or—who knows?—perhaps to celebrate the youthful screams, which must have penetrated the ceiling like a burglar alarm. He felt like flinging open the side door and shouting out, "Would you like a repeat performance tomorrow, ladies? Same time? Same place?" But his imaginary resilience proved very nearly nauseating, and he felt he had to stop to swallow, or be sick. Trust stayed with him, saying nothing as Oakes, head down, waddled, which was all he could manage to do, in the direction of his dormitory. He didn't know exactly why he was headed there, but at that point Trust's voice, rather shakily, but in unequivocal accents of pity and shared outrage that gave a moment's life to Oakes's spirit, said, "We'll go to the lavatory. Cold water will help a lot, and right away."

Trust brought up two empty wooden cases from the store closet opposite the empty lavatory, on which Oakes's

feet could perch. Then he poured cold water into the large washbasin, and once again Oakes pulled down his clothes, and sat. The relief was immediate, overwhelming, blissful. He perched there while Trust kept running in cold water. They said nothing, as Blackford's mind settled. It did so quickly. In ten minutes, he said, "Can I call you Anthony?"

"Sure."

"Well, I have to leave Greyburn."

"Don't. Chase has got it out of his system. Now Greyburn is *secure*." Suddenly Trust was less positive. "I don't think they'll keep after you."

Blackford went on without comment. "Anthony, I want you to do one thing for me, which I can't do for myself."

"What is it?"

"I want you to use the telephone in the prefects' lounge to order a taxi to meet me outside Caulfield Hall at one o'clock. I can't approach the housemaster and ask permission to use the telephone at this point."

Anthony's orthodoxy collapsed. Suddenly, willingly—enthusiastically—he was the coconspirator, sharing the wrath Blackford felt at the sadistic and xenophobic episode in which, the guilt began to assault him, he had somehow served as coexecutioner. He wondered, should he have *refused?* Told Dr. Chase that *no*, he, Anthony Trust, *declined* to opinion down a fellow American to accommodate one Briton's vindictiveness? But, he reflected—Anthony was always judicious—the anti-American animus was not really all that transparent until just before the punishment began, and on through the ferocity of it and the hideously redundant final blows. . . . There *was* that premonitory crack, at the beginning, about foreign aid. . . . For a wild moment Anthony thought of taking off with Blackford; but

reality quickly overtook him, as he tabulated the arguments, and reckoned that from such a flight he had everything to lose and nothing to gain, except a moment's satisfaction.

Meanwhile his enthusiasm for Blackford's resolution had become a commitment, at whatever risk to his own standing.

"Okay. I'll call Leicester Drivers. But why one o'clock? It's only eleven-fifteen. If you want to slip away earlier, I'll help you pack."

"I don't *want* to slip away. I can pack in fifteen minutes. Then I'll go to lunch."

"You must be nuts! Go to the refectory and advertise the fact that you're running away from school because you were beaten?"

"I am not running away from school. I am leaving school."

"Great God." Anthony wondered: Would the school forcibly stop him? He could think of no real precedent. Last year one of the boys in the Lower School ran away, but he sneaked off at night, taking the bus from Greyburn Town. He was back in two days, driven to the school by his irate father, was soundly beaten, and—Anthony vaguely remembered being told—was doing very nicely this term. Anthony could not conceive of a protracted, let alone ceremonial, departure from Greyburn when the departure was *itself utterly illicit.* He was certain only of this: He could either cooperate with Blackford or desert him; nothing in between. Anthony had not been invited by this strangely independent fellow-American to help formulate his plans, merely to help execute them. The boy sitting half naked in the washbasin gave off a nearly regal sense of rectitude and authority. Anthony had only to see how it would all proceed. He was not there to interpose.

"We'd better get moving. I'll help you up. It's going to

hurt again in a matter of minutes, after the cold wears off. After I call the taxi, I'll bring you some stuff I have left over from last year, which you can apply. It's for burns, and it dulls the pain."

Blackford stood up, shakily, stepped off the wooden cases, and drew up his trousers. The pain resumed, intensely, and his eyes were once more hot with pain.

He tried walking naturally. It was very difficult, but by the time he reached the staircase, he was managing a kind of deliberate and synthetically symmetrical gait.

"I'll make the call, then I'll come to your dorm—what number are you?—and help you. Five minutes." Anthony streaked out, and Blackford, his hand on the railing, moved himself, the left foot up, the right following, the left foot up again, the right following. He reached the landing and walked toward his little cubicle, along the neat row with the white hanging curtains drawn, the beds, the window sills on which personal belongings were permitted, pictures of parents and sisters, school photographs. He came to his own, halfway down the corridor, closed the curtain behind him, and, leaning against the dresser, wept convulsively. He must stop, he thought. Quickly. He leaned over, painfully, to open the drawers of the dresser, to take out his clothes. His suitcases were stored in the locker room, inaccessible. He would leave them there and pile his clothes into two laundry bags. He had already begun to do this when Anthony slipped through the curtains and whispered, "The taxi is all set." He helped Blackford stuff his clothes into the bags. Suddenly he stopped.

"Blackford, you'd better change your pants."

Blackford moved his hand behind him, felt nothing, and asked, "Why?"

"Because. Take them off."

Blackford did, and saw the spots. He removed his shorts, gazing with awe at the streaky bloodstains. He accepted from Anthony the proffered tube. With great care he applied the unguent first on one buttock, then on the other. He took fresh drawers and stepped into them. Then another pair of pants, and suddenly, the balm taking hold, he felt better, and his appetite increased for a last lunch at Greyburn College.

By the time he reached the refectory, promptly at 12:15, the word had obviously traveled to all corners of the school—it is so in schools—that the problem of Blackford Oakes had been disposed of, and all eyes were on him as he filed silently (the boys were not permitted to talk until the presiding master had said grace) to his customary place at the table. After grace, everyone sat down, except Blackford, who in any case could not have done so. Freshly birched boys routinely ate off the mantelpiece for a day or so, and it was expected he would go there, where a plate would be brought to him, and where he could chat with several survivors of Bleak Friday, the afternoon before. Instead he turned to the boy on his left, stretched out his hand, and said, "Good-bye, Dodson. I'm leaving Greyburn. It has been very good to know you."

Dodson, who found all things amusing, was tempted to laugh, but decided, his soup spoon barely out of his mouth, against doing so; instead he dropped the spoon and stuck out his hand. There was a terrible gravity in the good-bye he had just received from Oakes, who now was saying good-bye to Oldfield, continuing his tour around the table. The master, a young physicist called Mr. Brown, watched with fascination and suddenly found that it was his turn.

"So long, Mr. Brown. It has been very nice to know you."

The table was now quiet, and as Blackford walked off stiffly to say good-bye, selectively, to special friends here and there at other tables, the entire refectory gradually fell silent. Blackford appeared not to notice, and the whispering then began, in accents of awe, disbelief, and dismay. But no one did what Anthony most feared someone might do. Perhaps because everyone knew Blackford enough to know that to call him a coward would be implausible. And there was something in the precocious solemnity of the courtly tour around the large refectory that gainsaid schoolboy jeering. He did it all—from the lowly Dodson to the final occupant of the main table, the formidable head prefect, the Scottish aristocrat who, at age seventeen, was already a world-renowned equestrian—in six or seven minutes, his voice audible only to the person he was addressing. When passing by the presiding master—this week it was an utterly dumbstruck Spaniard, who taught his own language and Italian—he merely bowed slightly, stopping to shake hands with a genial prefect on his right. Then, without looking back, he opened the door of the refectory, and closed it on an explosion, the animated bustle of three hundred boys wondering whether they could believe their eyes.

Anthony rose from the main table, whispered to Mr. Castroviejo that he was suffering from a stomachache, left the refectory sedately, and then rushed down the hall, catching up with Blackford at the door. Together they crossed the quadrangle and climbed the stairs to Blackford's room, where Anthony insisted on picking up the two bulky laundry bags.

"I'll write to you, Anthony."

"But Blackford, your old man is bound to send you back. Oh God, what will they do to you then?"

"I won't be coming back," said Blackford, as they walked down to find a Leicester taxi waiting. There was no one else in sight. Blackford opened the door, put one of the laundry bags on the backseat, smoothed it out, gave the other bag to the driver, eased himself in, and, gently, lowered his weight on his cushion.

"We are driving to London," he told the driver, and returned Anthony's wave as the car pulled out.

Mr. Castroviejo, revived, rushed across to the headmaster's home to give him the news. Dr. Chase, caught at lunch with his wife and twenty-five-year-old daughter, clenched his fists on the seat of his chair, his mind racing. He *could* stop Oakes. But that would require physical force. And what then would he do? There were no *prison cells* at Greyburn. He could hardly, in Oakes's present condition, beat him again. He resolved that at best, by attempting to detain Oakes, he would risk indignity. Oakes would be back. If it required a few days, or a week, so much the better—he would be ready for another dose of the birch, he thought smugly.

But Dr. Chase experienced a real alarm. What if, on reaching London, Oakes should exhibit his backside to his parents? The nightmare took wings, and Dr. Chase had visions of Blackford Oakes reporting to Ambassador Kennedy or the American Embassy, and calling in the press to photograph his lacerated posteriors. What would the press in America do with that—the story of the American boy who spoke his mind in an English school!

Chase snapped out his orders to Castroviejo. He was to go fetch Mr. Simon *instantly.* He would get an affidavit, Dr.

Chase thought, and maybe signed statements from several of the boys in the class, testifying to Oakes's unparalleled insolence. He *did* wish now that he had beaten him a little less viciously, a little less . . . thoroughly. Too many people are too easily shocked by the stern discipline of fine public schools, he thought. But the trustees would *not like* the publicity. And what if, in America, it did become a cause célèbre? How he wished he had never consented to admit young Oakes. Trust! Trust!—he remembered. He had been witness to Dr. Chase's acid remarks about America.

"Geraldine," he barked to his daughter, "go right now to the refectory and get a prefect—any prefect—to find Anthony Trust. T-R-U-S-T. Have Trust come here *instantly.*"

He wondered whether he could strike preemptively by telephoning Sir Alec. It would be an hour and a half before Oakes reached London if he took the taxi all the way in. If he was headed for the station, it would take him—he looked at his watch—two and a half hours. Yes, that was it.

"Camilla," he said to his wife. "Get me the registrar on the telephone." She would have the home telephone of Sir Alec Sharkey.

He was not surprised, when he rang the bell, that his mother should open the door. It was obvious that Dr. Chase would report his absence and take the opportunity to vindicate Greyburn. He had steeled himself for this encounter, not knowing certainly whether her sympathy for him would be muted by dismay at his mutiny. Whatever she had planned to do, she in fact broke into tears as she hugged her boy, who had grown taller than she in the two months he had been away. He returned her embrace, but was dry-eyed.

"I'll be all right, Mother."

When she saw how he had to walk, ascending the staircase, she broke down again.

"Don't," he said, climbing slowly to the living room to face Sir Alec.

In the hour and a half's drive he had gone over it and over it, and he found himself strangely calm. He knew only that he *had* to communicate to his stepfather, early in their conversation, that he would go to a reformatory school before he would go again to Greyburn: that Greyburn was *out*. What to do then would be a matter of probably prolonged negotiation. He was ready to begin it.

Sir Alec was not. He looked awfully black and severe in his morning coat. But, rising, he extended his hand to Blackford and said, "We will go over the whole thing tomorrow. There is no point in doing it today. You are upset, I am upset, and your mother is upset. We shall have some tea, and talk about other matters."

Blackford feared that any extravagant gesture of caution, as he lowered himself into the sofa, might be interpreted as an appeal for pity. On the other hand, he guessed that his stepfather was practiced enough in the ways of Greyburn to distinguish between a routine, as distinguished from an abusive, punishment, by the precautions the victim had thereafter to take before sitting down. Blackford decided to do as he would if they were not in the room; so he sat down slowly, carefully. Even so, on the soft cushion, it was painful, as it had been in the taxi, and he yearned to go to his room and try to nap sleeping on his front.

"Tomorrow," his mother said, attempting cheer, "is your birthday, Blackford. I went out an hour ago and bought you one or two things, nothing in particular. We had sent a package to . . . Greyburn."

"Thank you, Mother."

There was silence as they stirred their tea. Sir Alec cleared his throat.

"The war news is uniformly bad. Unless we get a great deal of instant help from America, we are very probably lost. If the Russians don't check the winter offensive of Hitler, he'll have all of Europe. But the situation in America is coming to a head. Roosevelt has in effect given an ultimatum to Japan, and there is no reason to suppose that Japan will stand for it. . . ."

Blackford had tuned out. He was suddenly nearly sickened by fatigue, by the strain of the past four hours.

"Would you mind"—he paused—"Alec . . . if I went to my room?"

"Of course not. Carol, help the boy upstairs."

Mother and son walked up the second flight. His room was ready for him. His mother did not linger, kissing him lightly on the cheek and giving him two capsules and a glass of water. He disrobed, and lay down on his stomach, and awoke at eight the next morning.

At 9:45 they drove off to church. "Look, Alec," Blackford fought through his embarrassment, "I won't be able to sit in the pews. So when I stand in the back, please no fuss."

The church was very nearly full, and the minister prayed for national strength at this time of adversity. There were soldiers and sailors there, mostly accompanied by wives or mothers, and some very old people, fatalistic in the set of their faces, and in their routinized responses, and in the singing of the hymns Blackford missed—for a moment, until he decisively suppressed the nostalgia—the Greyburn College choir, half of it made up of boys from the Lower

School with their bel canto soprano voices, half from the throaty Upper School, under the spirited direction of Mr. Clayton, the gifted pianist, organist, and cellist, for whom the boys in the choir would do anything, so transparent was his pleasure when they did it right. He looked at his watch. The services at Greyburn would be over by now—they began at nine—and the boys would be free to do as they pleased for the balance of the morning, the balance of the blissful morning, that went so fast.

His mother had decided they should all go out for lunch. The awful hour was approaching when husband and son would discuss the future. Meanwhile there was a birthday to celebrate. The lunch was strained, but the food was good, and Blackford ate ravenously. In the taxi on the way home there was no conversation at all, and, once inside the door, his mother said she would be going up to her room; and so left the study, and the living room, for the privacy of "the two men"—"that's what I must think of you as, Blacky, now that you are sixteen."

They sat down.

"All right, tell me about it. You should know that Dr. Chase had me on the telephone for twenty minutes. So I know his side of the story."

Blackford related, without embellishment, in something of a monotone, the events that led to his session with Dr. Chase. He did not omit any detail of his drawing on the blackboard. But he repeated, exactly—the words were engraved in his memory—what Dr. Chase had said, before and after the punishment.

"He said, *'Courtesy of Great Britain, sir'*?"

"Yes."

Sir Alec had risen and was pacing back and forth.

"Blackford, stand up. Turn around, and drop your pants."

Blackford did as he was told.

"Take them up again."

Blackford did so, buttoned them, and turned around. His stepfather had left the room.

He saw him again at dinner.

"Blackford, we'll resume the discussion tomorrow. There's time, and your mother wants a proper celebration." In due course a cake with sixteen candles was brought in, and four gift-wrapped packages, a book of etchings, four ties, and a large box of chocolates sent over by Aunt Alice. The telephone rang, and Sir Alec answered it in the next room. They could hear him shouting and slamming the receiver down.

He ran into the dining room. "The Japanese," he said, "have attacked the United States Navy at Hawaii!"

They spent the rest of that night listening to the radio.

The next afternoon, the American ambassador was quoted in the newspapers as making an appeal to all American residents in England whose work was not related to the war effort to return home. Two passenger ships, under convoy, would leave on successive days, Wednesday and Thursday; and again, a fortnight later. Embassy officials were standing by, at the indicated numbers, to take reservations. Priority would be given to school children and the elderly. But men and women of any age would eventually be accommodated. The ships would ferry Americans until the last request for transportation was met. After that, there would be only irregular opportunities to leave the British Isles.

Late in the afternoon Sir Alec advised Blackford that he

would be on the S.S. *Mount Vernon,* leaving that Wednesday from Southampton. Sir Alec had two envelopes in his hand. He gave one to Blackford and told him to read it. It was a letter to Aunt Alice, endorsing a bank draft of five hundred pounds. He handed him the second envelope—a copy of a dispatch he had written the afternoon before to Dr. Chase. Blackford read it, lowered it, then rushed impulsively to his stepfather, hugging him tightly—his judge, vindicator, and protector. He wept one final time, with relief and gratitude, and prepared to leave his parents, whom he vaguely suspected he would not see again until the war was over; perhaps never again. On Wednesday, feeling strong now, and self-assured, he waved from the crowded, noisy, boisterous railroad car at Waterloo Station crammed with very young and very old Americans, until they were all gone. Sir Alec's bowler was the last object to slip from sight. He sat down with considerable aplomb, pulled out a chocolate from the recesses of his leather hand-case, popped it in his mouth, and sat comfortably, though still a little edgily, studying the sketches of Michelangelo.

Erika Chadinoff

THE PARENTS OF HER FRIENDS in America would make references to her "privileged" upbringing and now and then would imply, not without admiration, and not without envy, that she had been spoiled. Sometimes over a weekend visit or vacation, Erika's hosts, in the effusive style of the forties, would push Erika forward to exhibit one of her accomplishments, even as they might ask an older brother to show off a card trick. Erika went through the usual stages: she would be shy, she would be recalcitrant, she would use evasive tactics, but after her third year at the Ethel Walker School in Simsbury, Connecticut, she surprised everybody who knew her. Her fat friend Alice begged her after dinner one night to play on the piano excerpts from the first movement of the Grieg A-Minor Concerto, which Erika had played before the entire school at the annual concert only the week before—accompanied by the school piano teacher, who knew very little about music, but that didn't matter because it was recorded and rerecorded that in her youth she had actually studied under Clara Schumann. Erika surprised Alice, and rather dismayed Alice's parents, who went once every summer to the Lewisohn Stadium when Alexander Smallens did *Porgy*

47

and Bess and thought themselves thereby to have acquitted a full year's responsibility to music, by getting up without demurral and proceeding through twenty-two minutes of music, stopping only to sing at the top of her husky voice the parts written by Grieg for the missing orchestra.

"You certainly are a privileged young girl," Alice's mother said admiringly while the father, fearful that his daughter would suggest that Erika play an encore—had Grieg written another concerto? he worried . . . everyone knew that Mozart had written over, was it 400 concertos?—clapped loudly, looked at his watch, and said as a treat he would drive them all to the late movie with Bob Hope and Bing Crosby off and away on the Road to Morocco. The girls went happily to get their coats and Erika had time in the car to muse over her privileged upbringing, in Germany and England, before coming to the United States three years ago at age thirteen.

Of course, being the daughter of Dimitri and Anna Chadinoff *was* a privilege, this she did not deny, though she wondered—she truly wondered—what her parents would have done about her if she had not been . . . clever. She had picked up that word in England and thereafter used it—there being no satisfactory American substitute, as she told Alice. Her friends supposed that her early memories of Germany were of intellectuals and artists coming to her parents' elegant apartment to eat stuffed goose and read aloud each other's poems and short stories and argue long into the night the meaning of a fable by Pushkin. What Erika in fact remembered was the awful physical discomforts and the utter indifference of her father to them. She was very young when she learned that something called "money" was terribly important. When her mother looked

into her handbag, either there was money in it or there was not money in it. In the former event Erika would eat dinner, in the latter event she would not. Beginning in midafternoon, Erika would find that her attention was substantially given over to the question, Would there be money that night when her mother opened her handbag? Her mother, though not as stoical as her father, was twice as vague. If, on opening her handbag, she had pulled out a diamond necklace, she'd have said, "Dimitri, dear, I apparently have a diamond necklace here I hadn't reckoned on." Dimitri would have said, "That's fine, my dear," which he would also have said if his wife had announced that she had found an armadillo in her handbag.

Her mother did concern herself for Erika, and in the especially cold winter of 1936, washed dishes at the corner restaurant in return for bread and potatoes left over at the end of the evening's meal. Sometimes Erika had her dinner at one in the morning on her mother's return. Sometimes there was food left over from the night before. But sometimes there was no food at all. During these daily struggles her father was always reading or writing. He had access to the public library and spent much of his time there, often taking Erika because that way she could be warm. It was troublesome to do this at first because the guard at the door announced that the library was not a nursery in which to keep little girls. Dimitri Chadinoff asked just when could children be brought into the library, and the answer was: When they are old enough to read. Dimitri turned around, took Erika home, and was with her for three days, interrupted only when Erika could no longer stay awake. On the fourth day, triumphantly, he led her back and was stopped at the same entrance by the same guard. Calmly, Dimitri

made his announcement. The guard leaned over from his high desk, put a newspaper into the girl's hands and, pointing to the headline, said: "Read this, little girl." Her face solemn, Erika read, haltingly, but without error: "Roosevelt Sweeps Country/Dems Control Both Houses." She was three years old.

Her father showed no particular pride in his daughter, then or later when, at age seven, she earned a few pennies by drilling two dull teen-age boys, sons of a noble family, in English; or when Anna's friend Valerian Bibikoff, a fellow expatriate from Russia who taught piano and gave lessons to Erika, reported that the girl was singularly talented. Her father was as surprised as if he had been informed that his daughter was remarkable because she had ten fingers. He showed displeasure as rarely as he showed pleasure. When, freshly arrived in England, Erika returned to their flat to say she had made friends at school with the daughter of the Soviet military attaché, Dimitri looked down at her from his desk and told her that he would just as soon she did not associate with the children of barbarians.

"Why are they barbarians?" Erika asked in French, that being the only language spoken at the Chadinoff household on Thursdays (Monday, German; Tuesday, English; Wednesday, Italian; Thursday, French; Friday, Saturday, and Sunday any language save the language spoken in the country being inhabited).

"They are barbarians," said Dimitri Chadinoff, "because they wish to obliterate everything important that human beings have learned about how to treat each other in three thousand years."

"Why do they want to obliterate it?"—Erika had no difficulty with unusual words. Her problem, at school, was

in learning that some words *were* unusual: she had to study them attentively and learn to use them with great discretion, or preferably not at all, since at home they were used as nonchalantly as kitchen utensils. She got off to a bad start her first day at Blessed Sir Thomas More's School in Cadogan Square by asking a girl whether the policies of the school were "latitudinarian." It was years before she could explain to anyone—the solemn Paul, at the Sorbonne—that she had been guilty of affectation throughout much of her youth only by searching out simple substitute words for those that occurred to her naturally.

"They want to obliterate it," said her father, "because they are bewitched by the secular superstition of Communism, which is a huge enterprise that will settle for nothing less than bringing misery to all the people of the world."

"Why should they want to bring misery to all the people of the world?" Erika repeated her father's formulation piously.

"It isn't that they want to bring misery, though some do. They strut up and down in their baggy clothes swinging golden chains from their vests as if the keys to happiness were attached. All they have succeeded in doing is killing and torturing people and promising to do as much to people fortunate enough not to live in Russia during this period. To think that they have done it to Russia, the most beautiful land in the world," said Dimitri Chadinoff, and Anna agreed, recalling how the weather would be now in their native hills outside St. Petersburg.

"Did they take away all your money?" Erika wanted to know.

"Yes, they took away all our money."

Such an indifference as Dimitri Chadinoff's to money had not been seen since the natives begged St. Francis to

accept a copper if only to have the pleasure of giving it away. But he did not deign to express where, in the hierarchy of Soviet offenses, the loss of the family money had come. *Infra dignitate.* Erika, a thoughtful girl, assumed that her father was correct but promised herself one day to think the matter over more exhaustively, and turned to her homework in mathematics, which she was always pleased to express her concern with because she knew it was the single subject in which neither her father nor her mother could help her.

"What exactly is an integer? I don't understand."

"Ask your teacher. He's getting well paid," said her father.

Well, not so well paid by modern standards, but the school was well staffed and now Dimitri was making five pounds per week translating for a London publisher on a piecemeal basis, and that same publisher had sent out Chadinoff's fresh translation of Pushkin to be assessed by scholars at Oxford and Cambridge. "I could advise you," Chadinoff wrote to his editor, "which of the scholars at Cambridge and Oxford are competent to evaluate my work, but I suppose that if you agreed to accept my judgment in the matter the entire enterprise would be circular. Anyway, for the record the only man at either university who has the necessary background is Adam Sokolin at Cambridge. He studied under my old tutor, who beat some sense into him thirty years ago. Sokolin has done good work on Pushkin, from which we may safely conclude that he will not get very far in Cambridge." The editor took the letter by the corner, his fingers raised as if carrying a dead rat by the tail, walked into the office of his superior, dropped it on his desk and asked: "Have I your permission to tell this egomaniac to go and peddle his Pushkin elsewhere?"

The next day, manuscript back in hand, Chadinoff sent it

to the Harvard University Press. The following day, the London publisher dropped him as a part-time editor and then, after Erika had gone to sleep, Anna took Dimitri aside and, even though it was Tuesday, spoke to him in Russian and said that they had to do something to bring in some money, that all their friends and relatives were equally impoverished, that there was no money for the next week's rent, nor for the next month's school bills for Erika.

Well, said Dimitri—ever so slightly disposed to point out, by twiddling his fingers on the open page of his book, that Anna had interrupted his reading—did she have any suggestions?

Yes, she said, she had recently been talking to her friend Selnikov (former colonel in the Czar's prime equestrian unit). Poor Sergei Babevich had not only himself and his wife to look after but three daughters and a son. He had taken a position as a maître d'hôtel at a medium-priced restaurant where a knowledge of several languages was useful. "The trouble with you, dear Dimitri, is that your knowledge of food is really not very refined. You could write a scholarly book about the feasts of Lucullus, but you would not be able to distinguish the actual food from fish and chips at Lyons. So I have another idea."

Dimitri had sat without any show of emotion thus far. "Well?"

Anna couldn't, at first, remember what her other idea was, and Dimitri waited. Finally the newspaper caught her eye.

"Ah yes. There is an advertisement in the paper for a concierge. He must be presentable—here." She reached for the paper, shuffling through to the marked section. "Presentable, must be fluent in French and German. Some Italian and Spanish desirable. References."

Dimitri took the job. His hours were from one until midnight. He would sleep until six and then resume his own work. Erika was not permitted to see her father at the hotel during working hours. Once she decided mischievously to do so. She was small for twelve years, so that her head only just reached the counter. She had on a friend's hat, and her light-brown hair was knotted under it. She put on spectacles and, carrying a handbag, she said in a little girl's voice, imitating her father's own imperious accent and speaking in German: "Concierge, please get me a sleeper to the Finland Station!" Dimitri permitted himself a smile, and then in Russian said to her: "Get yourself out of here, Rikushka, before I invite the manager to paddle your behind." She went out roaring, and told her mother, who laughed, and then said not, ever, to do such a thing again. The following morning, when she went off to school, she found tucked into her notebook, in her father's unmistakable hand, a fable dedicated to her. It was called "The Little Girl Who Took the Train to the Finland Station, and Woke Up Lenin." That day, she thought, she was closer to her father than she had ever been before.

When the letter came from the Harvard University Press, Chadinoff was pleased, but not particularly surprised. He knew his Pushkin was superior. But he was surprised a month later to be invited by the Department of Slavic and Romance Languages to go to Harvard to lecture during the spring term. Chadinoff replied that, thanks very much, he would be happy to do so, and able to do so inasmuch as his job as concierge at the Basil Street Hotel required him to give only three weeks' notice, and February was still three months away.

They made reservations for the tenth of December on the

S.S. *Mount Vernon,* and it was well that they did, because after the seventh of December, which was the day of Pearl Harbor, no reservations were accepted save for returning residents of the United States. Chadinoff and his family carried Nansen passports, and his excited wife and daughter were apprehensive, up until the moment the gangplank was lifted, about having to yield their room to returning U.S. residents.

During the commotion Erika, snugly dressed in a white skirt, peasant blouse, and tweed jacket, excitedly accosted a tall, handsome blond boy—at least two years older, she judged—wearing an English public-school blazer, chewing an apple, and affecting the ways of the cosmopolitan traveler.

"Do you think we will pull out on time?" she began the conversation.

"Oh, sure," he said. She was surprised his accent was American. "They always pull out on time. Especially when there are submarines."

"Why should a ship be punctual for the sake of the submarines?"

Blackford Oakes looked at her pert face, and frank, inquisitive eyes accented by her austerely coiled braids. "Because"—he spoke just a little less casually than before—"there are escort vessels, and it is quite a muddle if every boat decides for itself when to start out."

She did not answer, but looked at her lumpy watch. She would wait—for what, later at Smith College, the philosophy professor would tell her is called "empirical verification." And, in fact, at exactly one forty-five in the afternoon the gangplank was pulled, the whistles and horns blew, the crowd at the pier interrupted its waving and yelling, and her

parents rejoined her. Before skipping off she turned to the boy, munching a fresh apple and looking very self-satisfied.

"You were right."

He smiled—it was a splendid smile, warm, animated. He reached into the brown paper bag and said, "Here, have an apple." She looked up at her mother, who nodded her head, so she took it and said, "Thank you," and then with her free hand grabbed her straw hat, which almost blew away as the great steamship slid out of the lee of the quay.

By the time Erika was sixteen her father was well known in the academic world and now held down a chair at Brown University, delivering learned, acidulous, witty lectures that would become famous. There was now money enough to pay the tuitions at the Ethel Walker School and, later, Smith College, and in her senior year her father gave her a secondhand car which Erika rejoiced in, traveling about New England tirelessly, to celebrate the end of gas rationing. She took on every challenge, competing for the classics prize, the philosophy prize, winning one, placing second in the other. In her junior year the dean had called her in to ask whether she would consider *not* competing for the Russian, German, French, and Italian prizes. She had won them all in her freshman and sophomore years, and now the teachers were finding it hard to persuade anyone to compete against so certain a winner. Erika said she would have to consult with her father, whose instructions to her had been to enter every competition. He wrote back and told his daughter that, noblesse oblige, she should allow other girls a chance at the prizes, but if she wanted to compete for the big Prix Giscard she might focus her energies on winning it. This prize went annually to four girls selected from applicants

throughout the country to study in Paris, all expenses paid, and its renewal, now that the war was over, had recently been advertised.

Erika competed and won without much difficulty, and without causing resentment. Though serious by nature, she could participate in gaiety and do so convincingly. Her friends now accepted matter-of-factly her prolix virtuosity and had long since ceased to think anything about it. She was like the boy or girl at graduation whose name recurs and recurs and who has to walk up to the headmaster fifteen times before he is done collecting the silver: Best Athlete, Best Student Leader, Best Scholar—Best Prig, often as not. But Erika got on well with her friends, all of whom assumed that she would either go on to become a professor of almost anything, or else that a very gallant and very rich man, desiring a beautiful girl of exotic manner and prodigious attainments, would take her off and make her duchess of something where she would preside over salons for a couple of generations of Princes of Wales. At home the night before leaving, in the comfortable house in Providence exploding with books and order, she actually managed to catch her mother's and father's attention at dinner by saying, "Are you glad we won the war, Father?"

Chadinoff, dressed in his velvet smoking jacket, finished chewing what he had in his mouth.

"I am glad we won. I am sorry *they* won. I am sorry that they now occupy Eastern Europe. I predict they will still occupy East Europe one, maybe two years from now."

Erika remembered the night her father so greatly embarrassed her during her last year at Ethel Walker, before two friends spending the weekend in Providence. It was the critical weekend when at first Stalingrad was reported cap-

tured by the Germans, and then the Russians were reported holding out. As the radio reports came in the girls cheered on all the news of Russian advances and hissed all the news of German advances. It soon became uncomfortably clear that their host, Professor Dimitri Chadinoff, was unmistakably cheering the other side. Alice, who was well known for her ingenuous candor, looked up during the late morning and said, "Professor Chadinoff, are you pro-Nazi?"

"No, Alice," said Chadinoff. "Permit me, are you pro-Communist?"

"Why, no," said Alice.

"Very well, then?" Chadinoff's eyebrows lifted, and he was evidently prepared to change the subject.

"But we are at war with the Nazis."

"Who is 'We'?" Chadinoff replied.

"Well, Americans . . ." Then she gasped. She hadn't thought about it before. She turned to Erika, hoping for help. But Erika's father was in charge.

"We carry Nansen passports, Alice. They are a kind of diplomatic Man-Without-a-Country passports. We are grateful to the United States for its hospitality and express our gratitude by paying exactly the same taxes we would be paying if we had been born and raised in Topeka, Kansas. We have not taken any oath to support America's foreign policy and, my dear Alice, if truth were told, no one's reputation for intelligence could survive the taking of such an oath."

Alice was a fair student of biology, a little backward in languages, including English, so she thought at least she could charm the famous linguist by trotting up a phrase from her Ethel Walker School French: "Well, Professor, *chacun à son goût.*"

"*Chacun à sa bêtise*," Professor Chadinoff retorted and returned to his reading.

That afternoon, when her guests were dressing for the Brown-Yale football game, Erika pleaded illness, sending her date off alone to the game. She then turned to her father as she had never done before and, fire in her eyes and a great ball of resentment in her stomach, she blurted out: "I think what you did to Alice was disgusting! Doesn't it matter to you that one million—*one million*—Russians have died in the last two months defending Stalingrad? They can't be as mad as you are at Communism for having taken away *their* landed estates!" She flung the door shut, went up to her room, locked the door, and wept. She wept fitfully through the afternoon and her intelligence alerted her, after a while, that her discomposure was deeply rooted. She did not know exactly what was the cause or causes of it, and now, three years later, she still did not know. Characteristically, neither her father nor her mother had ever again alluded to the incident.

This time she said, "Father, do you believe in God?"

"No. But I believe in some of the things attributed to God."

"Like what?"

"Like the Ten Commandments. Most of the Ten Commandments. One or two are arguable, explained by Jewish cultural idiosyncrasies."

"What do you believe in?"

"I believe in the life of the mind, and in human fancy, and in the everlasting struggle against vulgarity."

"What do you mean, you believe in *the struggle against vulgarity?* Does that mean you believe that that struggle is going to happen, or does that mean that you believe that that struggle is worth winning?"

"It is obviously worth winning. But it will never be won. That is why I qualify it by calling it an everlasting struggle."

"The Communists believe more than you do."

"That is certainly correct. So do African witch doctors."

Her mother was following the argument, but was now distracted by something, and she could not remember what it was. She had mistakenly begun the meal by serving the chocolate soufflé because she had found that, by mis-reckoning, it was done when they sat down, and obviously would not wait, whereas the lamb would.

"As a matter of fact," broke in Anna Chadinoff, her points of reference not immediately clear either to her husband or to her daughter, "lamb will wait very nearly indefinitely."

"What did you say, Anna?"

"I said that lamb would wait very nearly indefinitely."

"Do you mean, like the everlasting struggle?"

"What do you mean by that, dear?"

Chadinoff, knowing when the door was finally closed on any possibility of nexus, pronounced the chocolate soufflé quite excellent, and wondered whether they would now be served kippered herring.

No, Anna said. Now there would be lamb. And Chadinoff then understood. Erika understood. God, if he existed, now understood. Erika thought that, really, her parents were quite splendid, but how wonderful it would be to be gone from them for a while: for a long while, she thought that night.

Erika arrived in Paris in the awful, depressed postwar season three years after the war. She was loaded down with letters from her father and mother commending her to the attentions of their numerous friends in the expatriate world.

She began dutifully with the first names on the list: Mr. and Mrs. Valerian Sverdlov. Mme. Sverdlov was a niece of Tolstoy; her husband had commanded a czarist cavalry regiment; both had known Erika's parents since childhood and both greeted her warmly once communication was effected.

This proved difficult because although Erika rang the telephone number her father had given her and, after a few days during which there was never an answer, checked it against the telephone book to find it correct, *still* there was no answer. So she sent a letter and got back a prompt invitation to come to tea, which the following day she did. Mr. Sverdlov, quite bald, with a mustache, bad teeth, pink cheeks and twinkling eyes, was always laughing, and he rejoiced at seeing his beloved Chadinoff's daughter, rejoiced at being able to speak in Russian to her, and several times emptied his glass of vodka to celebrate the general celebration. His wife, though more reserved, was also warm. She worked as a tutor in Russian and found now in the postwar world a considerably increased demand for her services. Beginning the following week, Valerian would return to his job as driver of an American Express tourist bus. Erika was faintly surprised to learn this, but then reminded herself that, until a few years ago, her father worked as a concierge and her mother as a dishwasher.

When she alluded to the difficulty in getting through to the Sverdlovs on the telephone, he laughed and laughed and said several times that the French were the *silliest* people in the *whole* world. You see—he adopted a conspiratorial voice—I was a *collaborator!* Yes! I worked for the Germans! One day I traveled with the German Army as far as St. Petersburg. Not *into* St. Petersburg, but as *far* as St.

Petersburg—and there—he stood theatrically, and waved his arm forward, "there from the hilltop I could see—my house. My father's house. My grandfather's house. Where your father played with me when we were boys."

But, he said, that was as far as they had got. Russian resistance proved effective and the retreat began. He returned to Paris and resumed his clerical work as translator of Russian war documents and radio communications—it was understood he would work only against the Soviets.

"Now," he said with delight to Erika, who struggled to conceal her chagrin at her father's friend's collaborationist activity but little by little was caught up by his ebullience—"now," he said, "the French know that I was a collaborator. And *they* know that *I* know that *they* know that I was a collaborator. But!"—he stood again and howled with glee, his mustache high over his white, crooked teeth, his wispy hair tousled, cheeks pink with mirth and stimulation—"they cannot prove it. And the reason they cannot prove it is that before the Germans left, I said to Colonel Strassbourg: 'My dear Colonel, you can have very little use for my file in Berlin, so be a good chicken and let me have it.' And he did, and I burned it, right there"—he pointed to the shabby little fireplace with the four pieces of coal warming, or trying to warm, the whole apartment.

"So what do these silly Frenchmen do? They take away my telephone! They do not tell me: 'Mr. Sverdlov, you are a traitor, and we cannot send you to jail, and we cannot send you to the firing squad, so we are going to take away your telephone.' No. They just disconnect it. Everything else is the same. And when I ask about it they just shrug their shoulders and say I must wait!" He laughed at this trivialization of treason, although of course he too, Erika knew,

would have used the same arguments her father used about the Nansen passport, so she did not catechize him. She enjoyed him most unabashedly, and he offered to take her the next Monday to Chartres; and, on the bus, where he wore a chauffeur's cap without any apparent self-consciousness, he buoyantly situated her in the seat directly across from him and they chatted as he drove.

When, like her parents, he had run out of money, he had applied to American Express for a job as a bus driver, stressing his knowledge of French (perfect), German (excellent), English (shaky), and then he qualified his application by saying he would be interested in only a single route: to Chartres. His employer was puzzled until Sverdlov explained that the cathedral at Chartres was the most beautiful sight in the world, more beautiful even than any sight in Russia, and if he was destined to drive a bus every day he might as well drive it to the most beautiful sight in the world.

"Why not?" he exclaimed, his whole face and shoulders rising in interrogation. When after a month the dispatcher told him that that day he would have to drive the bus to the cathedral at Rheims, Sverdlov said that under no circumstances would he go to Rheims—the cathedral there, for all its reputation and pretensions, being simply inadequate. American Express tried suggesting that he was, in fact, under no obligation to join the tourists in the cathedral, but Sverdlov was so affronted by the implied mechanization of his role, American Express quickly retreated, undisposed to discipline the driver who was the favorite of the tourists. By now, even after the war's long interruption, his title to Chartres was secure and no one would question it, he said happily. Later, in a whisper, he told Erika that after seeing

the cathedral, he would take her to a little Russian delicatessen where they would have some vodka and some cheese and sausage while the other tourists had their regular lunch.

Erika's reaction, on seeing the cathedral, gratified Sverdlov: she found it was everything Henry Adams said it was, in the book she was assigned to read by one of her art professors at Smith; and other things that Henry Adams had failed to say it was. She asked Sverdlov, whom now she was told to call Valerian Babeyevich, whether he had read Adams's book on Mont St. Michel and Chartres, and he replied that he had not, that he did not want to read about the cathedral, only look at it. Erika mused that her father, who would much prefer reading about a cathedral to seeing it, would scarcely approve of Valerian's attitude: and in the course of the afternoon she discovered that Valerian really knew nothing about her father's career except, vaguely, that he had become a success of sorts in America.

"When he writes me letters"—Valerian laughed, as he tipped his fifth jigger glass of vodka down his throat—"he writes about obscure poets or writers he has discovered, and always he forgets to tell me about Anna and his darling and beautiful daughter."

He looked at his watch and said that they must go back to the bus now, the tourists would be assembling as instructed. He insisted to Erika on paying the bill, which proved painless when the old Russian shopkeeper in turn insisted on refusing payment from his old friend, who had brought that day such an "elegant"—he bowed to Erika—"and beautiful daughter of an old friend."

From the American Express bus terminal it was a short walk to the apartment Erika rented at Rue Montalembert: a

bedroom, study/living room/dining room, kitchen, and bath—for thirty-five U.S. dollars per month, on the Left Bank almost but not quite overlooking the river. From there she could walk to the Sorbonne, and did now regularly, even though the weather had turned cold, attending classes in philosophy and the history of art. The classrooms were cold and dirty, the students poorly dressed, and on the faces of many of the boys there was a premature gauntness of expression. Erika noticed a sharp divergence in the attitude of the students. Half, perhaps more than half, diligently took notes on what the instructor said, particularly in the class taught by Jean-Paul Sartre, who when he spoke did so with a precisionist nonchalance, a quiet and perfect engine of volubility whose words, transcribed, could have formed completed chapters of books, indeed regularly did so. But other students, though they might make a note occasionally, were studiedly skeptical, as if to communicate to the instructor that no presumptive respect was owed either to him or to the words he spoke. During the exchanges these students, when they said anything at all, tended to challenge this or that generality of the teacher, or ask whether, by this inflection, he had meant to say such and such. M. Argoud, who had written a history of art, answered questions, however provocative, neither with indignation nor with servility. If the question was barbed he would ignore those parts of it that were provocative, giving unadorned answers to whatever was left. "Would you not say, M. Argoud, that you slip into confusion when you suggest there are similarities between the theoretical defenses of abstractionism and of primitivism?"

"The similarities to which I alluded are listed in the chapter on Braque in my book."

Next question.

M. Argoud did not care for his students, and did not care if his students cared for him. But he would do what he had contracted to do so that as quickly as possible he might get back to his own work. He broke his rhythm on one occasion to notice Erika, with her tweed skirt, blouse, and sweater, her full bosom—perhaps she reminded him of something Braque had said, or painted, or loved? Erika looked at the teacher, still young, but utterly unconcerned. If he could look ten years younger by snapping his fingers, she thought, he would probably not take the trouble. But to inquire into the authenticity of a Del Sarto in a museum, he had devoted seven months—and came up calmly with the pronouncement that it was a forgery. Erika guessed that, on the whole, M. Argoud would probably prefer coming up with a forgery than with an original: the whole exercise would somehow reinforce his misanthropic inclinations.

Except, of course, for Paul. M. Argoud obviously cared for Paul. Paul's (infrequent) questions were answered in a tone of voice distinctly different. M. Argoud was even seen, on at least one occasion, talking casually with Paul in the cold, high-ceilinged corridor. Since Paul was young and beautiful and intense, Erika wondered whether the relationship was unnatural, but when Paul sat next to her in the cafeteria one day at lunch and they fell to talking she discovered that Paul Massot was François Argoud's stepbrother and that they had belonged to the same guerrilla unit during the resistance. Both had been tortured in the same cellar at the same time, she would learn weeks later when she and Paul were lovers, and Paul whispered to her early one morning, stroking her breasts with his chin, that if he had known her then, he'd have probably told them

everything, done anything, espoused any creed, incurred any risk, performed any treachery, lest they deprive him of her—his—Erika, no one else's, ever, ever—his rhythms were matching now the words, and her responses were elatedly fused to his own, as he repeated the word, ever, ever, ever, ever, ever, more excitedly, more quickly, almost shouting now, as she closed her eyes and moaned, then opened them to observe her beautiful Paul, EVER!

Whenever he left her apartment, whether to fetch a book in the library or perform an errand or check the mailbox, there was prolonged discussion. Exactly how long would he be gone?

Twelve minutes?

That was too long, Erika said, and Paul would agree. And he would say that perhaps if he ran both ways he could manage it in eleven minutes. As often as not, Erika would suggest that the safest way to handle the problem would be for both of them to leave together. His solemn young face would light up with pleasure and, taking her hand, he would open the door, pausing on the stairway, now for a passionate, now for a tender kiss.

Paul Massot's stepfather, the elder Argoud, had died during the war. Since he wasn't shot by the Nazis and did not die in a military prison, he didn't qualify for the Vermork; but he was listed officially as a "casualty" of the war because, suffering from diabetes, he was medically undernourished owing to scarcities that were an undisputed result of the war; so that his impoverished widow, Paul's mother, received a little pension on which Paul now drew a few francs every month to finish the studies interrupted when, at seventeen, he withdrew from the university to devote himself to the resistance.

He had gone then, instinctively, to his austere, normally unapproachable half-brother, older by eight years, with whom he associated during the nearly three years before the American troops, General Leclerc heading the procession, entered Paris. There were long, tedious hours of joint activity. On one occasion, Argoud and Paul were responsible for checking the movements of a Gestapo official. They huddled in a single room across the street with their stopwatches and notebooks, clocking the monster's goings and comings for nearly three months. In the long stretches of inactivity Argoud undertook two missions, the first to teach his half-brother something about the esthetic history of the world: it would prove, before long, a substantial history of the Renaissance. And the second, to convince Paul that the only hope for humanity lay in acknowledging the truths of Marxist analysis and historiography and in backing the Soviet Union's lonely, and acknowledgedly often brutal efforts to export to the world that which only Russia was experiencing.

Paul knew about Erika's background and had even read some of the works by Chadinoff, whose fame had come to France. Neither he nor she was perturbed by Chadinoff's reactionary politics. Why should one expect Chadinoff to feel or reason otherwise? Paul said. How natural! If it were *easy* for the world to accept communism, it would have done so by now. The forces aligned in opposition to communism aren't merely those specifically identified by Marx. There are all those other accretions of man: his nostalgia, his fear of the unknown, his conservative temptation to resist change.

"But, Paul, there *are* other things." They were at dinner, in their favorite restaurant where, unless instructed other-

wise, the waiter brought them the same appetizer, the same entrées, the same house wine, and the same bill, but no longer any cigarettes (Paul having told Erika she must give up smoking), which came to seventy-five U.S. cents apiece. "There's the suffering in Russia."

"There has been suffering everywhere. Look at the suffering in Germany and Italy. Even in the United States, one hundred years advanced over Russia industrially, they could not manage their Depression. Stalin is not a gentle man, and he has made many mistakes, and will make other mistakes. But unlike the Catholic Church, the Marxists do not claim infallibility for their leader. We claim only that history has imposed a responsibility on him, and we must help him discharge that responsibility. There is no way of getting around the fact, Erika, that millions of Russians fought for Stalin and for their country: and no one disguised from them that they were fighting for communism. Of course it has been bitter and hard. And it will be harder and more bitter if we are to prevent the forces in opposition from gainsaying the effort of all those years, all those lives, because"—he dug into his meatloaf with his knife; he never used a fork—"that is exactly what will happen if, just because the formal fighting is over, we think of ourselves as other than at war."

Erika heard the arguments but could not say, really, that she had listened to them. All through her life she had resisted only that one intellectual challenge, an examination of the ideology that had banished and impoverished her father. She did not, really, want to go into the arguments now, though she would if Paul wanted her to. She would do anything Paul wanted her to. She could not imagine that it was possible to know such joy as she knew, whether at the

table listening to him, seeing his straight dark hair fallen over his brow, his sad brown eyes, his pointed and delicate mouth deftly retrieving the morsels of food from the knife, his long tapered fingers, explaining his position to her, sensitive to every sound, every inflection, or in bed during those long bouts of ardor and tranquillity. Or sitting next to him, listening to his unprepossessing but acknowledgedly brilliant half-brother. She could admire her father, but she could not ever really *believe* in him. In Paul she believed— entirely. And she knew that she would never betray him. If it should happen, in a final philosophical revelation, that his ideology was wrong, and the contrary of it right, it would matter far less that she had taken the wrong course, than that she had followed him. He was her ideology, her idyll, her lover, her friend, her counselor, her Paul, forever for- ever forever.

"Do you understand what I'm talking about?"

"I understand what I need to understand. If you want me to study Marxism, of course I'll study Marxism. And"— she smiled at him—"I'll even win the Marxist Prize if you want me to."

No, he did not want her to study Marxism, he said. He would like it if she read Marx, but that didn't matter so much; he, Paul, would tell her everything she needed to know about politics. What he did not want was for her to associate openly with Marxists, because that would put her in the way of unnecessary harassments. The anti-Commu- nist French were mobilizing against the French Commu- nists, and there were divisions already even among men and women who had worked together during the resistance. The Croix de Feu, which drew from the militant wing of the anti-Communist coalition, were talking violence. The

forces of American fascism were everywhere. There was no need to alert anyone, save his own special friends, to her new political allegiance. He himself had been careful not to enroll in the Party, and not to attend any of its official functions—François, though himself an active Party member, had so counseled him.

And thus it was left, during that golden autumn. One day every week he was away, by himself, pursuing duties which, he told her, he could neither neglect nor explain. One other evening per week he required her to share with his political intimates, who, after the briefest experience with her, were all of them happy that Paul, whose star was so manifestly ascendant, had found so accomplished and lovely a companion. She liked especially Gerard, and when one day he actually stopped smoking long enough to make it possible to see through the smoke to his wry face, she was surprised to notice how much he looked like her own father, though younger of course. He presided over the meetings, which is what they really were, and there was a worldliness but also a spirituality in his analysis of the French contemporary scene that touched Erika, which she found wanting in her own father. Gerard was especially kind to Erika and one day surprised her by addressing her in a Russian which, though clearly not native, betrayed a convincing knowledge of Russia, a knowledge the details of which Erika did not feel free to probe; these were, after all, clandestine meetings. She did not know Gerard's surname, nor where he lived.

It had proved difficult to locate Gerard, but finally Erika succeeded in doing so, exactly one week after the day when, groceries in hand, she had opened the door, exhilarated at the prospect of seeing Paul lying there as she so regularly

came on him, dressed only in his undershorts, reading easily in the dim light. He was there exactly as she had anticipated, but the book rested flat on his olive-skinned chest and his head was slightly turned, by a bullet that had entered his brain.

Erika was released from the hospital just in time to attend the funeral three days later. Scant attention was given to the extraordinary shooting—execution?—of young Paul Massot. Paris was inured to death and terror, after five years of it. The detectives came, but eventually they left, without formal findings. Still white when she tapped the doorknob of Gerard's apartment, she waited, and Gerard came and, on opening the door, beheld a grown woman ten days after knowing her as a university schoolgirl.

"Who did it?" she asked.

"I don't know," he said.

"You do know"—she looked him in the eyes, and the psychic pressure was greater than the torturer's that nightmare night in 1944. He yielded.

"It was almost certainly the work of the Croix de Feu. Paul was assigned to penetrate the organization." Gerard held out his arms to her but she was past tears, and simply took his extended hand in hers and said good-bye, and told him that if ever he needed her services, he might have them.

Axel Wintergrin

WINTERGRIN WAS TWENTY YEARS OLD when Hitler marched into Poland. A first lieutenant in the lead reconnaissance battalion, he reached Warsaw ahead of the shock troops that would crush the city. Twenty-four hours after he was in Warsaw, Lieutenant Axel von Euchen Wintergrin disappeared.

For a few months the relevant people tried to find out what had happened to him, but notwithstanding the diligence of German record-keepers, interest waned, and it was supposed that Axel Wintergrin, the gifted young Count of St. Anselm, was the casualty of a Polish sniper, or that he had been kidnapped and killed. After six months, during which the German prisoners held by the Poles were liberated or killed as the resistance movement was smashed, Wintergrin was officially reported Missing in Action and Presumed Dead, and his widowed mother was sent a decoration of sorts which she hung around the photograph of her son but only after prying from the medal the disfiguring swastika. The absence of it was noticed by the mayor of St. Anselm's on the feast day of St. Anselm, when the countess, observing tradition, entertained local officials at the castle; and the countess, her graying hair in perfect trim, her leath-

ery face handsome and resourceful, sipped her tea, then said Yes, decorative swastikas are not safe these days when the patriotic fever causes them to be so greatly coveted. She would not be surprised to see it materialize on the charm bracelet of her silly little maid, Nona.

Did the countess—the subject could now safely be raised without opening the year-old wound—have any private opinion what might have happened to her son? Yes, she said, she did have a private notion, but it was so ridiculous, she did not really want to share it. We are old friends, said the mayor: Confide in me. The countess leaned over to him and pointed to the little gray kitten, asleep near the fireplace, and whispered: "Do you believe in reincarnation?" The mayor changed the subject, and went gladly back to the village to resume the war. The countess, a lifelong clairvoyant, knew Axel was alive, though no word from him or of him had reached her. Moreover, she was sure that he was well; and altogether certain that—wherever he was— he was risking his life in the fight against the Nazis.

It had been, in fact, a very near thing. Axel was roughly treated when, in civilian clothes taken from a corpse, he presented himself to a Polish captain in command of a rearguard outpost. Axel understood only enough Polish to gather that the captain had calmly given orders to take this German lad out somewhere and shoot him. But he had anticipated some such possibility, and accordingly had memorized the Polish words necessary to communicate a willingness to mark on the map the two major repositories in Warsaw of Nazi ammunition laid up by foreign commercial agents before the invasion began, one of them in a part of the city as yet unoccupied. It took less than three hours to verify this, and from the jubilation Wintergrin briefly won-

dered whether he would be made to stick around and serve as grand marshal of the Pulaski Day Parade. What he wanted was to be escorted out of the country. The Polish captain promised to guide him to Sopot whence, assuming Nazi airplanes did not completely close off the traffic in the Bay of Danzig during the next two or three days, he could be infiltrated by ferry into Sweden, whereafter he would become a Swedish problem. Axel's guide, Zinka, was a woman who spoke no German, and after the first two days of walking and bicycling north toward Olsztyn, his vocabulary failed him, he ran out of variations on hidden ammunition dumps, and so they walked (and sometimes ran), and ate, in silence, the stocky forty-year-old gym teacher from Warsaw, and the angular twenty-year-old Westphalian aristocrat.

Approaching Malbork, Zinka suddenly motioned Axel into a barn when she spotted the checkpoint down the road. The uniforms were Polish but confused reports, snatched here and there from overheard talk, from fragments of broadcasts on municipal radios blaring the grim news into village squares, suggested to Zinka the possibility that units of Polish troops had been conscripted by their captors. The word was that no one carrying papers unfranked by the Gestapo would be permitted to travel, and that anyone without papers of any sort would be detained. Zinka, alone, ran toward the two soldiers. Axel strained to discern what was happening but succeeded only in seeing the indistinct figures apparently in commotion, and then both soldiers racing in their motorcycles up the road over which he and Zinka had just bicycled. The girl motioned Axel to come on, and as the motorcyclists disappeared, he did so, and she described, miming rather more graphically

than Axel required in order to catch the gist of her story, her complaint to the patrol that five kilometers back, a young German in soldier's uniform, jumping her from the side of the road, had raped her. Axel wondered whether the chivalrous pair of Polish soldiers was prepared to challenge the entire Nazi Army, rape being the sport in which, at this point, he assumed the German Army to be substantially engaged. He even considered the possibility that *he* would be apprehended and hanged as a rapist.

So they left the main road and traveled cross-country. As they came closer to the coast Axel's well-disciplined face brightened, even as Zinka's grew pensive and sad. *He* was moving away from the Nazis, *she* would return to their most recently occupied European capital. At the garage near the commercial pier she extended her hand, but her eyes looked down. Axel took it, bent his head formally, touching his lips to her graying hair, and, in English, said, "Goodbye, Zinka. I will never forget you."

Axel made his way through Sweden to Norway, where he presented himself to Norwegian intelligence. After the Nazi invasion of Norway he joined the resistance. For five years he made no effort to be in touch with his mother or any other relatives in Germany or England: he would not risk retribution against his family. When the war was over he received from the Norwegian monarch the highest decoration for bravery in a simple ceremony to honor all the surviving heroes of the resistance. "Like lining up for food stamps," one veteran grumbled. Axel returned to Germany with an undetailed story of detention in Sweden, whither he said he had escaped after a brief period of captivity in Poland and where he was held incommunicado. The story was routinely, indeed listlessly, accepted by a society

crushed under the events of recent months. In such a season Marco Polo could not have commanded an audience of six people to hear out his exploits.

Axel resumed his studies, pursuing philosophy at Heidelberg under Karl Jaspers, and receiving an advanced degree after three years, working long days in the library and long afternoons in the gymnasium, where he boxed with some success as a middleweight. He was serious, but not fanatical or even obsessive in his pursuits, and though he led an apparently carefree life it was true—as later was widely remarked when every commentator in Europe undertook the definitive portrait of Axel Wintergrin—that strain was etched into a face otherwise that of a healthy twenty-eight-year-old: the calling card of Gestapo torturers in Norway who, pity the poor innocents, never even discovered that the man they were mutilating was a German. But he could smile through his calcified sadness, though nobody could quite remember when last Axel had been seen laughing. This is a very serious world, he told his closest friend Roland Himmelfarb, who as one of the few surviving German Jews—he sat out the holocaust in the strangest, strongest sanctuary of them all, serving undetected in the records department of the Gestapo in Berlin—hardly needed advertisement of the fact. Indeed, in his circle no one disagreed with him, because no one applied to Axel the conventional criteria.

It was not expected of Count Wintergrin that he should join in beer-drinking contests or take his turn entertaining his associates with accounts of bawdy adventures or attend the games to cheer on his university team. Even as a boxer, he fought with a certain detachment. Although he was first-rate, adversaries and acute spectators got the impression he

had a disinterested concern with the sport: often he eschewed the opportunity to cripple his opponent after maneuvering to do so—rather like throwing back into the stream the trout you have labored so hard to land. And after the match, though always affable and sportsmanlike, he would leave rather than stay on to see the other matches or join the team at refreshments. He would return to his studies, or write a letter to his mother or a friend, or write in his journal, which he never shared with anyone.

His desultory romantic life was of concern to his mother, since Axel was her only child, and heir to the huge landed estate of his father. At first he obligingly escorted the ladies proffered by his mother for his attention: the neighboring blue bloods. Then others came from remoter parts of Germany. When he traveled with his mother to England in 1946, he saw for the first time, since graduating from Greyburn in 1938 after six years of English public-school life, his second cousin Caroline, herself first cousin to the reigning monarch, whom she succeeded as queen a few years later after the fatal accident. Caroline was imperious by nature and undertook to find the perfect girl for her glamorous, studious, wealthy, driven German cousin. Axel obligingly affected to be quite taken by the three girls (beautiful, literate, witty, in differing mixes) he escorted during the summer, all of whom were deeply attracted to him (Lady Leinsford in particular, though it had not amused Axel when she said to him, sighing in his arms, "For you, Axel, I'd even become a Nazi"). Axel's treatment was perfunctorily ardent. He would systematically contrive to seduce them (four days, three days, eleven days respectively), and then with much tenderness announce that he had to get back to his work, the nature of which he never specified.

"Has it ever occurred to you, Axel," Princess Caroline once said, "that it isn't absolutely clear whether you are a nice man? I mean, I love you very much—you know that, Axel—but you are very distracted. And your interest in people seems, somehow . . . abstract." She searched his eyes. "But I am certain you are going to do great things in European politics. If you don't mind, Axel, when you take over Europe could you please leave this little island to its own idolatrous pleasures? Don't forget now, Axel. That can be your bread-and-butter present to me on leaving Stamford House." Axel smiled—and then actually appeared to . . . think about it. ("I do believe," Queen Caroline said, recalling the incident in 1952 when Axel Wintergrin announced the foundation of his political party, "I do believe," she repeated, "that when I made that flippant—that ludicrous—'request' of Axel, back when he was a mere child [Axel had been a mere child of twenty-six], he hesitated *precisely* because he was trying to decide whether to *grant* it!") Back home, after two months' summer indolence in England, Axel drove himself in his studies, adjourning altogether that part of his romantic activity that could be said to be oriented toward a possible marriage. "All in due course, Mother," he comforted the countess.

After submitting his thesis and taking his degree, he spent his time traveling throughout Germany. He would know, on arriving in a city or town he had never been to, just where to go: always he would find the man, or woman, who shared his obsession. And—always—in a matter of days he had made fast friends, who as often as not became disciples. As his movement grew it became easier for him because he would come to town, check in at a hotel, and there he would be reached by those who had word of his

coming. They would seek him out, sometimes a single man or woman, more often two, three, or a half-dozen people, and talk with him. He would be asked to speak to a gathering, but always he stipulated that not more than a roomful should be there. He was not ready to address large audiences.

He spoke quietly about the genuine idealism of the German people who had become united less than a hundred years earlier, and now were sundered by a consortium of powers, one partner in which had designs on human liberty everywhere, while the other partner, fatigued by a war that had roused its people from a hemispheric torpor which they once thought of as a part of the American patrimony—an American right, so to speak—was confused now and disillusioned by the ambiguous results of so heroic an effort. The Americans saw a Europe largely enslaved by Allied victory—and unconcerned about Germany. No, never count on allies beyond a certain point, he said: only Germans can reshape their own destiny. Only Germans can come, would come, to the aid of their brothers in the East. Faced with such resolve, the Russians would necessarily yield; even as, eventually, the Nazis had yielded.

Always the questions were practical, always he gave the same answer: How, in the absence of armed help from the West, could he effect the liberation of East Germany? Always he answered: by spiritual mobilization.

Did he mean the satyagraha preached by Gandhi?

Spiritual mobilization, Axel said, means the mobilization of all one's strength. Foremost is the will to live as free men. Any means appropriate to the realization of that end are licit—from peaceful resistance to ultimate weaponry.

Would he be more explicit?

In due course, he would say, and his smile was without smugness, without affectation, though he would then fasten or unfasten (his only mannerism) the two bottom buttons of his rusty-green tweed jacket, a perfect cut on his tall frame, and his light-brown hair would respond sluggishly as he shook his head to the right, his lightly chiseled, sensitive features, and sad eyes, struggling in coordination with his thoughts to frame the answer in a way so many of his followers sought.

All in good time, he answered, as if to say: Allow me to trouble myself, on your behalf, on these technical matters. I shall not let you down.

When he rose at his alma mater to announce that if the Occupation Forces would not deliver an ultimatum to the Russians to reopen the road to Berlin, the German people should do so, he was suddenly a conspicuous figure on the European scene, a man not yet thirty years old. Until then no national notice of him had been taken, only here and there a character piece in a local newspaper about the aristocratic curio who dreamed of irredentism and talked as if he would smash the Red Army with the might of his left fist, trained at the gymnasium at Heidelberg. These efforts at caricature failed when undertaken by reporters who went to hear him talk. They could no longer bring off conventional ideological denigration. ("Count Wintergrin seems to have forgotten the horrors of war . . .") But after Heidelberg, all the major papers in Europe suddenly began to take notice of Axel Wintergrin and his—his what? they asked themselves. Here was someone who, biologically, could have been the grandson of Adenauer, the *de facto* leader of the country (with his Christian Democratic Union, serving as chancellor under the authority of the joint occupation com-

mand). And when direct elections came in November 1952, Adenauer would surely win—with the Social Democrats under Erich Ollenhauer taking perhaps one-third of the seats. Germany's future would be a generation's oscillation of power between these two parties, the analysts joined in predicting. There was no room for the so-called "Reunification" party of this Wintergrin. Why so much fuss over a quixotic Heidelberg Manifesto? Why had groups in every major city in Germany suddenly invited the young count to address them: elated veterans' organizations, cynical student associations, inquisitive business associations, wary labor unions—even, here and there, always discreetly, organizations of civil servants . . . why the fascination with him?

The disciplined left, and of course the papers in East Germany, had the ready answer. Wintergrin was this season's Hitler!

In late December of 1949 *Neues Deutschland* ran a large feature section triumphantly announcing that a search in Sweden revealed that there was no record that Axel Wintergrin had been detained in a Swedish concentration camp. The article suggested he had feigned opposition to Hitler for the sole purpose of sparing himself the rigors of military life and the dangers of service on the eastern front, and had spent the war years in Swedish dissipation. The story, given wide circulation everywhere in Europe, and intensively circulated within West Germany, brought a tide of curiosity and evolved quickly into dismay in his camp. Wintergrin's failure during that heavy week to answer questions about the sensational charges caused apprehension among even his closest followers, though those who knew him did their best to reassure everyone that he would be vindicated, as they firmly believed, somehow, he would be.

Finally he scheduled a press conference—and limited attendance to six journalists. What he had to say—he gave out in a general release—was not easily said in the hectic circumstances of a general press conference. ("Shee-yit!" the dumbstruck, excluded *New York Times* correspondent in Bonn reacted, on receiving the notice. "Who does this young kraut think he is? Immanuel Kant calling a press conference to explain his *Critique of Pure Reason?*") But clearly there had been no political favoritism in making out the list—one was the correspondent of *Der Spiegel,* a journal whose hostility to Wintergrin was rancorous and sustained.

The meeting took place in a private dining room in the Rheinhotel Dreesen at Godesberg, where ten years earlier Hitler had talked Chamberlain out of hunks of Czechoslovakia. The reporters arrived on time, and there were a score of others outside the room, patiently but firmly denied entrance by Wintergrin's friend Roland Himmelfarb. One reporter-photographer from *L'Humanité* pressed for admittance, and three burly figures, manifestly at his service, added their pressure to the reporter's attempt at a forced entry. Surrounding photographers snapped pictures of the contest. Himmelfarb, holding the door, called out for the help of hotel personnel. Axel Wintergrin, disembarked from the small Mercedes driven by a student volunteer, entered the hotel lobby at the height of the commotion. An aide, rushing to relieve Himmelfarb, paused to brief Wintergrin in telegraphic bursts. "Communist bastard . . . *L'Humanité* . . . here with thugs . . ." Wintergrin reached out, collared the French reporter, and lifted him whole up on his toes, his nose within a few inches of Wintergrin's, holding him there silently until the noise abated. "Go back

to your commissar in Paris. Or, better still, head that way"—Wintergrin pointed his nose to the east—"to the Soviet Union, and tell them that force in Germany will be used only *against* tyranny, not to promote it." He dropped the paunchy reporter, whose swagger had diminished as, one by one, his companions had been subdued by Wintergrin's partisans, and he fell almost to the floor before salvaging what he could of his aplomb and, muttering something about how Nazis will always be Nazis, scurried out of the lobby, the most photographed photographer of the season. Wintergrin walked into the room and apologized to the press for detaining them.

Wordlessly he distributed a copy of the citation he had received from the King of Norway. He gave the names of three Norwegians with whom he had associated in the resistance. He would prefer, he said, to answer questions after the press had satisfied itself of the validity of his representation. The first questioner asked why had he not revealed his actual story, instead of saying that he had been detained in Sweden.

It was precisely because he had in fact been active in the anti-Nazi resistance, he said.

"What was there to hide then?"

"The German people know now that it was wrong to support Hitler. I did not want, in 1945, to lecture my countrymen, most of whom, after all, were Germans fighting under Nazism, not Nazis fighting under Hitler. Their punishment was heavy enough without adding to it the reproaches of a twenty-five-year-old."

"Are you then saying that Germany now, the Germany of 1949, is different from the Germany of 1945?"

"Even in 1945 the support for Hitler was largely inertial. If

the war had ended, and Hitler had faced a free election, he would have lost. There is no significant nostalgia for Hitler today. Those unhappy Germans in the East who continue to live under tyranny do so because they have not—yet—been given another choice."

The meeting ended. In a matter of hours, Norwegian reporters tracked down the former resistance fighters. Olin Justsen was now a naval architect, living in Kristiansand, and he said to the reporter, Yes, he had known "Alec"—he knew him by no other name, but recognized him on seeing his photograph in the paper—and had participated with him in two missions.

"What were they?"

"Well," said Justsen, puffing on his pipe, his eyes glazed, his hand trembling slightly, "one of them required attaching an explosive to the hull of a freighter sent over by the Germans to take a load of heavy water to Germany. That mission was accomplished."

"What was the other?"

"The other," Justsen said, in measured accents—he had consulted his own conscience rigorously on this, anticipating the question—"involved the elimination of an individual."

"Who?" the reporter asked.

"We do not give out his name."

"What had he done?"

"We do not describe his crimes."

"Was he a German?"

"We do not give out his nationality."

Neither of the other two Norwegians questioned knew about the assassination. They had served with Wintergrin on other missions. Pooling their information, reporters

counted two parachute jumps into German bases in Norway, three demolition jobs, two intelligence sorties into Nazi installations, plus the mysterious assassination. Rhitto Heitger, the grand old man of the resistance, would not talk except to say that from the time Wintergrin presented himself in 1939, occupying a desk in routine intelligence work, through the occupation, until liberation, he had refused no assignment except one that might take him to his native country, betraying his identity and imperiling his mother.

The information, consolidated in the major newsrooms of Europe, was sulkily reported by the hostile press and, dispiritedly, the newsmen gave up that line of attack on Axel Wintergrin, which would have taken care of so many problems, if only *Neues Deutschland* had been right. When next Wintergrin spoke, on Wenceslaus Day in Frankfurt, he was given a standing ovation before he uttered a word. He received this by fastening the two bottom buttons on his coat, and smiling his half-distracted smile. His speech was on the usual themes, and later, at the press conference, he spoke the words, in answer to a question, that caused the phone to ring at the home of Pyotr Ivanovich Ilyich in Moscow, even though it was almost midnight there; and, in the United States, where it was late afternoon, caused an aide to walk right into the office of Allen Dulles. What, the reporter at Frankfurt had asked, were Count Wintergrin's plans? Why, he said, his plans were to organize his movement into a political party to compete in the elections in November, which elections he was certain of winning.

Having won them, he would proceed to liberate East Germany.

Vadim Platov and Viktor Kapitsa

VADIM PLATOV wondered why, on that day, the train had moved only for a half hour. But then he also wondered why he continued to spend time wondering about anything, let alone evidence of logistical irrationality. The reason—he concluded—was that his mind continued to work. How long would *that* go on? He had been given a tenner under Article 56, Section 10, which was directed at nonspecified forms of "Anti-Soviet Agitation." Instantly his mind had gone to work to collate the random statistics he had begun idly assembling when, two years earlier, Stalin had reintroduced the draconian *katorga*. Would he *live* ten years?—under the conditions in Vorkuta? As a scientist, he warned himself sternly, he had to deal scientifically with scientific evidence: It never pays, in science, to deceive oneself. "What is the point in building a bridge which will fall down?" the professor at the engineering school at Kiev had once observed.

Not that Vadim Platov had ever been interested in building bridges, but he was very much interested in the scientific principles involved in bridge building. It was in physics, not engineering, that he had distinguished himself, graduating with honors in the class of 1938 and winning a fellowship to study under Academician Pekrovskii, the as-

trophysicist. He wished instead that he had devoted all those thousands of hours to the study of hypnotism. He couldn't quite remember whether hypnotists could hypnotize themselves—or just other people . . . Perhaps, he ruminated, he might have succeeded in hypnotizing himself by looking at a mirror and practicing on himself the same skills he practiced on others. Then, then, after hard concentration—he might succeed in causing himself to lose consciousness. Consciousness of the cold.

In about a half hour it would be his turn to lie on the floor, and the turn of his two companions to sit on him, one on the legs, the other on the torso, thus providing him a little extra warmth. In approximately a half hour Glinka— the illiterate Glinka, little Glinka with the eye patch, the two missing front teeth, and the perpetual smile—Glinka would advise them that a half hour had gone by. Their watches, those of them who had watches—Vadim had had a watch, won it as a prize after his paper was published—had been taken from them at the processing center at Riga, but one of the men, the big Kurd, had hidden his. A clumsy guard had forgotten to make him open his mouth. Glinka told the men that all his life he had had the gift of time, that he never used a watch nor needed the summons of a bell but would come in from the fields to receive his lunch and his supper at exactly the specified hour even as a young boy, and his parents, who had a radio, would show him off to their family and friends, saying, "Tell us when it will be six o'clock, Glinka." In due course he would raise his little hand and say in a high happy voice, "It is nearing six o'clock, Father." Whereupon the father would turn up the volume and, inevitably, within a moment or two, Radio Moscow would announce that the hour was six o'clock.

They had found the man who had hidden his watch. And soon after that the Armenian began smoking cigarettes which he had now mysteriously come by, and the big bearded Kurd whose watch had been discovered and who had been beaten for concealing it observed the Armenian with ill-disguised suspicion. Shortly after Glinka called out the hour of midnight, the sixty occupants of the railway car heard a stifled cry followed by a gurgle followed by silence, and the next day when the door was opened and the five pails of gruel were slid into the car, the prisoner nearest the door jerked his thumb behind his shoulder and said, "The Armenian is dead." From behind him the prisoners passed up the corpse and flung it over the side. The guard called for an officer from the command car. A captain came, looked at the corpse, and up again at the impassive faces he could see framed by the space opened up by the door. He hesitated, whispered instructions to an orderly, then removed a whistle from deep inside his vest and blew three times on it. In a few seconds six guards with semiautomatic AK-47s stood behind him at attention. The officer looked up at the men huddled about the railway car opening.

"Tonight," he called out in a rasping voice, creating clouds of steam in the subzero cold, "you will not get your rations." The prisoners were silent.

"And right now," the officer's voice achieved a mechanical stridency, "we shall teach you that executions are a privilege of the Soviet State, not of counterrevolutionaries."

The orderly returned with a sheet of paper. The officer looked at it, turning it around so that the typed roster faced his orderly, to whom he said in a loud voice: "Place your finger on one number." The orderly did so.

"Call out that number."

"V 282."

"V 282, present yourself."

There was no motion from within the car.

"For every minute I am kept waiting, I shall add another number."

The silence, thought Vadim, whose own number was V 280, was profounder than any he had ever heard, profounder even than the silence when the colonel had risen to pronounce sentence on him at Riga.

In exactly one minute, the captain repeated the ritual with the orderly, who now called out, "Number V 295!"

At this point there was a shout from the end of the car, and the men moved to permit the Kurd passage to the open door. He looked down at the officer, spat, and said: "Let them alone. It was me."

With dignity he managed to lower himself to the siding. The officer pointed to a telephone pole ten meters away and the Kurd was led there. His hands were tied behind the pole and, immobilized, he faced his comrades. Three of the six soldiers, on command, hoisted their rifles and fired. The officer withdrew his pistol from its holster, approached the Kurd, slumped now over to one side, and shot him behind the head. Vadim looked across the width of the car at the young man of his own age who had not uttered a word in the three weeks since their common journey began. His hair was blond, and a bandage of sorts was wound about his left ear. His eyes were streaming tears.

On noticing that Vadim was staring at him, Viktor Kapitsa turned his face away, but in that railway car there was no privacy, and Vadim Platov knew that although he had not studied hypnotism, or extrasensory perception, he had succeeded in communicating to the young man that he,

Vadim, was forever grateful to him for this comment of tears. Vadim himself closed his eyes, and suddenly the words appeared before him which he had not thought to utter since he was twelve years old and his grandmother died, thereby relieving him of the (counterrevolutionary) task of a daily recitation. He prayed: He prayed for the Kurd, prayed for the stranger across the way, prayed for the executioners, prayed for Stalin—but his scientific training then asserted itself. If he prayed for Stalin—prayed that Stalin should mend his ways—then Stalin might become commendable, and if he was commendable, Vadim would logically be obliged to revere him. But all he could ever do was hate the monster, so he must *not* pray for him, otherwise he would face a terrible dilemma. He remembered suddenly that his grandmother, who had actually traveled abroad before the Revolution and studied philosophy in Germany as a girl, once told him that not even God could ordain a contradiction. He was very hungry. But the five pails of gruel with the long-handled spoons sat there in the silence, untouched. The guard, looking briefly over his shoulder in the direction of the officers' car, slid the door shut without removing the pails, as he would normally have done. The door would not open again until the next morning; captain's orders.

It was, Vadim reckoned, the warmest day of the summer. The temperature was above freezing and, at midday, he even found himself unbuttoning his heavy jacket, experiencing a sensual thrill felt not more than a dozen days in the year. He sat with his back to the great pile of frozen wooden railroad ties—the weather would never be warm for long enough to thaw them out, and in his gloved hand he fon-

dled the eleven-ounce lump of bread which was the whole of the day's hard rations: At the end of the day they would be given a pint of a fishy gruel, and, at breakfast time, nothing. Vadim said to his companion, "Viktor, today I think, I think that we are going to make it."

Viktor Kapitsa had begun to chew on his bread. He ate very slowly, with deliberation, and did not speak while he chewed. "I don't know, Vadim. We have five more years. Shall we play again at our game?"

Statistics, with improvisations on numbers and concepts, was their principal diversion. Viktor had been what they called a "calculating prodigy." At age five he could give out the sum of a list of figures, each with as many as four digits, of whatever length. His father felt it his duty to report this peculiarity to the party secretary at the 8th District of Kharkov where Viktor's father worked as bookkeeper at the shoe factory that was the center of commercial life in the 8th District. The secretary was held in awe because he had been present (he was a railroad porter) at the Finland Station when Lenin arrived there on that great day in April. Vitkovsky amused himself for a half hour interrogating the little boy and giving him longer and longer lists to add. The boy's little voice without hesitation gave the answer to the first question: How much is 578 plus 624 plus 1,009 plus 333? The secretary painfully added the figures to corroborate the boy's accuracy.

After the next question, he stopped, confident that Viktor was giving the correct reply. He tried then the multiplication tables. "How much is 381 times 411?" On these Viktor would hesitate, closing his eyes and shaking his hair slightly, but the delay was never more than for a second or two. There were conferences, and it was decided that when

he became seven years old, the state should take Viktor to a special school in Moscow where he would keep company with the brightest young sons of Lenin's associates and develop his skill in such a way as to be of maximum use to the state. The elder Kapitsa felt free to urge on the secretary the comparative advantages of keeping the boy in Kharkov, but the secretary by this time spoke as though it had been the personal decision of Lenin himself that Viktor should go away to school.

Happily, Lenin died before Viktor was seven and the secretary disappeared without a trace, leaving his successor with no known file on Viktor Kapitsa, who, accordingly, went to the regular Soviet school. There his precocity was acknowledged enthusiastically by a stocky, imperious woman in her sixties who had taught the children since before the inauguration of the last Czar. She took over Viktor's schooling and arranged that at age thirteen he should indeed go away—to a special school, fashioned after the German *gymnasia,* where Viktor was introduced to physics. His avid pursuit of it carried him through the university at Kharkov and then to the Lenin Institute for graduate work and, finally, experimental work under Perelman and Fortikov, disciples of the great Tsiolkovskii, who had founded GIRD—in Russian, the Group for the Study of Reactive Motion. By the mid-thirties GIRD had evolved into a rocket research program where, at age twenty-one, Viktor Kapitsa, fair, lithe, even-featured, slightly distracted in demeanor, was acknowledged as a young man of established achievement, having already published an astonishing paper on the aerodynamic problems of space flight which was distributed among laboratory technicians of the Moscow Military Air Academy.

"Ah, Viktor," Vadim now replied, "in your company, of what help can I be to you with statistics? Besides, are we not equipped to deal with measured competence with respect to the variables? It is not likelier ever to be colder than it was during Christmas week of 1948. They have not increased our rations since the day we arrived here. We have managed, between us, to steal an average of 280 ounces of bread per month. Your special relationship with our dear captain's wife, whose quarters you scrub, has netted us an average of twenty-four ounces of cod-liver oil per month. I don't know what I weigh, but I don't think I weigh one ounce less than I weighed one month after we got here. Looking at you, my dear Viktor, is a singularly unpleasant experience: Your skin is yellow, your lips are blue, your face is freckled with frostbite scars, your blond stubble is uneven—it is fortunate I don't have to look at your face except at night" (both men wore balaclavas the bottom part of which they moved up to nose level when they ate), "but you do not look worse than you did soon after we got here. We have put in our twelve hours a day seven days a week and neither of us has had dysentery in over a year. What have you got to say to that?"

Viktor pointed to the horizon on the left, where the wooden profile of Vorkuta's barracks could be seen and, one hundred meters to the right, a mound, taller than the tallest building, and stretching a kilometer off to the right like a huge ice dirigible beached in the snow.

"That," said Viktor, pointing to the corpses of ten thousand men who had passed through Vorkuta, "is my answer."

"Ah," said Vadim, who felt today a strange elation, "but look at this, my doubting Thomas," and he raised his hand. "That is not the hand of a corpse. That is the hand of

Vadim Platov." He lowered his hand. "And who decided that I should lower my arm? The Gulag Archipelago? Captain Popolov? The Great Shithead in the Kremlin? No, it is Vadim Platov who decided just now to lower his arm. And listen, listen carefully"—the nearest guard was nowhere within hearing distance, but Vadim lowered his voice theatrically—"listen: 'Our Father, Who art in heaven, hallowed be Thy name. . . .' Nothing that they have done to us has kept me from remembering those words, and I know that they mean more than"—by instinct, he turned his head to one side—"than everything ever written by Marx and Lenin."

Viktor's teeth flashed into a smile, and he ripped off his balaclava, and the lines of an old man's face were visible, corrugating the sunken cheeks, but the eyes were young. "Ah, Vadim, how would I have survived except for you! My beloved Vadim, you know nothing about fate, or historical necessity. You don't allow yourself to remember now, with a few ounces of bread in your stomach, that you will wake at midnight from the cold and from the awful pain from your parched stomach. They will call us out, as usual, sometime between twelve and two, for a roster-check, and you will experience, for the thousandth time, a little fire of indignation. And you will return to the bunk and spend half an hour trying to contrive your body and the rags we have collected over five years into a position so as to make sleep possible. And then both of us, I know, will play mentally with figures, and our theories of spaces, trying to think, think of something except that we have lived a lifetime, every night is a lifetime, every night we have no reason to expect that our lives, our bodies, can accept one more day of . . . this. But now you speak as if you were lying at a beach

on the Black Sea wondering whether you would go to the smorgasbord before, or after, lying with your girlfriend. . . . Vadim—"

The whistle blew. The conversation stopped in midsentence. All over the area men rose—220, in this detachment—and lifted their picks, their shovels, the ties, the wheelbarrows with the rock and gravel, and at that slow, deliberate pace from which no prisoner ever varied, they went back to the railroad bed to work a second six hours, during which no conversation was permitted except to ask questions of a supervisor. A cloud suddenly occluded the sun, which was not seen again on that day in July.

At five-thirty on that memorable morning the following March the great bell did not sound. By habit, most of the prisoners in Detachment D woke anyway. There were no watches, so that nobody could say with certainty that the hour was past when the guard would unlock the door and shout out to the men to move outside to relieve themselves in the open latrine before lining up in the dark to march out to the work area. But an hour went by, and through the crack in the door a prisoner announced that he could see traces of light, and the word spread through the barrack to the two hundred men who lay in their bunks dressed in exactly the same clothes they would wear marching out the door to work, the temperature inside the barrack being forty-five degrees. Something was up.

Vadim whispered to Viktor. "Perhaps there is another hunger strike?" The reference was to the strike in 1949 in Detachment L. The spokesman for the men had announced, when the guard opened the door in the morning, that the detachment would not go out to work without

receiving food. The demand was for five ounces of bread in the morning. The other detachments were kept locked throughout the day, eighty thousand prisoners ignorant of the ongoing drama.

It was not until that evening that the routine was resumed, and although the barracks' doors had opened only to admit the kitchen zeks with the great cans of gruel, and they—supervised, as ever, by two armed guards—said nothing, everyone suddenly knew; in the way that, in a prison, everyone knows when a prisoner has been executed.

The hunger strikers had been told in midafternoon that their request was granted. Joyfully they had filed out toward the work area, two kilometers distant, where they had been told the baker's truck awaited them. Exercising caution, the prisoners' spokesman specified that the ration would have to include the normal midday ration of twelve ounces *in addition to* the five ounces bargained for during the morning, and the commandant said that he understood the terms well.

The men marched toward food, their spirits exuberant because of this unheard-of victory. As they marched forward toward the railroad bed the guards, normally abreast of the detachment, began casually to fall behind until there were, in fact, only the two columns of prisoners. It was then, from hastily improvised foxholes in the snow, that the machine gunners went to work.

There were of course no survivors, and the commandant had issued crisp orders that the corpses would remain where they had fallen, as monuments to the incivility of the criminal class and the expeditiousness of Soviet justice. That was four years ago, and although the population of

Vorkuta was constantly refreshed, there were still enough old-timers to ensure the unlikelihood that another detachment would attempt a hunger strike.

"It has got to be something else," said Viktor.

It was noon before the guards opened the door and called out the men. Vadim squinted, the sight being unusual. It was dark when the men rose to go to work, dark when they returned—only during the summer was it still light. So it had been seven months since Vadim had seen the endless files of scruffy men, as far as the eye could see, in double ranks, shuffling their arms and feet to gain protection against the zero temperature. No noise was tolerated, not even the clapping of gloved hands—in order that the commands of the detachment captains might be heard clearly. But today they heard the rasp of the amplifiers, posted on high telephone poles at intervals of about fifty meters in all directions. These were infrequently used, but were the instrument by which the commandant occasionally addressed the entire population of this island of the Archipelago.

"Prisoners of the Soviet State! Hear this! Silence! Hear this! Yesterday, the great father of our beloved socialist republic passed away. I know that your grief will incapacitate you"

—*"that sadist is incapable of sarcasm,"* thought Vadim, his heart pounding with joy—

"so that in memory of our beloved Marshal Stalin, we shall suspend the work requirement for the balance of the day so that you can mourn his passing. You will all return to your barracks."

And here—never mind that the noise would be overheard—there was no restraint. Men who had not smiled in

years broke out with laughter that became nearly hysterical. Men who had not spoken to each other embraced. They shouted and they sang in uninhibited dissonance, each man yelling out whatever hymn of thanksgiving occurred to him. The jubilation would have gone on into the night except that the biological instinct so highly developed in survival circumstances—to husband one's energies—gradually asserted itself, and the men fell gradually into a kind of comatose silence. But Vadim and Viktor, sitting on the lower bunk, talked on excitedly. Vadim whispered that surely the death of the monster would affect their prison terms? Playfully he asked Viktor: "It is 2,928 days since I was sentenced. What percentage of my tenner have I done?" Viktor closed his eyes, grinned, and asked: "To how many decimal places do you want your answer?"

"Four!" Vadim answered coquettishly.

"80.0022 percent," said Viktor.

"Well, don't you think our new masters might consider remitting the . . . 19.9978 we have left over?"

"No," said Viktor. "Probably they have forgotten we exist."

It was several months before the folkways of Archipelago began gradually to change. The first sign was the commandant's advising the men that they would each be permitted to write one letter, on not more than two sides of a sheet of paper, which, together with one pencil, would be issued the following day. The rations were increased by four ounces with very nearly miraculous physical effect, Viktor and Vadim agreed, most noticeably permitting sounder sleep. It required a huge act of will, but both men regularly husbanded one-third of their noonday ration, and ate it the following morning. They noticed before many weeks had

gone by that the ranks of Vorkuta were diminishing without any significant bloating of the ice dirigible. Still, in their own detachment, though six men had died in July and there were no replacements, no one was called to the processing center, the staging area for torture, execution—and release.

But the day came. Viktor and Vadim had not dared to give voice to that which both feared most: that one should be released while the other stayed. The prospect of one day in the Archipelago without each other was a thought neither could permit himself to express. They were both, in fact, summoned from their work area one Wednesday in August and led by a guard to the processing center where they were directed to a cubicle in one of the administrative buildings. Pictures on the wall were of Khrushchev and Bulganin, and the bulletin board was thick with communications from that huge spectral building in Moscow, the ganglion of the Archipelago. Viktor was called in first and told to sit down on the stool opposite the clerk, who was dressed in a shapeless brown corduroy and wore a heavy vest and rimless glasses and a trim mustache. He studied the papers on the unpainted table.

"Kapitsa. Yes, anti-Soviet agitation . . . protested deportation of traitors on eastern front in a letter to the rector of the University of Kharkov. Hm. Well, Kapitsa, the Soviet State, exercising its customary mercy, has granted you an amnesty. Moreover, the Moscow Military Air Academy has . . . requested . . . that you report for duty there. Within thirty days. You are to go to General Bolknovitinov. Do you agree? Sign here." Viktor Kapitsa, his hand shaking, took the pen and signed his name on the form without bothering to read it.

He was given a release order, a train pass to Kharkov, and

ten rubles. Vadim Platov was dealt with similarly, and told to report to an institute in Kiev whose name he did not recognize. He was emboldened to ask what it was that was needed of him. "The state requires the services of all its trained scientists." When could they leave? The clerk looked at his watch. It was eleven. "There is a train at one o'clock. You change at Ust for Moscow."

One o'clock! The station was a mere one-kilometer distant. Clutching his release papers, Vadim left the cubicle for the anteroom, where Viktor was waiting for him. They did not speak, could not speak, but walked silently to their empty barrack. To put together their belongings was the work of five minutes. They must not misgauge the time, but the bell at noon summoning the camp personnel to lunch would give them exactly one hour's advance notice of the train's departure. Feverishly they set about writing, with the stubby pencils they now possessed, notes of farewell to their companions, having agreed to write joint notes so as to cover as many as possible.

They reckoned what they supposed must be half an hour after the bell. They had written a total of forty notes, which they distributed on the frayed canvas bunks of the addressees. They picked up their satchels and went out the door at the usual pace and turned, this time not east toward the endless railroad line but west toward the building from which smoke always rose, in the direction of their youth. They could see the outlines of a dozen railroad cars. Simultaneously both men began to walk at a brisk pace unexperienced in years.

Their bearing was now erect. Viktor with his topcoat of sorts, sewn together from three separate remnants of jacket material, and the shawl wound about his head and ears,

Vadim with the heavy jacket, a coarse piece of string girding it tightly about his fleshless waist, patched trousers, heavy shoes much dilapidated. Suddenly Viktor paused, laid down his satchel, and ceremoniously removed his balaclava; Vadim did the same. Cautiously they inserted these life-saving face masks in their satchels, and resumed their march. At the gate, so ferociously guarded with high turrets, machine guns, and dogs, their documents were accepted routinely and, giddy with the sensation, they walked out of Gulag and climbed the staircase to the station level unsurveilled, for the first time in eight years, by armed guards.

Inside, a sergeant at the ticket window inspected their travel passes and issued them a stub for the journey to Ust. Was the train leaving on time? Vadim asked, as if he were a boulevardier asking a routine question at the Gare du Nord. The clerk stared at him incredulously, uttered a profanity, and returned to his chair by the stove. Vadim looked at Viktor, who said, "There's the train. Why not board it?" Intoxicated by their authority over their own movements, they moved up the steps of the car, half expecting that at any moment they would be recalled. Timidly Vadim opened the carriage door and was overcome by the heat within. He had not experienced such comfort since leaving the courthouse where he was sentenced. Two dozen men, half of them prison personnel on leave, half of them liberated prisoners from other detachments, were sitting on the wooden slatted benches *with backrests*. Vadim and Viktor sat opposite each other, lowering themselves carefully onto the unaccustomed chairs. A guard approached them. He bore a large heavy covered tray at waist level, strapped behind his neck.

"You have money?"

They nodded. He uncovered the tray and they saw rolls, sausage, cheese; enough, Vadim thought, to bring the whole of their detachment to delirium.

"How much?" He struggled for urbanity.

Five kopecks bought them each as much as they could eat. That was not a great deal, because their stomachs rebelled at such unaccustomed richness. They finished just as the train began to move. They looked out the window. The sky was a curdled yellow, the ground specked by snow, the squat barracks gray and frostbitten and bleak. The ice dirigible had assumed a perfect symmetry.

Viktor looked at Vadim and said, "You were right, Vadim."

Vadim looked up curiously, as if to say: Right about what?

"You were right," Viktor repeated. "We did survive. But I would not be here except for you," and the tears came down again, and Vadim thought back on the boyish face of that very young man, in the other railway car, with the tears, which would take a lifetime to dry.

Benni Bolgiano

BENNI, AS EVERYONE CALLED HIM THEN, was the guest of honor at the party—it was his birthday. The year was 1939. Benni was thirty-nine, and a considerable figure in Alturgia, the little suburb southwest of Rome where Benni was born, schooled, and now worked. Though still young, he had inherited his father's role as something of an informal ombudsman for the workers who kept afloat the massive enterprise that sustained Alturgia, a subsidiary of the giant firm of Etzione Srl. whose cash registers, to point to only one of Etzione's products, supplied half of Italy's needs, and were exported worldwide. These were made in Milan, but the firm had many products, including typewriters and sewing machines. At Alturgia the principal product was the renowned Etzione Stapler, and Benni was the shop steward of the craft union, which called on him to do much of the paperwork for the six hundred–odd employees who looked to him for help in those little matters that can mean so much, like getting an advance before the new baby. Benni would get it, and with the check, more often than not, came a letter offering, however prematurely, the congratulations—of the Italian Communist Party, Etzione Stapler division.

Soon after the advent of Benito Mussolini, back when

Benni had just begun to work, the sales in staplers had risen dramatically. It was not only because under fascism the paperwork was enormous; Mussolini, who was given to variable and episodic enthusiasms, had on one occasion elected to dwell on the virtues of husbandry by speaking of the staple as a symbol. This had been during a long and robust address delivered over state radio and blared into all public buildings and town squares. His researchers, Mussolini had recounted, his voice rising with triumphant enthusiasm at the discovery, had calculated that for every paper clip, Italians could, at the same expense, manufacture *ten* staples. "I ask you, my fellow citizens," Mussolini had said, coming to the climax of his address, "I ask you, are you willing to serve the motherland to the extent of substituting a little physical exertion, in return for a saving of ninety percent?" Mussolini then dilated on the general theme of Italian physical culture, to which he was strenuously devoted. "Is it not," he asked in his most seductive accents, "something of a symbol to ask all Italians to exert themselves physically to the extent of applying a little pressure on a stapling machine, rather than to slither on a paper clip, requiring no physical exertion, causing the arm muscles to become flaccid, replicating the obviously degenerate ways of our anarchic neighbors to the west?"

He ordered that henceforward the stapler should be recognized as the agent of the energetic in body and spirit. He did not want to see a paper clip in any office of the Italian government, he warned, his voice now not only paternal, but menacing.

The next day the orders had, of course, outrun the capacity even of Etzione, and there developed a six-week delay in delivery; but the demand proved constant, and the Alturgia

division flourished, bringing finally the promotion of Benni to the position his father had had when suddenly the old man died, in his sleep, from a heart attack. The handsome, diffident, hardworking Benni was all but unanimously elected, on the fourth round, and shortly after a visit to the only other contender by two heavily muscled Party representatives from Rome, the other contender announced that he had decided to withdraw from the race so that Benni Bolgiano would receive the backing of all the workers, united.

The negotiation process with Etzione followed a preset course, every three years. The managers would meet with Benni and his lieutenants and announce exactly what the terms of the new contract would be. Benni would decide which terms of the new contract the management should fail to enumerate in its public message to the workers. Benni would take that clause—in 1938, it was two weeks' vacation with pay after two years of work—and publicly insist that the company yield on the point. Much pressure would be mobilized. The managers would respond that the concession was economically crippling, but Benni would stick to his guns. Then, when there were only minutes to go before the old contract ran out, management would tearfully yield and there would be a noisy celebration among the workers. Benni would join in their celebration, and make a speech about the goldenwork of the bargaining table. He was careful not to say what actually was on his mind, namely that one day there would be no bargaining table, because the workers would own and operate the enterprise—that was for tomorrow, and at the last several Party meetings in Rome he had been cautioned against any public declaration that might attract the attention of Mussolini's fascist police.

At the birthday party, Benni wished that the meeting in

Rome had been this morning rather than yesterday, because the other historical event of September 1, 1939, was the attack on Poland by Hitler. Benni was not certain how to instruct his friends in the local Party on the proper reaction. Hitler was the enemy, of course; but Mussolini had twice, in recent months, professed a fraternal devotion to Hitler, and since the Party was cautious about provoking the opposition, Benni thought it wise to caution against any public comment, "pending developments."

The great Togliatti would have to instruct them on this one, for Benni knew the importance of rank, and discipline. So when he raised his glass, which he did frequently, both giving toasts and receiving others', he spoke the usual generalities, and when he got home to his wife and ten-year-old son and saw that they were safely asleep, Benni got down on his knees, secure from detection. Benni and the Party disapproved of prayers, but he was a man of some sentiment. "Although, Almighty God," he whispered tonight, "I know that you do not exist, there is no reason to hold that against you; and accordingly I address you simply as a matter of courtesy, to ask you to look kindly on the workers of the Etzione Syndicate, Stapler Division, to bless the efforts of the members of its affiliated unions, and to give special guidance, in his all-important role, to Comrade Stalin, to help him in his campaign to bring freedom and peace and justice and brotherhood to the peoples of this world. All this I ask, and especially that you look after my precious Maria and Michele." Benni now lapsed into the boilerplate of his youth, from which his mother, proudly Jewish, would ostentatiously desist when Benni's father conducted the prayer meetings, "through the blessings of thy son, our blessed Lord, Jesus Christ."

It wasn't until two years later that the Nazis came. They were technically there to help convert a part of the factory to the manufacture of parts for automatic weapons. At first Benni was treated with some deference, although he was not consulted on all of the decisions reached by the new military-technological hierarchy, even those decisions that directly affected working conditions.

He spoke to Maria about this one night in June, while Michele was fiddling with the radio. He said he would have to make an official protest, to which end he would have to see Captain Kreisler, who seemed to be the man to deal with, notwithstanding that he had no specific title; it was to his office that, increasingly, one went in order to get authoritative decisions. He would, he assured Maria, see him tomorrow—indeed, he had already made the appointment for three o'clock. Maria, pretty, always shy and a little frightened, turned her eyes toward Michele and asked Benni to be careful. He smiled, kissed her, and whispered that she might coach him better on how to behave—upstairs, in the bedroom.

Benni was astonished, on being admitted into the office of Captain Kreisler, that he was not invited to sit down. He stood, awkwardly, his opening remarks rather scrambled by the social clumsiness. Captain Kreisler, his black military jacket on, the heat of the afternoon notwithstanding, sat behind his desk, in front of a photograph of Mussolini and Hitler embracing at Munich. He had a sheaf of papers before him.

"I am glad you made this appointment, Bolgiano, because I had it down to see you."

Benni said nothing, but could not remember when last he had felt so awkward.

"You are the son of Eva Moravia Bolgiano?"

"That is correct, Captain."

"The records show that Eva Moravia was Jewish."

Benni, finding a sudden equilibrium returning to his body, looked down at the pale blond person with the wispy mustache and broad, hunched shoulders.

Benni weighed his words carefully. "What business is that of yours? Besides, my mother is dead."

Captain Kreisler's cheeks flushed.

"I am aware that she is dead. I am also aware that you are one-half Jewish. I am also aware that a Jewish conspiracy, worldwide, is engaged in attempting to frustrate the great war effort binding your country and mine. You are as of this moment relieved of your duties at the Etzione Company. Empty your office by five o'clock, and hand the keys to the clerk in my office."

Benni did not move.

Captain Kreisler looked up at him. "Should I make myself more clear? We do not want a Jew in our enterprise. Now get out."

Benni leaped over the desk as if catapulted by a huge sling. His hands were on the throat of the captain, who had gone crashing to the floor, toppling the chair and the type-writer table to one side.

The captain screamed in German. Benni released one hand, closed it, and delivered a smashing blow on the nose which instantly swelled and bled. He had delivered four blows, and started a fifth, before they pulled him away and held him outside pending the arrival of the military police. Benni said not a word, lowered his eyes, and looked at the ground: he did not wish to see the faces of any of his co-workers; even as he knew that they, frightened, would not

want to see Benni. The wait wasn't long. There were three men in the heavy black car that drove up. Two came out, and one of them with his stick, belted Benni in the stomach. He doubled over, and the guards took the opportunity to toss him into the backseat, separated from the front by wire netting.

The sergeant, preparing to enter the front section alongside the driver, turned to the four men from whom he had seized Benni.

"I am the adjutant of Captain Kölder of the military police. Send the official complaint by Captain Kreisler to the Office of the Advocate General at the Palazzo Venezia. We're taking him right to Rome."

During the next three days, in which twice each day he was taken to the "courtyard," as the prisoners called it, and there beaten, without any observable passion, by two huge young loutish-faced men both stripped to their T-shirts, then dragged back to his cell, no one asked him any questions at all, and to his mumbled request to see a lawyer, a doctor, or a priest, no answer whatever was given. In or out of his cell he felt only a single pain: Maria and Michele. Michele, age twelve, would be—Benni almost had to stop to calculate it—one-fourth Jewish. Would harm come to him? To Maria? For having married a half-Jew? His resentment during those days, which were followed by the mockery of a trial (at which a gratifyingly mutilated Captain Kreisler gave evidence) when he was unable to wrest from anyone information about his family, let alone cooperation in transmitting any communication to Maria, caused a radical change in his easygoing nature. He felt hardening in him a resolve altogether incompatible with anything he had felt

before. A resolve that left no room for compromise. It sustained him during the trip to the penitentiary near Naples, administered now by the Nazis, appearances to the contrary notwithstanding. He hardly noticed his surroundings. What had been the sentence? When last had he eaten? On the second evening Salvatore, his cellmate, doused a piece of bread in the cold soup and flagged Benni's attention. "Eat this for the sake of Maria and Michele." Benni was startled. Who was Salvatore? How did he know?

Salvatore anticipated the question. "You talk about them in your sleep."

Benni looked at the mushy piece of bread as though he had never eaten before. He chewed at it, consuming about one-half.

Salvatore spoke. "I have got word out on Maria and Michele."

Salvatore was speaking in whispers. "The Party will look after them."

"How do you know?" For the first time Benni felt he could focus on the problem. He looked at Salvatore, who was smoking a cigarette made from rancid prison tobacco rolled in newspaper. His voice was husky, but his words were authoritative in tone.

"I do not know. But the message has been passed along, and sometime soon you will hear."

Benni, unfamiliar with the sinfulness of being part Jewish, asked Salvatore, who was obviously more cosmopolitan, whether it was now the active policy of Mussolini's government to persecute the Jews.

"The answer to your question, Benni, is: Yes. It began with the October 1936 edict against Jews in the civil service and the armed forces. But the policy now fans out."

"Would it affect my son?"

"He would be better off elsewhere. His father," Salvatore spoke fatalistically, "is after all a political criminal who attempted to kill in cold blood the German representative of the Joint Military Command. They could have executed you."

"Why didn't they?"

"The workers at your plant stayed home until you were sentenced."

All this was news to Benni. "But it must have been—four, five days before they tried me?"

"Your . . . attack was on a Tuesday. You were tried on Friday. On Saturday morning the workers went back to work their half day."

Benni was visibly pleased, and proud; but then he wondered whether his coworkers' contumacy might enhance the danger to his family.

He asked suddenly, "What was my sentence?"

"Seven to ten years, in a labor camp. This is an administrative center. Soon they will take you away."

"And you?" Benni asked.

Salvatore, lighting another cigarette, said, "Me? Unhappily, I am to be shot."

Benni stood up, but dizziness and weakness brought him back to the bedside. He began to speak, but his voice failed to function. Finally he said in a whisper, "What did you do?"

Salvatore, twirling his cigarette in his hand, said, "I blew up the refinery at Ostia." He paused, and inhaled deeply. "It will take them three months to set it right."

"How did they catch you?"

"That is the only reason I will die without peace. It can

only have been one man who betrayed me, and he will survive me. But not"—Salvatore crossed himself—"for long. I gave his name to my friend."

"What friend?"

"Never mind. The same friend to whom I gave the name of your wife and son. You must not ask for names in this business."

"What business?" Benni asked.

Salvatore looked pityingly at his cellmate. "Benni, we are both members of the Party. The Party was forced to make an ugly alliance with Hitler. But that alliance will not last. And what you must realize now is that there is only one thing that matters, and that is for the Party to prevail. *That* is our business."

Benni repeated, as if liturgically, "That is our business."

"Do you understand what I am saying?"

Benni said he understood.

"In that event, your imprisonment will cause you less suffering."

Benni then said, in accents he normally reserved for Maria and Michele, "Salvatore, what can I do for you?"

"Benni, you are a sentimental fool. What are you in a position to do for me? You cannot even provide me with a plate of fettuccine, let alone a bottle of brandy, let alone an hour with my bitch Teresa—curse her philandering soul— let alone cause these walls to dissolve, let alone bring on the death, by the slowest available means, of Il Duce and Der Führer." Salvatore paused. "You can tell them—don't ask who they are; they will make themselves known to you— that Salvatore Gigli died like a man, but that his soul will not rest in peace until his betrayer is brought to citizens' justice." Salvatore slowly, lasciviously went through the

motion of cutting his own throat, sticking out his tongue as if in extreme agony.

He was quiet then, and Benni did not want to initiate any conversation. He would not sleep for the few hours Salvatore had left to live, in case he wanted to talk. But he didn't; he simply smoked one cigarette after another, and when the smoke reached the level of the single window, ten feet up on the side of the wall, the moonlight illuminated it, rising torpidly in the night air in the hot, humid cell.

They came when the moonlight, though dissipated, could still be seen. An officer, six men, a priest.

"Dismiss him." Salvatore pointed imperiously at the priest. "I am a Marxist, and need no opiate before leaving this wretched world."

The lieutenant and priest spoke to each other in whispers. The priest drew back, but did not leave the detachment. His head was bowed in prayer. They put handcuffs on Salvatore, who turned then to Benni and said in a resonant voice, "The revolution will bury these bastards." They yanked him out then; moments later, Benni heard the fusillade and was sick, though all that came from his impoverished stomach was an ill-digested crust of bread. Was this, he wondered, what was meant by casting bread upon the waters?

Benni found, at the prison in Basilicata, that he was happiest in the company of those who discreetly shared his own secular passion. One month after his arrival the news had been passed that the Resistance, under Party leadership, had smuggled Maria and Michele to America; they were safe, living in Washington. From time to time the Red Cross would bring him a letter from Maria, reassuring

Benni that she would wait forever for him, and that Michele—now "Michael"—was doing well in school.

The days and weeks and months went quickly—the summers hot, the winters cold, the food all but inedible, the spirits kept alive only by news, which would trickle in, of defeat after defeat, the deposition of Mussolini, then of course talk of a military invasion by the Allied powers, in anticipation of which the Nazis descended in large numbers. Would they—there were three hundred in the work detachment—be moved north? Perhaps even as far as Germany? Or might they be shot? That, Benni reflected, probably depended on whether the relevant orders were given by the Germans or by the Italians, whose loyalty in the southern provinces was less than rigorous. The Germans would be more expeditious in their approach, the Italians more nonchalant; besides, the Italians would be around after the surrender to answer for what they had done, while the Germans would be retreating to their northern fastness.

All the talk was about what was looming; finally, during the summer of 1943, the guards permitted them to listen to the radio broadcasts. It was not difficult, after a week or two, to get the hang of it. The announcers spoke in an Aesopian mode: thus, "The Allied expeditionary force, led by General George Patton, suffered severe losses in the fighting outside Palermo, as the valiant armies of Italy resisted wave after wave of assault on the capital city." This meant that the next day the Americans would take Palermo. The prisoners did not bother to disguise their enthusiasm for the invading armies, and the morale of the guards was visibly disordered.

By October all the Germans had been detached to the front in Calabria. The Italians did their work listlessly, under officers who at first were younger and of lesser military rank than their predecessors. These in turn were replaced by men who had clearly been yanked by the Nazis from retirement, and now the prison camp was under the command of Colonel Nicola Paone, who must have been overage in grade during the *First* World War. The colonel knew nothing about the manufacture of barbed wire, which was the principal production of Campo Spirito Santo, and there weren't enough old hands about to notice the general slowdown. The manuals had always specified that the barbs should be four-point half round, wrapped around both cable wires. So it had been from time immemorial, with the wire coming in from the die at one end of the long, ill-heated building. But the loss of supervisory controls began to bring on difficulties. The lubricant box was neglected, or the fiber washers went too long without replacement, or the holding screws were unregulated. At the other end, waiting for the naked wire, those in charge of the barbing process were often idle. And when the wire was passed through the feeds into the spinner head, as often as not a single worker would insert the barb, resulting in two-point, rather than four-point, barbs. Instead of precisely measuring the specified eight centimeters between barbs, the prisoner pulling the wire would merely approximate the distance, then nod to the spinner operators. However, no one in Rome complained that production quotas were not being met, indeed were down by fifty percent.

Benni, by now the acknowledged leader of the ideological militants, acted in effect as spokesman for all the prisoners, since it was only the Communists who were organized; and

it was he who was called into the office of Colonel Paone on the evening of February 4, 1944, and invited to sit down. Benni did so warily, refusing the proffered cigarette. The colonel said that he had listened to the shortwave radio the evening before and had done considerable thinking. The war—at least the Italian part of the war—was, he said . . . well, was over. In a matter of weeks, the Americans would reach Rome—and here, at Campo Spirito Santo, the prisoners were halfway between the beachhead and Rome— what would be the point in pointless resistance? Benni's heart began to pound, but he did not change his expression. The colonel went on to say that American radio had put on the air a general who, speaking in perfect Italian, announced that any Italian or German officers found guilty of brutality or acts of savagery against civilians or political prisoners would be tried by American military courts and held responsible for their acts. "When we take Rome," Paone quoted the American general, "we will have ammunition left over for firing squads."

Benni permitted himself to nod his head slowly, weightily, as though the American general who spoke Italian had been meticulously transcribing Benni's orders.

Colonel Paone then asked a direct question. He wanted to know whether Benni would be willing to testify to the effect that under Colonel Paone, he and his fellow prisoners had been fairly and humanely treated?

Benni decided to take a long gamble.

"On one condition, Colonel."

"What?" Colonel Paone's voice was anxious.

"That you permit all prisoners to leave within twenty-four hours."

Colonel Paone looked at Benni as if he were utterly mad.

He rang for the orderly, motioning him to lead Benni back to the barracks.

The next morning at dawn the usual bell didn't sound. The men began, out of habit, to stir. Most were fully dressed against the February cold. The prisoner nearest to the door which should have been unlocked at 6:45—so that they could walk, under the watchful eye of the guards with the automatic weapons, pacing up and down the elevated walks to the refectory—pounded on the door. "Hurry up! I'm hungry." There was no answer. Playfully, he pulled on the handle. The door swung open. The men fell silent. Apprehensive, he motioned to Benni, who walked purposefully to the gray-lit aperture, sticking his head out the door. The light was sufficient to see. He looked up to the commanding patrol tower. There was no one there. Benni looked to the right, toward the mess hall which would be bustling with the preparation of the soup and gruel they would be given for breakfast. It was silent.

And so he knew. Looking neither to the right nor left, and followed silently by his ragged barracks mates, he walked to the huge gate under the control tower. Confidently he turned the handle and pulled. It opened squeakily. For Benni, the war was over.

Henri Tod

HENRI TODDWEISS (they called him Heinrich in those days) and Clementa (Clementina) had always shared the same bedroom, and did so even now, aged thirteen and eleven. It wouldn't be until the following year that they would get separate quarters, their mother said: so it had been in her own family, and in that of her husband. Henri and Clementa had privately sworn never to sleep other than in a single room. Moreover, they swore according to the sacred rites of a society so secret that it had only two members, Henri and Clementa, and even beyond that, so secret that no one else in the entire world knew of its existence, not even Hilda, who knew most things about her little charges, and in whom they confided most things. But not about their society.

They called it The Valhalla, because everyone who was a member of it was, if not quite a god or a goddess, a king or queen. Clementa, when she was ten, had presided over the coronation of Henri, and it had been a most solemn occasion, conducted in the bathhouse outside the swimming pool at Pinneberg, where they lived then. And the very next day, King Heinrich had presided over the equally ceremonial investiture of Queen Clementa. Each now had a staff of

office, for which purpose they had taken two golf clubs from a discarded set of their father. Clementa had complained that her wand was unwieldy, but Henri had reassured her that she would grow into it: so at least twice every week, usually on Wednesday afternoons and Saturdays, they convened the royal court—not, during the summers, in the bathhouse, which was otherwise engaged. But their court was mobile, and met sometimes in the attic, sometimes outdoors, in the little glade at the end of the property. On such occasions they heard petitions from their subjects, discussed matters of royal moment—for instance, whether Hilda should postpone the hour at which she turned off their reading light. Always, they would refer to themselves with proper respect. "Is Queen Clementa satisfied with the service Her Majesty is getting, or does she desire King Heinrich to behead anyone?"

"Sire, I would not go so far, but Stefan [Stefan was the groom] I think should be given forty lashes, because he was not properly dressed yesterday when Her Majesty went to the stable to ride."

King Heinrich would write in his notepad, and move his lips as he spelled out the sentence he would mete out: Stefan, 40 lashes.

Every Saturday morning they were given their spending money, and in recognition of Henri's seniority he got two marks, while Clementa got only one mark fifty. But Clementa knew that she could confidently expect to find, that Saturday night under her pillow, an envelope with twenty-five pfennigs. And, written on the envelope, with crayons of different hue, a note. Last week's was, *His Majesty King Heinrich has ordered that this purse be put at the disposal of Her Majesty, the Queen.*

The messages would vary. And once, when Clementa was eleven, she found on the envelope a note advising the Queen that her purse this week would come to only twenty pfennigs, because His Majesty had seen her eat an American hot dog at the school picnic, and at age eleven the Queen should know that Jews do not eat hot dogs, under any circumstances. But the King added that he did not intend to report the infraction to their parents.

They didn't know what time it was that night when Hilda roused them. They had been asleep, and it was dark outside—it might have been eleven in the evening, or four in the morning. Hilda had turned on the lights and quickly placed on their beds a set of clothes and told them to get dressed instantly, not to utter a single word, that she was carrying out the instructions of their parents, and that the success of the enterprise absolutely required that they utter not a single word. "We will talk later," she said.

Confused and bleary-eyed, but with a sense of adventure, they dressed, and looked at each other, exchanging The Valhalla signal pledging secrecy to their proceedings. Hilda had two suitcases in hand, and outside a car was waiting. Not one they had ever ridden in before, or even seen before, and the driver was a stranger to them and spoke not a word, even as Henri and Clementa kept their silent pact. What was distressing was the near ferocity with which Hilda embraced them, each in turn, as she shoved them into the car. "I will see you tomorrow," she said. But when the car drove off Clementa whispered to Henri, "Hilda was crying!"

"Shh," Henri said, removing himself to the corner of the seat. By the time they reached Tolk, a two-hour drive, it was dawn. Clementa began to cry, and so the spell was broken

as they drove, finally, into the little farm where they were met by the Wurmbrands.

Mrs. Wurmbrand told them that they would be staying here at the farm for a while, that such were the instructions of their parents, who would be absent for a spell, but soon they too would come. Meanwhile, Mrs. Wurmbrand had said, they must refer to their hosts as Aunt Steffi and Uncle Hans. Now they must go to bed, and she would talk to them more later in the morning.

If asked when did he and Clementa realize that they would not again be seeing their mother or father—or Hilda—Henri could not answer. For the first few months, Aunt Steffi simply kept postponing the day on which they could expect to see their parents. When, after the first fortnight, Clementa had asked why her parents had not written a letter, Aunt Steffi said curtly that where her mother was, there was no post office. At the time, Henri had not known how to interpret this retort. Aunt Steffi was kind, but not demonstrative—but this time she had put down the telephone in the kitchen during dinner, after an exchange of only a couple of minutes, during which she had contributed practically nothing except to say, "Yes . . . Yes . . . I understand . . . Yes." She had then, inexplicably, leaned down and embraced first Clementa, then Henri, and had left the kitchen so quickly that, though Henri could not absolutely swear on it when he and Clementa discussed the episode, he thought she was in tears; certainly there had been a noticeable heaving of her bosom. By the time Henri had reached age fourteen, he had guessed that that was the conversation at which Aunt Steffi had got news of his parents' annihilation. When he was fifteen he would find out: at Belsen.

In those early days, Uncle Hans told them that the war had brought on a number of difficulties and hardships, and that it was important to take certain precautions. For instance, under no circumstances must they discuss politics, not with anyone. This instruction Henri found extremely easy, because he didn't know anything about politics, except that there was a war going on, and Hitler was the head of the country, and Henri was quite certain his father didn't like Hitler. A few weeks later, Uncle Hans told them he was going to enroll them in the little school at Tolk. He told them that—"now listen to me very carefully"—they were to pass as orphans, the children of a Danish mother and Uncle Hans's brother. Their parents had died in a car crash when they were very young children, they had been brought up by a cousin near Hamburg, and when that cousin died they had been brought to Tolk. Their surname was Tod.

This deception they managed without difficulty, and without difficulty they mingled with the children, most of them, like Uncle Hans, sons and daughters of farmers. The schoolmaster, after two months, was called away to serve in the army, and passed along the teaching job to a widowed sister, who was a proficient disciplinarian. Her attention gravitated toward students in whom she detected curiosity, and before long Henri was reading special books assigned by her, and handling English with considerable fluency, as was Clementa.

And so it was that, gradually, the profile of Nazi Germany transpired in his mind, and Henri gradually came to know what it was all about. He and Clementa were Jewish; they were being protected, for some reason he did not know, by "Aunt" Steffi and by "Uncle" Hans, and if it were known that they were in fact Jewish, they would be taken away, perhaps

to wherever it was that their mother and father had been taken. All this he passed on to his sister, but only after he had thoroughly digested the data and it had become clear to him that Clementa could take the news with fortitude.

They were never apart. The schoolhouse had only the one room for the forty-odd students. When they returned from classes they worked, side by side, helping Uncle Hans with the cows or with the hay; or Aunt Steffi, in the kitchen. She quickly noticed that they liked to be together, and for that reason did not separate the chores by assigning kitchen work to Clementa and outdoor work to Henri. They were put to work together, indoors and out. When it got dark they went into Henri's bedroom, which doubled as a study, and did their homework, Henri helping Clementa with her work, she, occasionally, with his. Supper was increasingly unimaginative fare, as shortages multiplied, but they were never hungry. After supper they would resume their home-work and then, for one-half hour, they were permitted to play games, and there was a checkers set, and some playing cards. After a year or so they were permitted to listen to the radio, which broadcast news of one Nazi victory after an-other, although they did finally conclude, after a few weeks of trying to sort it all out, that the Nazi army had *not* un-dertaken an amphibious operation against England; and descriptions of enemy bombers shot down suggested that there were considerable Allied air raids going on. In Tolk, so near the Danish border, it wasn't often that they saw enemy aircraft overhead, although blackout precautions were rigorously observed.

One day, two months before Henri's sixteenth birthday, just before noon, the children heard the sound of a motor-

cycle, the roar diminishing to the whine, then the little stutter, as the engine was turned off, directly outside the schoolhouse. There was no knock on the door. It opened, and an elderly man—someone had once pointed him out to Henri as the mayor of Tolk, also its postmaster and undertaker—escorted in a hulky young man dressed in a Nazi uniform.

The mayor approached Mrs. Taussig at her desk in front of the blackboard and whispered to her. The Nazi officer was meanwhile scrutinizing the children and taking notes. He said nothing. Mrs. Taussig addressed the class. "Children, the gentleman from the army here has been sent to check on draft registration." She was interrupted by the officer, who spoke to her in a quiet voice that could not be heard. Mrs. Taussig then transcribed the order: "The captain wishes all the girls to leave the room."

They did so, rather in a hurry. Clementa managed to grip Henri's hand on the way out.

Now the captain took over. He was very young, perhaps twenty-five. His brown hair was clipped short, his frame husky, his voice metallic. "How many of you are sixteen years old or over sixteen, raise your hands."

Two of them did so. "Move to that side of the room." The captain reordered the seating.

"How many of you are fifteen years old?" Henri and one other boy raised their hands. "All right, the rest of you are dismissed. Wait a minute"—he pointed to a boy leaving, who looked older than the others—"you. What is your name?"

"Paul, sir."

"Paul what?"

"Paul Steiner."

"Steiner? Stay here."

The captain was interested in four things. He wanted to know by documentary evidence whether either of the two boys who had given their age as fifteen might actually already be sixteen. And he wanted to know whether Steiner was Jewish. Concerning the first point, the captain wanted supplementary proof, more than that which school enrollment records provided, so Henri and Siegfried were sent home to consult their parents. Steiner, with the name suspiciously Jewish, was asked where he had been baptized. He replied that he didn't know. Mrs. Taussig intervened and said that the boy's parents were Lutherans, to her certain knowledge, as she regularly saw them in church on Sundays. The captain was finally satisfied, and now needed from Steiner only proof that he was not yet sixteen.

Uncle Hans had two years earlier foreseen the need for papers. Having through sources established that St. Bonaventure's Church in Hamburg had been bombed and all its records destroyed, he procured on St. Bonaventure's stationery a baptismal certificate, dated December 7, 1928, which listed Henri's birthdate as one year earlier. In longhand he wrote that his nephew had been born in Denmark, at his mother's home, and that when Henri's mother and father were killed in the auto accident, they had merely been visiting in Germany, so that no papers concerning their son and daughter were in hand, and that he had never known where his dead brother had kept such papers. "Give this to the captain, and if he wishes to see me, tell him I am here, at work, and would be glad to see him."

It worked. But the captain had made careful notes, and told Henri, Siegfried, and Kurt that they would receive notices within thirty days of their sixteenth birthday telling

them where they were to report for induction into the army. The senior boys would be receiving their notices right away. He put away his writing materials, bowed perfunctorily to Mrs. Taussig, and left the schoolhouse.

After dinner Uncle Hans informed Henri that he needed to talk with him. The spring evening was warm and Uncle Hans said they might take a little walk. It was then that he told Henri that he must go abroad, that contingency plans had been made to take him to England. The following day, right after dinner, a resistance member would pick him up and take him to Tönning, on the North Sea. He would be delivered there into friendly hands, and by the end of the week he would be in England. Once there, a Mr. Wallenberg would look after him. When the war was over—as, Uncle Hans said, surely it would be over, within a year or so—he would be reunited with Clementa.

Henri, up until now compliant in attitude, stopped dead in his tracks. What? Leave without Clementa? He came close to hysteria. He would do no such thing, ever ever ever ever. Uncle Hans replied calmly that he had no choice in the matter, that resistance leaders made such decisions, that they had evidently reasoned that Clementa, as a girl, was in no danger, unlike Henri, who stood to be drafted in a matter of weeks. Henri replied that he would rather be drafted than leave Clementa. Hans Wurmbrand replied that to be drafted would hardly put him any closer to his sister. Henri threw himself into a mound of hay at the side of the pathway, and half swore, half cried that he could not leave Clementa. Hans Wurmbrand reasoned correctly that he should let the matter drop for the moment and confer with Clementa.

And of course he did; and of course Clementa went to Henri and told him that if he truly loved her he would leave, and be safe, until the war was over. He had cried, inconsolable at the thought of their separation; but agreeing, finally, to go. They stayed up until early in the morning, talking, exchanging endearments. At school that final day he could not bear to look in her direction, or she in his, and halfway through dinner, after removing the soup plates, Clementa crept upstairs and shut her door. Aunt Steffi handed Henri a note. He opened it. Clementa had written, "You must not say good-bye to me. I will see you very very soon. I know I will. Besides, that is the royal command of Queen Clementa, who loves her King Heinrich so very much." Henri lunged out of the door, and wept uncontrollably until the car came, and after hugging his adopted parents he went off with the stranger and two weeks later was enrolled in St. Paul's School in London as a boarding student.

Mr. Wallenberg told Henri that he had been a friend of Henri's father, that he would look after Henri until the war was over, that Henri was to be extremely careful not to divulge to anyone the circumstances of his departure from Germany or give any clue concerning the practices of the apparatus that had brought him to safety, and above all he was not to breathe a word of the existence of his sister, or of the Wurmbrands. Special arrangements would be made to instruct him in the Jewish religion, but this was to be done during the vacation period because his Jewish background, combined with the obvious fact that he was German, might arouse curiosity in someone capable of making mischief.

To all of this Henri of course assented, but he was astonished on being told that there was no way in which he might

communicate with Clementa, that the resistance was simply not willing to run risks in order to deliver correspondence. The day he heard that—the day before entering the school— he resolved that he would write her a letter every single night and, after the war, he would give her the whole collection to show her that he had not let a day go by without thinking of her.

St. Paul's School could not remember when last it had received a student of such energy and talent. Although the curriculum was very different from what he had got used to at Tolk, it was only a matter of weeks before the necessary adjustments were made. Before the semester was over, Henri was receiving all A's—in Latin, Maths, English, Geography, Greek, and History. He was permitted to stay at the school during the summer vacation, during which he studied and did chores twenty hours every week. By the beginning of the Michaelmas term he was jumped in grade to the fifth form. Several months later, soon after his seventeenth birthday, he was elected school captain, his office to begin in the Lent term, after the holidays of December 1944.

That was the night. It was traditional that the captain-elect and his prefects should be taken by their predecessors to the Aldwyn Chop House, next door to the school, a favorite and handy restaurant for visiting parents. It was the unspoken tradition of the school that on that night the captain and outgoing prefects would entertain their successors and dip deep into the Aldwyn's inexhaustible supply of ale. The headmaster of St. Paul's had himself staggered out of Aldwyn's sometime after midnight thirty years ago, and so—on that one night—the school's stern rules were, very simply, overlooked.

Henri had not tasted beer before, but of course as captain-elect he was the special object of the revelers. The incumbent captain rose with toast after toast to Henri Tod, the German boy who in a little over a year had had such a meteoric career at the same school as the great General Montgomery—Montgomery, who would be the first to reach Berlin (cheers!), by God, and show those Krauts (nothing personal, Tod) who was who, and maybe General Montgomery would bring back Hitler's mustache to frame in the school's museum (cheers!). Are you willing to drink to that, Tod?

Henri lifted his glass solemnly to the defeat of Hitler. To the defeat of Hitler *and* the Germans, corrected Espy Major.

Wait a minute, wait a minute, Henri smiled, jug in hand, there *are* some good Germans, you know, please don't think that they are all like Adolf Hitler.

Well, said Espy, there are certainly a lot of Germans who are taking orders from Adolf Hitler and a lot of Germans who have been cheering Adolf Hitler all these years. Perhaps, he said, Tod was so engaged in his studies while in Germany that he didn't have a chance to find out what was happening to other people?

Henri at this point could not quite focus, either on his companions or on the question. But he felt a compulsive need to straighten Espy out, and so, as the boys began filing out to cross the street to the campus and to their dormitories, Henri approached Espy and asked him to come with him for a minute to the corner of the room, as there was something he wished him to know. Espy good-naturedly did so. "But first," Henri said solemnly, trying to remind himself how one was supposed to look when one looked

solemn, "first, you must promise me that you will never tell anyone what I am about to tell you." Espy promised, solemnly, that as long as he lived, Tod's secret would be safe. Well, said Henri, he *had* suffered. He was a Jew. His parents had been taken away and killed in a concentration camp. He had a sister, her name was Clementa. She hid out in a town called Tolk, with a family called Wurmbrand. They pretended that Clementa and Henri were their niece and nephew. They had looked after them since he was thirteen, and they were in touch with the Resistance. And the Resistance had brought him safely to England. Was this not evidence that there were indeed good Germans?

Espy Major whistled, and whispered that he'd had no idea that Tod had gone through so much, and that he wished immediately to modify any suggestion that Tod had not known danger. Whereupon they shook hands, rose, and Henri was very sick. Espy led him to his bed.

Three weeks later, Henri was surprised to be called out of his Greek class. Mr. Wallenberg had secured permission of the headmaster to interrupt him, and was waiting for him in the reception room.

He was pale, and told Henri that he needed to talk with him privately. And so they drove to The Boltons, at Number 7 of which Wallenberg lived. Inside, he told Henri to sit down.

"Have you spoken to anyone about the Wurmbrands and your sister?"

Henri's lips quivered, and for a moment he did not reply. Wallenberg repeated the question.

"I told one boy."

"When?"

"The night I was made captain. Three weeks ago."

Wallenberg turned his face to one side. "The day before yesterday, the Gestapo went to the farmhouse. They took the Wurmbrands out and shot them. They took your sister away in their car. She was driven to Hamburg and put on a train with all Jewish people rounded up in a general sweep. The train left Hamburg, and headed toward Poland."

Henri Tod left St. Paul's the next day and took a job in Leeds as a coal miner. His curiosity about Espy was limited, because he knew that Espy himself would not wish harm to come to Henri's sister. He did inquire about the profession of Espy's father, who was a journalist, wholly engaged in covering the war. It crossed his mind only fleetingly to ask Espy Major whether he had told his father (or anyone else) the story of the new school captain's secret family in Tolk, but decided against doing so. Of what use that line of questioning? On whom could the blame be put, other than himself? And so all he did was to collect, wordlessly, his personal materials, and leave a note in the headmaster's office. He did not leave a forwarding address with Mr. Wallenberg, whom he never saw again.

In the spring of 1950, he knocked on the door of the dean of admissions at Trinity College in Cambridge and said he would like to enroll to do advanced studies in philosophy. The dean looked at the young man, deferential but proud, mature beyond what the dean had experienced in young men of twenty-three or -four. He was clean-shaven, strong, even-featured, brown-eyed, with perfectly shaped white teeth, slender nose and lips. The dean told him, somewhat more courteously than he'd have addressed a young man

less striking in appearance and behavior, that there were conventional ways of applying for admission to graduate schools—where had he attended college?

He was surprised to be told that the applicant had not even completed his public schoolwork at St. Paul's, five years earlier. However, the applicant said, he had done concentrated reading while working in the coal mines, and was prepared to submit to examination. Rather intrigued by all this, the dean excused himself, left the room, and telephoned to the taskmasterish Russell Professor of Philosophy, James Jamison, and told him he would be grateful if Jamison would examine an applicant who was there under unusual circumstances.

Three years later, with an advanced degree in philosophy, Henri Tod recrossed the Channel he had only once before crossed, as a frightened fifteen-year-old sick at heart at leaving his sister who, however, had promised him she would be seeing him soon, very, very soon.

Cecilio Velasco

CECILIO VELASCO drove back toward Chapultepec Park, then turned to the right, up Asalto Boulevard. He was headed toward Coyoacán. He had known many years ago that if ever he returned to Mexico he would need to go there. Perhaps, by merely sitting in the car and looking at the site, he would sort out one of the residual confusions he still harbored about his long experience worshipping that awesome god. Or was it simply a morbid desire to revisit the scene of a crime?

A great crime. But then, really, that was one of the questions that continued to vex him, whether it was a "great" crime in other than the conventional sense. The assassination of Leon Trotsky had been "great" in that it had been the center of international attention for weeks, with months, even years of ripple effect. It had been a great crime in that Trotsky's legion of followers had lost, irretrievably, their leader, who proved irreplaceable. And it was a crime formally defined to take a man's life, inasmuch as Velasco, and Hurtado, and Mercader—it was Mercader who had planted the mountaineer's pick in Trotsky's skull—were hardly engaged in executing a civil commission. The phrase normally used in such situations, Velasco reminded himself as he

turned west toward the district of Coyoacán, was "killing an innocent man." But he was no longer certain that such a phrase described what he had engaged in. Trotsky was perhaps—probably—innocent of having committed any capital crime under Mexican law. Was he otherwise innocent?

1922: When at age twenty-two in Barcelona Raúl Carrera was told that he would have to leave the law school because there was now no money, his father having left nothing but the tiny, heavily mortgaged house in which Raúl's five sisters lived with their mother, he was saddened at the prospect of not finishing his law studies. But he was desolate at the prospect of losing touch with those of his companions who, like Raúl, had been inflamed by the great events in the Soviet Union. They had taken, ever since Lenin's April theses, to meeting at least four times a week. At first only three or four of them, but now as many as twelve or fifteen, and the growth was steady, in order to discuss developments in Russia and the opportunities that surrounded them to universalize the great energies they were discovering among the disaffected—however few—with all those Castilian encumbrances, most notably the Christian God and the Bourbon king.

Raúl admitted that he found it most difficult to break with the Catholic Church, to which his mother was passionately devoted. But he recognized that the rupture with old, traditional Spain could not be merely formalistic. He needed not merely to drift away from belief. He needed to disbelieve. To know that man is an accidental chemical-biological concatenation of cells that somehow, along the way, developed a will. And that the great narrative cycle of history was coming to a climax during this very century. Perhaps during

the next ten or twenty years. That Lenin was showing his disciples how it could come about, that centuries of class consolidations could be wiped away; the poor would find that the future lay in their hands and that the exploiters and the imperialists were forever bereft of the slaves they were so accustomed to oppressing.

Raúl's earnestness combined with an unusual analytical eloquence, which he exercised in small circles only, and infrequently. He would never think of addressing a large public gathering. He had once been invited to develop formal forensic and oratorical skills by Beatriz, with whom he shared his vision, his meals, and his bed. She had offered to pretend that she was a great crowd—they could just go off to Blanes, toward the cliffs of the Costa Brava, and there in the pastoral wilderness where no one could possibly overhear them Raúl could mount a rock, use a makeshift lectern, and practice public declamation. Raúl did this three times, but always he tended to speak as if engaged in a seminar, and eventually even Beatriz was forced to admit that the project had failed, that Raúl's golden tongue must be reserved for exercises more intimate than public orations.

His companions, especially Antonio Durán, whose seniority (he was twenty-four) made him ex officio the leader of the group, were as torn as Raúl by the news that he would need to withdraw, and so Durán and three of Raúl's special friends met on the Monday night before Raúl's scheduled departure on Friday, the end of the term, to inquire what might be done. Every semester the cost of tuition and board came to a thousand pesetas. But however often they reviewed their collective resources they could think of no way of coming up with that much money, particularly not by

next Friday when the payment for the next semester was inflexibly due.

They sat about an austere, dilapidated empty classroom lit by a single bare bulb. It was getting cold—Barcelona gets fearfully cold in January—as the conversational hubbub mounted, and then Rico banged his open palm on the desk, demanding silence. Rico did not speak often, and so was presumed to have something worth listening to when he sought attention. It was also Rico who, of them all, was the most inventive, as when he had got up the idea of the anonymous letters alleging that the dean they all hated was a practicing homosexual, practically a capital offense in Spain in 1921, thus bringing on the dean's premature retirement.

"I have it! I have it! It not only is no problem, it gives us an opportunity to exercise the revolutionary arts! We will rob a bank."

There was a moment's silence, followed by excited cross-talk. Rico was quite carried away. "By robbing a bank not only can we put Raúl through school, we can begin to finance the revolutionary movement to which we are consecrated. Robbing a bank is an excellent place to start since there is no greater affront to socialism than banks."

"Which bank?" Héctor wanted to know.

"What does it matter which bank, my dear Héctor? They are all the same."

"If it is all the same to the rest of you," Héctor said, "I would like to rob the bank that owns the usurious mortgage on my father's house."

"Which one is that?"

"It is the Banco del Sagrado Corazón, on Calle Marina, near the bullring."

And so the plan was conceived.

Rico, because he had thought up the idea, took charge. He assigned Antonio the job of monitoring the bank's activities from outside the building, minute by minute, from nine in the morning when it opened until one, when it closed down for the midday break, to take note, for instance, how often and when policemen patrolled by and at which hours patronage of the bank was heaviest. It had been resolved to stage the robbery in the morning, and now they had to determine at exactly what hour in the morning. Héctor, who regularly delivered his parents' mortgage payments to the bank, was assigned the job of surveying security arrangements inside the bank, in whose chambers he could find excuses to dawdle by making a mistake in the mortgage vouchers, an innocent mistake but time-consuming to correct.

They would concert their findings the next afternoon. Meanwhile Concho was to lay his hands on firearms. "Handguns would be preferable," Rico observed gravely, stroking his beard—all four of them wore beards and moustaches, in the style of Lenin—"but if we can't get them, then rifles or, better still, shotguns will do. We need"—he paused, not without a sense of the drama that accompanies armed struggle—"a proletarian arsenal."

On Wednesday, at Antonio's home because his parents were visiting his sick aunt at Santander and the house was empty, they convened to pool their information. Concho began by producing triumphantly, from a large bag, one .32-caliber pistol. "I got this from a policeman's holster while he was taking a crap in the railroad station."

"Did he see you?" Rico asked.

"Yes, but he was in no position to get up and chase me," Concho laughed, with the air of a grand strategist. "Don't

worry, he'd never identify me. These beards can be useful."
He then brought out of the bag his father's militia rifle and
the old family shotgun with which his father shot an occasional rabbit or dove.

Héctor reported that there was an armed guard who sat
near the entrance to the bank and occasionally would stroll
about; moreover that he deduced from his intensive concentration on the cash teller's window and the movements
of the teller that there might be a pistol hidden but within
reach of the teller. Antonio reported that he had observed
only two policemen going by, always between nine and ten.
He reported that the customers were relatively few between
ten-thirty and eleven-thirty, after which they began to crowd
in again.

It was resolved that Rico, using the pistol, would on the
stroke of eleven jab it into the back ribs of the guard and
disarm him. At that identical moment Antonio would rush
through the door with his shotgun, followed by Héctor
with the rifle. Héctor would threaten any bystander who
obstructed the operation, while Antonio would aim the
shotgun at the chest of the bank teller, demand the money,
and scrutinize him carefully lest he reach for a weapon.

"How much money should Antonio demand?" Concho
asked. "One thousand pesetas?"

"No, you fool," Rico said. "This is no longer merely an
enterprise to pay for Raúl's semester. It is a venture in
revolutionary justice. We shall demand all the money."

There was discussion about this, and it was resolved to
compromise by taking all the money in the till, but not to
risk asking the teller to dip into the reserves in the bank's
vaults. "Remember, we have to act quickly," Rico warned.
"In and out."

Concho would be waiting outside in a getaway car that would be stolen that morning, hardly a problem since half the cars parked for a few blocks past the great square outside had keys in the ignitions. Car theft was virtually unknown in Spain in 1922. They would dispose of the car, and then, moving separately, unite in Antonio's house by three o'clock in the afternoon. Later in the day Héctor would make a deposit with the bursar for the account of Raúl Carrera, and Raúl would be told that an anonymous donor had made it possible for him to continue in school.

It was in high mood that they broke out one of Antonio's father's 1917 gourds of good red wine—"an appropriate color," Concho said, smiling, "to toast the beginning, in Barcelona, of true revolutionary activity." They all resolved to sleep in the same house to anneal their fraternal bonds and consecrate the singularity of the historical occasion.

"Perhaps someday," Concho whispered to Rico, who was preparing to sleep on the couch, "this house will be a shrine." Rico nodded solemnly.

The money in a pillowcase gripped in his left hand, the shotgun in his right hand, Antonio ran to the revolving door through which they had moments before entered the bank, but the hard thrust of his elbow into the glass pane had the effect not of causing the door to turn, but of rupturing the glass. At that point a shot rang out. The bullet appeared to go right through Antonio's arm, because he dropped the shotgun in the shatter of glass. Héctor rushed to help Antonio but he too found the revolving door adamantly shut. He wrestled with it while Rico, his own pistol and the guard's in his hands, ran to help his comrades. Now a second shot rang out, this time penetrating Rico's right

hand, causing him to drop both pistols. Héctor stopped wrestling with the door after a calm voice rang out from somewhere high above them. "You. With the rifle. Drop it."

Héctor dropped the gun, and looked over at Rico, who was thrusting his wrist against his sweater to staunch the bleeding. Sitting, his back against the revolving door, Antonio only moaned.

The voice had come from behind the balcony on the second floor, where the offices were. It was the voice of José Luís Cambray y Echeverría, the sixty-five-year-old president of the Banco del Sagrado Corazón.

It all had been very easy, he later explained to the press, puffing on his cigar and leaning back in his armchair. The teller, when accosted by the bandit, had simply put his foot over a special buzzer. The president, hearing the alarm ring in his office, depressed a switch that electrically bolted shut the revolving door. He had then reached for his rifle, conveniently situated right by the entrance to his office, opened the door, surveyed the situation below, aimed one shot at the fellow with the shotgun, a second shot at the fellow with the pistol, and was ready with a third shot to take on the rifleman; but that proved unnecessary, Don José said, tapping his ashes into the brass cuspidor.

At the trial, Rico, Antonio, and Héctor were given ten years of hard labor. Concho and Raúl were given five years as accomplices, never mind that everyone swore that Raúl had been ignorant of the entire proceeding. After searching Raúl's room and finding all the revolutionary literature, there simply could be no reasonable doubt of his involvement, the prosecutor had argued. The judge, pronouncing sentence, asked that God should forgive the young brutes,

and Raúl's mother, sitting diffidently in the second row, glad for once that her husband was dead, bowed her head and crossed herself.

Raúl and Concho were sent to work on a mountain tunnel designed to penetrate the Iberian Mountains to permit the construction of a highway. During the day, under heavy guard and dressed in distinctive uniform, they would work in the seemingly endless tunnel, hewing rock and pulling out earth, and at night they would be driven by truck to the prison site at Altamira. A routine deprivation of the Altamira prison was the denial of any reading matter whatever. This vexation very nearly drove Raúl out of his mind, and he and Concho arranged to loiter outside a guard's office in the few minutes they had, after work and before their supper, to hear the news over the radio. On the day that Lenin died Raúl felt as though he knew what it must have been that the apostles experienced at Calvary. He swore that he would dedicate himself when he got out to avenging Lenin.

Concho said he did not understand this. "What did Spain do to Lenin that you should avenge Lenin?"

Raúl explained to Concho that he was not well schooled in revolutionary rhetoric. Any defiance of Lenin—and the whole extra-Soviet world had been in defiance of him—was a defiance that needed to be avenged. Indeed, the cruel treatment given to Rico, Héctor, Concho, and Antonio, to say nothing of Raúl who had been entirely innocent, was so to speak a profanation of Lenin who was not only a leader but a prophet. Concho nodded his head. He said he wished Lenin would be avenged, but that in point of fact he had to confess that during the past three years he had found his revolutionary appetite abated, and he wanted most awfully

first to spend a night with a woman, second to have a decent meal, and third never again to have anything to do with the police.

"Does that mean," Raúl asked, stroking his clean-shaven chin (the prison authority did not permit beards: "You never know what a beard is hiding," the warden had pronounced), "that you never want to have anything further to do with me either?"

Concho tried evasion. "You were not involved with the police."

"Answer me, Concho. Have you lost your communist faith?"

"Well, no," Concho said. "I'll be glad when the revolution happens. It's just that I don't feel quite as . . . creative about it as I used to. I certainly"—he added this with heavy enthusiasm—"wish you the best of luck."

Raúl knew that but for one factor he would be bitter. That factor, of course, was that Concho had got into this difficulty only because of Raúl. At least that had been the initial impulse behind what had evolved as a comprehensive revolutionary gesture. Although he continued to be friendly with Concho, Raúl Carrera had experienced disillusion.

When he emerged from prison Raúl Carrera was five years older, on the record. But he was much older than his twenty-seven years, and his political faith was wholly matured. At the railroad station in Barcelona he inquired about the fare to Madrid. He owned one hundred pesetas, his dismissal bounty. The fare to Madrid was one hundred and twenty pesetas. He turned then from the station and walked to Calle Carmen and entered the public library, where he asked for the periodicals desk.

He read hungrily the papers for that day, and then the day before that, and then the magazines. The papers, he had noticed excitedly, had made several references to the Communist Party, whose headquarters were of course in Madrid, which was why he wished to travel there. But then he stumbled on what he had subconsciously hoped to find. It was in *El Standard:* a story about a threatened strike by electrical workers. Their spokesman was Gabriel Ponzillo. And Gabriel Ponzillo was listed as leader of the Electrical Workers Union—and Vice President of the Communist Party of Barcelona.

Raúl Carrera stood up.

The Communist Party of Barcelona!

He looked about him. There was no one in sight. With his fingers he tore out the column from the newspaper, stuck it in his pocket, and walked out, past the great obelisk to Colón, south toward the working district. He went into the Cantina de Milagros, and sat down and asked how much was a liter of red wine, and then put down the seventy-five céntimos on the table. The newspaper column in front of him, he drank the wine, one glass after another, his spirits soaring. The Communist Party of Barcelona!

One hour later, Gabriel Ponzillo was testing the voltage of one of the auxiliary generators in the hot engine room of the principal electrical plant in the Jardín region. A clerk entered the room and, shouting to be heard against the generator's loud whining, repeated that a young man demanded to see him and would not leave the premises until Ponzillo spoke to him.

Ponzillo, a huge man in his late thirties, bearded and sweating in his T-shirt, put down his voltage meter without any change in expression.

"Where is he?"

"This way. Just outside the bursar's office."

Wiping his hands and chest with a towel, Ponzillo came out into the dark. It was after ten, and Ponzillo would be on duty until midnight. He stared at a short, slim young man with straight hair and thin lips and eager eyes.

"What do you want?"

"I want to help you, Señor Ponzillo. I was framed by the police and have been in prison for five years. I was a law student. I have read all of Lenin and Marx. I wish to join your cause."

Ponzillo paused, and stared down at Raúl. Another plant? he wondered. He said to him, "I live at 322 Calle Hércules. Meet me there at 12:15."

"Tonight?" Raúl pressed.

"Tonight."

Raúl Carrera was there at 12:00, but waited outside, across the street. He saw Ponzillo walk into his own house at 12:10. He waited five minutes and knocked on the door.

Ponzillo had washed, and now, wordlessly, led Raúl into the kitchen. On the table was coarse bread, red wine, and cheese. Ponzillo sat down and began to eat and drink, making no gestures toward Carrera except to point to a kitchen chair where he might sit down, which Carrera didn't do.

"Tell me your story."

Raúl did so, giving also one or two details about the gruesome regimen of prison life. He did not speak of the attrition of Concho's revolutionary stamina.

"All that for robbing a bank?" Ponzillo commented—his mouth was full of bread and cheese, but his eyes were on Raúl.

"No sir. All that—without having robbed a bank."

"Very well. Tomorrow morning we are going to rob a bank. Will you join us?"

Raúl Carrera turned pale. He thought of the 1,825 days at Altamira, of five years of rock hewing, of forty thousand hours without reading material. He wavered, but for only a moment.

"Yes, señor."

Ponzillo pushed his plate of bread and cheese to Raúl's end of the table.

"Sit down, comrade."

Comrade Raúl Carrera rose rapidly in the fledgling hierarchy of the Spanish Communist Party, and because of his special, quiet eloquence was much used in the academies, which were hot with sentiment for the overthrow of the dictatorship backed by the king. In the turbulent years that followed the overthrow of the dictatorship and the abdication of the king, the election of a Popular Front republican government, and the outbreak of the civil war, Carrera was specifically engaged in attempting to win over, or win back, those who had gone to the Trotskyist party or to the Anarcho-Syndicalists. The pressure from Moscow was considerable to discredit the Trotskyists, and by the summer of 1936 when the war came, Raúl Carrera had been trained to identify the Trotskyists as the principal enemy. Without their sundering influence, he reasoned, the communists would grow in power, take over the anarchists, and then simply swallow up the republicans. And after all that had been accomplished, taking on General Francisco Franco should not be so difficult, though he acknowledged that the opposition was increasingly united and that just as the republicans were receiving massive arms support from the

Soviet Union, so Franco was receiving shipments of arms from Mussolini and Hitler.

In early April of 1937, Raúl Carrera was advised by Party Secretary José Carrillo that he was wanted in Moscow. He went, of course, with great though subdued excitement. Raúl Carrera, as he grew older, grew quieter; in manner, more nearly clerical than flamboyant. But the ideological fires were well banked.

In Moscow, Carrera was taken to an army barracks which had once been used for junior officers. He was assigned a small room and told that he would be interviewed the following morning by Major Boris Bolgin of the KGB. He spent the late afternoon and evening worshipping at Red Square. It required a two-hour wait in line before he could get in to view the corpse of Lenin. He reminded himself of the pledge he had made thirteen years earlier to avenge Lenin's death. He stared at that pale countenance with the austere beard, at the black suit and bald head, and but for the guard who brusquely told him to move along, he'd have stayed there throughout the night, or for as long a vigil as was asked of him.

Outside the monument, Carrera wished that he knew someone who might show him about. He had been studying Russian and could manage to read Russian guidebooks. Indeed he had proved adept at languages, becoming competent in English and in French. As if drawn by a magnet, he thought to move toward the university, and so after studying the subway map he made his calculations, as usual with exactitude; he emerged at the Omsk station and walked over toward the Student Union Building.

There on the vast ground floor he saw a number of

posters against the wall on the left: Stalin with a little girl presenting him flowers on his birthday; Stalin with a peasant, head bowed in reverence as Stalin paternally touches him on the shoulder; Stalin with the troops cheering him at an armed forces festival; Stalin dedicating a naval vessel. Something stirred in Carrera's memory. It was the talk the year before of Lenin's "Testament," in which the communists were warned against Josef Stalin. But he was satisfied to believe that this was a forgery, probably composed by Leon Trotsky, the great enemy of communist unity. He spotted a studious-looking girl, her head bent over a reading table, the day's paper spread out before her. Perhaps it was because of the exotic circumstances and the loneliness that had hit him that Carrera addressed her.

"Excuse me, I am Comrade Raúl Carrera from Spain. I am here on official business. May I speak with you?"

The girl glanced up, unsmiling, and looked at the slim young man, a trace of the Moorish in his complexion and skin. She did not smile, but neither was she clipped in her response.

"Can I help you?"

Raúl wondered whether he should ask the routine questions—How to Get to the Main Book Section, or Where did one go to Get Tickets to the Ballet. Instead he said:

"Would you consent to having a cup of tea or coffee with me?"

Without hesitation she rose, bundled her bag of books into a canvas case, buttoned her rough woolen sweater about her—it was April and chilly, though not cold. She spoke.

"You have a little difficulty with Russian, and I do not speak Spanish. Do you speak German or French?" Raúl answered delightedly that he could speak French and so,

conversing in French, they went outdoors. She led him to a little shop a few blocks away frequented primarily by students. The service was cafeteria style; there was a choice of several coarse breads and pastries, sausage, potatoes, carrots, Ukrainian wine, vodka, beer, and tea. Raúl watched to see what his companion would take, intending to follow her example, and was agreeably surprised to see her take some of almost everything available, save the alcoholic drinks. Raúl Carrera took sausage, cheese, and a tenth of vodka.

Three hours later he had refilled his vodka glass three times, and Katia had taken a glass of wine. She was twenty, studying European history and literature, and she intended to pursue her studies and to teach, preferably back in Kiev where her divorced mother lived.

"You can hardly blame my mother. Father was sent to Siberia eight years ago and after three years she didn't hear from him anymore. Dead, I suppose."

She had then waited for a complementary recital by Raúl so that they would advance with knowledge of each other more or less pari passu—"My birthplace is Riga, what is yours?"

"It is Barcelona. I was born on January 13, 1900. When were you born?"

"December 1, 1917."

That kind of thing. Prudent.

And Raúl complied, while taking care to edit his biography since leaving law school. And she maintained this demand for conversational parity for a full hour when suddenly she found herself free of any suspicion of the intense young Spaniard, whose words were so nicely framed in a French obviously learned at the academy, yet learned with idiomatic finesse.

She began then to speak with some abandon, express-
ing frustration at the difficulty of getting books on modern
French and German authors she wished to read, for
instance Thomas Mann. Carrera volunteered to attempt
to get those books—"though it is not easy today to 'get'
things in Barcelona, but I have a few contacts outside
Barcelona." To which Katia had replied, looking rather
patronizingly at her companion, never mind that he was
old enough to have fathered her, "How would you, assuming you got the books of Thomas Mann, arrange to get
them to me, here?"

Raúl said he did not know about the difficulties attendant
on these matters, that he had always thought of Thomas
Mann as a thoroughly progressive writer, to which she
snorted that a progressive writer was defined as someone
Stalin happened to approve of on that particular day, and
Thomas Mann had said or written something a year ago
that had got him proscribed in Soviet Russia. Raúl smiled
and said that perhaps the Trotskyists were spreading some
of these rumors. At which Katia had got thoroughly impatient, and for a full hour she berated Raúl with the intellectual difficulties of conducting higher studies in a Soviet
university. All this without, however, condemning the communist system. Had she done this she would have prompted
Raúl, however ruefully, to put an end to the discussion,
because he did not engage hospitably in schismatic talk. It
was all in the day's work to contend polemically with fascists and liberals, but with fellow communists he felt a
theological bond, the bond that made so very conspicuous
and outrageous the heresies of Trotsky.

They agreed to let the matter of Thomas Mann rest, and
Raúl again offered her a cigarette which again she declined

for herself, but this time she requested one for her room-mate. She deposited it carefully within the neat folds of a handkerchief in her tan woolen purse.

Raúl noticed her heavy Slavic features, and the warmth and intelligence of her face. She expressed now a curiosity about developments in Spain and, lighting his own ciga-rette, Raúl Carrera told her about the awful chaos in his own country, while she listened. He felt she wanted to make more pointed comments than the conventional ones she used. But she did not again slip into overdrive, and before long Raúl's words felt desiccated in his mouth. There was a moment's silence, neither of them spoke; then Katia said that she would have to go now as she had a long subway ride ahead of her. Raúl said that was true also of him, but he would be grateful for her address, as he would like to endeavor to send her some books by Thomas Mann. At which she had abruptly risen and hissed that it was all very well for foreigners to undertake to send forbidden books into the Soviet Union, but it was not safe for Soviet citizens to receive those books, could he not understand that simple point?

Raúl Carrera apologized. And he thanked her for being so kind. They shook hands at the eastbound station.

"I am going the other way," Katia said and half smiled, tucking the wool collar of her sweater about her neck. "Good-bye, Raúl."

Carrera received rigorous training by the KGB. Special attention was given to the need to weed out of potentially influential positions in the republican government and army those who might have ties to the Anarcho-Syndicalists or—especially—to the Trotskyists. Already Raúl had had train-

ing in physical defense, and a Catalan physical education instructor sympathetic to the Electrical Workers Union strike in 1927 had given him training in karate. Considerable time in Moscow was given over to the study of foreign languages, in particular English, in which Carrera became fluent. Heavy attention was given to ideological orthodoxy, and this of course was made difficult with the frequent changes ordered by Stalin. The shifts had sometimes to do with the party line—there were changes in emphasis on industrial development and agricultural development. But mostly the changes seemed to center on men who had been heroes of the young Soviet Republic but were now demonstrated to have been traitors, men like Zinoviev, Kamenev, Bukharin. Carrera had taught himself to accept the word of higher authorities in these matters and when it became known that the word had come down from Stalin himself in the matter of prosecuting the principal betrayers, Carrera accepted the verdict dutifully if sadly. Carrera was saddened by diluted loyalties, even as he had been saddened by Concho, at Altamira.

He was back in Barcelona just after the great uprising there, the so-called civil war within a civil war that resulted, finally, in ejecting the Anarcho-Syndicalists from the republican government. Carrera's mission was now specific. He was to provide information to his superior, Colonel Glukansk, on the activities of the Trotskyists and their party, the Partido Obrero de Unificación Marxista (or P.O.U.M.), with the view to getting as many of their leaders as possible liquidated, on the grounds of putative treason. Colonel Glukansk was not given to disquisitive talk and told Carrera it was simple: the republican government of Spain would succeed or not against the fascist forces depending

on whether the Social Democrats acquiesced in the leadership being given by the Communists. But the Communists could not make common cause with the Trotskyists, who served only to undermine the philosophical integrity of the movement.

Late on the hot September afternoon of the following day, a hastily mobilized tribunal whose members were dominated by Colonel Glukansk heard the case against Juanito Lorca, cousin of the poet. The prosecutor, parading up and down the abandoned cow barn on the hillside near Valencia as though it were the supreme courthouse of Spain, inveighed against Lorca, charging that he had been seen at the post office staring at the fascist poster offering a reward for the capture or execution of Captain Diego Brujo, the heroic republican guerrilla fighter who in the previous six months had ambushed a half-dozen fascist columns, capturing a trainload of arms and ammunition.

The very next day, emerging from the house of his betrothed where he slept when in Valencia, Brujo was shot by a *pistolero* who had fired from a speeding car. An accomplice in the front seat next to the driver had snapped a photograph, thus obtaining evidence of Brujo's assassination, obviously needed to collect the fascist reward. The prosecutor then triumphantly produced a deaf-mute who had been walking the street at the critical moment. The prosecutor sat him down on a bale of hay that served as a witness stand and wrote out on a pad of paper, *"Point to the man you saw taking the picture last Monday when Captain Brujo was shot."* The deaf-mute, wearing coat and tie and sweating, pointed to where Lorca was standing, handcuffed. The prosecutor rested his case.

Lorca gave as his defense that indeed he had been at the

post office on the day in question—but so had he been in the post office every day of the week, since occasionally a letter from his sister and mother in the south reached him. And yes he had seen the poster, but then he habitually looked at all the posters in the post office; indeed it was from a poster that he had first learned that his cousin, García Lorca, had been shot by the fascists. Far from wanting to kill Captain Brujo, he had great admiration for him, and on the fatal morning was at the other side of town, sound asleep, as he had had watch duty from midnight until four in the morning. Moreover, he owned no camera, had never used a camera, and did not even know how to operate a camera.

The major asked sneeringly if he had any witnesses to his story, and Lorca replied that he slept alone. The major and the two captains rose and went to the corner of the barn where they smoked cigarettes for fifteen minutes. They returned to their makeshift seats behind the old door that had been propped up as a table and pronounced Juan Lorca guilty of treason and murder, and sentenced him to death. The two guards who watched over the prisoner knew what to do, walking Lorca back to the end of the barn where the hay was stacked. Lorca demanded to see the regimental commander and began to shout out charges of political persecution. The major told the three riflemen who had stood guard outside to get on with it. The guards refastened Lorca's manacles through the thick wire that bound a hay bale together. The major, putting aside his judicial robes and donning executive dress, gave out the order to fire. After which he walked forward, discharged the ritual pistol shot at the head of the corpse lying on the floor, and walked back to his companions.

"Really, Ramírez," he said to the prosecutor, "can't you come up with something better than a deaf-mute?"

Ramírez, smoking his cigarette, shrugged his shoulders. "It is a question of supply and demand," he said. "The demand is very heavy these days."

He offered Carrera a cigarette, but Carrera declined it. He would report now to Colonel Glukansk that there was one less Trotskyist in the Republican army.

In due course it was all over; General Franco took Madrid and Raúl Carrera, reporting for the last time to Colonel Glukansk at the railroad station in Bilbao, was given an address in Paris. "There you will be equipped for your next mission." Which proved to be to look after not Trotskyists, but Trotsky.

Now, twenty-one years later in Mexico City, Raúl Carrera, though now he was Cecilio Velasco, drove slowly up Calle Morelos, as far as the corner of Calle Paris, where he had stopped that night. They would walk softly the last three blocks to Trotsky's villa, there to give assistance to the executioner—Carrera preferred this word to assassin—Mercader, who had infiltrated the household. They would wait until they saw the light in the room on the first floor turn on and then off again. That meant that in exactly five minutes Mercader would walk out of his door down the hallway, thrust himself into Trotsky's study, and swing down the weapon designed to drive holes into mountain rock. Human skulls, to the mountain climber's ice hammer, are as apples to a nail. In exactly five minutes—Carrera held the stopwatch, and he could hear the heartbeat of Julio on his right and Texco on his left—they would create the

disturbance that, if all went according to plan, would distract Trotsky's guards and provide the assassin with the opportunity, the deed done, to slip away.

Cecilio Velasco, after staring at the site, the place where he had helped carry out a spectacular mandate of Josef Stalin, drove back toward the flower market off Chapultepec and then, slowly, past the huge Soviet Embassy. It was now even more massive than when he had known it, had worked in it, during those five years after arriving from Spain. That building—he had parked his car and sat down at the coffeehouse diagonally away from it—had housed his superior, Colonel Igor Ochek. It had also housed the ambassador, Dmitri Oumansky. And Mariya.

He had never liked Colonel Ochek. It wasn't so much that he was ruthless—Colonel Glukansk had got him used to that: a job was a job. There was something extraclinical about Ochek's ruthlessness. Operating in a foreign country not engaged in civil war, the colonel had to proceed more carefully than his counterparts in Spain. Besides, the problem of a Trotskyist party standing directly in the way of the Communists during a military operation wasn't there to dominate his attention.

There were, accordingly, far fewer direct victims—or, better, fewer objects of Colonel Ochek's mission. There was occasionally a matter of discipline within the embassy itself. It was the largest embassy Stalin maintained, during the war years, in Latin America, and it was the headquarters for communist operations throughout the hemisphere, excluding the United States.

Mexico itself was extremely hospitable to the Soviets. General Cárdenas was still president. Cárdenas was a com-

munist-populist at heart—he had endeared himself to the socialist world the year before by expropriating American oil holdings. Mexico was the very special haven for refugees from Spain, and a great many of these were Party. The heaviest concentration of Spanish communists stayed in Mexico City; indeed the heaviest concentration of everything in Mexico was in Mexico City. Ambassador Oumansky was responsible for maintaining discipline among the migrant population of communists and this job, of course, fell most directly on the shoulders of Colonel Ochek.

So that there was nothing like the quotidian executions back in Spain. The foremost objective, during that first year, had been of course to monitor Trotsky's activities. Then there was the abortive expedition, led by the artist David Siqueiros, that had failed to kill Trotsky. Ochek had erupted with rage over such an enterprise's having been undertaken other than under his direct supervision. The cable received from the Kremlin did not disguise the primogenital fury of Stalin. True, Stalin had had to bear the brunt of the international democratic uproar over an attempted assassination carried out by acknowledged communists who were presumably acting on instructions from communist superiors. To face all this—and then to fail! Trotsky, it seemed, had simply hurled himself under his bed. His bed! Safe under his bed against a machine gun! Colonel Ochek's fleshy face writhed in pain.

Trotsky had been the first preoccupation of Igor Ochek. But Raúl Carrera noticed that, in exacting discipline here and there, unlike Glukansk, who had been matter-of-factly concerned with discipline, Ochek took manifest delight in enforcing discipline. Utterly routine requests from subordinates were gleefully rejected. Carrera remembered the day

in May when María Socorro had asked permission to take three days off to attend her brother's wedding in Monterrey. Ochek said no. Not, Carrera knew, because he feared that María Socorro, in Monterrey for a few days in festive circumstances, might indiscreetly divulge what slight knowledge she might have had about the extent of the activities of the Soviet Embassy; and not because for three working days she was irreplaceable—there were several secretaries to share her clerical burden. Ochek simply liked to say no. And liked especially to say no when he could experience the distress he had caused.

The pain was not always psychological deprivation. There was young Valerian, the day he was brought in drunk by the police. Inside the embassy he was searched. Ten thousand pesos were found in his coat pocket.

Where had Valerian, whose salary was 250 pesos per month, got hold of ten thousand pesos?

Valerian, brought down now to the cellar quarters of the embassy, was interrogated directly by Ochek. He had answered lamely, persistently, that he had won the money at the state lottery and gone out to celebrate.

Where had he purchased the ticket?

From a street vendor outside the embassy.

What was the ticket number?

He did not remember.

Where did he go to cash the ticket?

To the central office, right by Bellas Artes.

Who had witnessed his cashing the ticket? No one besides the cashier herself.

Had he told anyone in the embassy about his good luck?

No, he had kept it quiet—but he intended to give a big party for his associates.

Had intended to give a big party for his associates.

Ochek had him taken to what they called the library—
"We conduct research there," Ochek, his thick glasses especially prominent when he leered and his eyes narrowed,
had chuckled to Carrera when he first came to work. After
viewing Valerian's condition when he was carried out, Carrera was grateful that he had never had any business to
transact in the library. And then suddenly, unexpectedly,
because he long had been accustomed to the style of Bol-
shevik justice, he had asked himself a question the reso-
nance of which would become haunting. He asked: But *was*
Valerian guilty? *Maybe it was exactly as he said it was*—he
had bought a winning ticket on the national lottery.

Merely to frame in his mind the question *Was Valerian
guilty?* was an invitation to conjugate retrospectively the
phrase: Was Valerian guilty? Was . . . A. "guilty"? Was B.
"guilty"? Yes, all those men were indeed guilty, guilty of
Trotskyism. Oh how much better off the world would be—
he had finally put his doubts serviceably to one side—when
Trotsky was no longer there to poison the wells.

A month later Mariya was brought in to take the place of
Valerian, whose broken body was sent back to Moscow on
"suspicion of treasonable relations with foreigners."

Valerian was a cryptographer, but within the KGB there
are levels of cryptography and Valerian had handled only
the routine work. He had sat for eight hours every day
behind a large machine, the protruding center of which
berthed a typewriter keyboard of sorts. A large collection of
newspapers and periodicals from all over Latin America
went through a kind of intelligence assembly line. Four
KGB officials would mark those columns or articles they

thought would be of interest to KGB-Moscow. Before the arrival of Colonel Ochek it was thought perfectly safe merely to clip and photograph these oddments and send them off in the weekly diplomatic pouch on the military transport plane that ambled up from Buenos Aires to Santiago to Lima, Bogotá, Mexico, Havana, Bermuda, Terceira, Lisbon, Stockholm, and Moscow, carrying diplomatic personnel and mail. Colonel Ochek had ruled that all such matter had henceforward to be encrypted. The material, because it was not of urgent security value, could then proceed as before to go forward to Moscow not by radio code but in the pouch, in those bizarre and theoretically inscrutable taped sequences into which the machine converted Russian.

So that Mariya's job was first to translate the Spanish material into Russian, and then to encrypt it. She was a graduate of the KGB academy, trained in Spanish, English, and cryptography. She had been orphaned during one of the early purges in the thirties and brought up by an older sister who—Raúl would learn all this—resented her younger sister's superior looks. Mariya had attempted to be dutiful and behave inconspicuously, and had worked for eight years, after leaving the academy in Moscow, under the supervision of her sister, who occupied a supervisory position in the KGB. Glinka was her name, and Glinka apparently desired above all things that Mariya should have no social life whatever. And so Mariya worked during the day, and then went home to the apartment where the two sisters lived, and did the housework. Thus it had been until suddenly a Spanish-speaking cryptographer was needed in Mexico.

Mariya was overweight, but Raúl found her very attractive; and already, after only a few months, she seemed to be

slimming down—as though the nervous tension caused by her sister's surveillance, now removed, freed her to find distraction other than in food.

Raúl took to sharing his lunch hour with Mariya and they practiced languages together, her English, his Russian. They went one night to the movies at the Cine Chapultepec and saw a rerun of *Gone With the Wind* and were quite dazzled by it. They went then to take a late dinner at the Hotel Géneve, right by the American Embassy, and Mariya drank some wine while Raúl had rum and cigarettes. She spoke of her sister, and of the academy. He spoke of Spain, and of his year in Moscow.

Six months later he asked Mariya if she would marry "an older man—I am forty-four, but I am healthy, and I know how to look after . . . somebody"—he found it hard to use the words modestly, so he went into French, the least secure of Mariya's languages—"somebody . . . *que j'aime.*" She looked at him with a face Raúl had never seen before. What he saw was something he adored. She told him she would marry him tonight if he asked her, that she never wanted to be away from him, not ever. That night they walked in Chapultepec until dawn.

The next day Colonel Ochek was utterly unambiguous on the subject. "The answer," he said in his office to his two subordinates, the short, wry Spaniard and the plump, wholesome Russian who stood stiffly in front of him, "is quite simple. It is No. The KGB does not run a dating service or a marriage bureau here in Mexico. We are engaged in a great revolutionary struggle. I expect you not only to remain unmarried but to see less of each other so that you will not be distracted in your work. Otherwise I shall simply transfer you."

Oh how they had talked about the alternatives, that night at dinner, and about the need to exercise great care. But the central objective was taken for granted. They would marry.

This required clerical footwork inasmuch as, in Mexico, foreigners who work for embassies require employer approval on their applications for a marriage license. But Raúl Carrera had become accustomed to the ways of Mexico, and he surmounted that problem with a mere one hundred pesos. The next problem was to consider living quarters that would not come to the attention of the colonel. They resolved, forlornly, that it would be necessary to continue to maintain their separate apartments. They could not afford a third apartment. They would need to run the risk of visiting each other in their separate abodes, always careful not to arrive, or leave, jointly. And, at work in the embassy, they would affect a gradual alienation from each other. No more joint lunches or shared jollity. Ochek and the general staff must be given the impression that it had been a temporary infatuation.

On the twenty-third of September a magistrate in Villa Obregón issued them a marriage license, and they spent the weekend, beginning at noon on Saturday, in Xochimilco, among the flowers, holding hands, and the two nights in each other's very loving arms.

Carrera was surprised when he was reached by telephone at his home by Colonel Ochek four months later—Ochek seldom telephoned. "You are to meet me in Room 51 of the Hotel del Valle in Cuernavaca at 10 P.M. tomorrow, Tuesday night. You will make no reference, during office hours tomorrow, to our forthcoming meeting. If anyone suggests any meeting with you after hours you are to say that you

have made plans to do work in the library and will not be home until very late. Is that clear?"

Carrera said that that was clear.

"There are buses, as you probably know, every hour to Cuernavaca. You should be able to make the six o'clock bus after work, but even if you take the seven o'clock bus, you will arrive in plenty of time to make our engagement."

At exactly ten, Raúl Carrera knocked on the door at the Hotel del Valle. There were three men in the suite, two of them strangers to Carrera. Ochek did not give out their names. He merely pointed to one, then to Carrera: "Carrera," he said. And to the other, the same thing: "Carrera," he said. And then to Carrera, directly: "Sit down."

He deferred now to the first of the two men, younger than Ochek by perhaps ten years. Forty, Carrera guessed. But Ochek referred to him as "General." He was smoking a cigarette, as was the third man.

"Your record shows, Carrera, total fidelity to the Party for a period, now, of over fifteen years."

Carrera nodded.

"We have a most grave commission to execute. You will, I assume, be satisfied of my credentials if I inform you, as I have Colonel Ochek, that the orders I bring were given to me by—Comrade Stalin himself."

The mere mention of the name caused the voice of the general slightly to alter. He cleared his throat. And went on to say that evidence, of an incontrovertible character, had come to the attention of the KGB in Moscow that Ambassador Oumansky was a double agent.

Carrera was astonished. He had seen pictures of the great Oumansky with almost every dignitary in Moscow, including Stalin himself. He was the ganglion of communist activ-

ity in the hemisphere. Everything that happened in Latin America happened because Oumansky authorized it to happen, or didn't happen because Oumansky did not authorize it to happen. He had been at least twice to Washington to confer there on matters of common purpose—for instance nazi submarines fishing in Mexican and Caribbean waters. The whole idea of Oumansky as double agent was unimaginable.

The general continued. He was seated now, peering at papers on a desk.

"Your record shows that you received training in Moscow in demolition. Is that correct?"

"Yes, General, that is correct."

"Your instructions are to prepare an explosive force of about ten pounds of dynamite. The decision, you will have gathered, is not to stage a public trial. It would be too demoralizing to too many of the comrades who have trusted the traitor Oumansky."

The traitor Oumansky. Carrera breathed deeply at the force of this apparent oxymoron.

"Do you have the necessary matériel?"

Colonel Ochek interrupted. "General, please. Of course we have access to it."

"Where is it to go?" Carrera asked.

"It is to go in the diplomatic pouch, having been set to explode on reaching eight thousand feet of altitude. The altitude in Mexico City being seven thousand feet, the plane will reach eight thousand feet in approximately three minutes, at which point the bomb will go off."

Carrera did not need more details.

That was Tuesday. On Wednesday after work Carrera, ever so careful to tell Mariya nothing of what it was that

would keep him from going to her apartment that night, even as he had not told her why she must not come to him the night before, went to a designated street corner where a car waited. Colonel Ochek was in it, and together they drove to a remote, inconspicuously guarded shed in the Guadalupe area near the railroad station.

It might better have been designated a small armory. Everything anyone could need in the way of explosives. "And all of it made in America," Colonel Ochek said, with a leer. "Useful, in case fragments are picked up."

It was simple enough, as Carrera retained what he had been taught and on several occasions, retreating from General Franco's juggernaut, a bridge or a railroad would need to be bombed, and if the regular people weren't there they would call in Carrera.

Carrera selected one of the wooden boxes, of which there were several in different sizes. This one would have berthed two magnums of champagne. He grouped together thirty-six sticks of dynamite, which would occupy about three-quarters of the space within the box. With great care to make the opening smooth, he detached the lid from one end of a soup can, lightly filing the edge to remove abrasive surfaces. He cut with metal shears a thin metal strip ten inches long and just under a half-inch wide from the same tin can. And a second piece six inches long. Again, light strokes of a fine file to smooth the surfaces.

He cut cardboard into a disk that would fit snugly inside the can, and clipped out two one-foot sections of insulated light wire, removing the insulation from an inch at either end. With care he applied strips of tape inside the can to strengthen the explosives' insulation. He took the shorter metal strip and bent it in half, rounding the insulated lip of

the soup can like a clip. He completed the taping and then, forming a kind of U shape out of the original strip, inserted it into the can, seating it across the bottom. He fastened a wire to the outside end of the first metal strip, anchoring it firmly into place. Now the current between the two wires could be made to flow only through the junction of the two strips at the rim of the can.

He blew up a child's round balloon to its full capacity to test it. Letting the air out, he slipped it into the can's center and blew up the balloon until there was enough pressure to press the bent tip of the wire to within a tiny distance of the contact on the can's edge. He had calculated that approximately 1,000 feet higher than the current altitude, air pressure would swell the balloon, bringing together the firing cap's leads. And effecting the explosion.

The bomb finished, Carrera was escorted to within a few blocks of his apartment by Colonel Ochek, who was friendlier to him than he had ever been before. (That often happens, Raúl ruminated, when someone shares with you, however unwillingly, a major secret.)

Raúl learned on the car trip home that he would serve yet another function on the following day. He was one of four officials who had personal clerical access to the pouch, both after it arrived—when it was Carrera's responsibility to pull out and distribute material for the KGB section—and when it left, it being Carrera's responsibility to insert material compiled by KGB-Mexico. The pouch, as it was loosely called, was more like an indefinitely expandable canvas sack. Indeed sometimes it was several sacks, as it was frequently used by high officials as conduit for small gifts; Ambassador Oumansky regularly received his caviar in the pouch. Colonel Ochek explained to Carrera that he did not

wish the bomb to be placed in the pouch in the embassy, as there was always the possibility that someone else, at the last minute, might desire to put something into the pouch and trip across the lethal parcel. Carrera's instructions were to take with him the office seal, go out to the plane when it was almost ready to board the ambassador, and go to the pouch with his package, advising the plane orderly that Colonel Ochek had neglected to enclose a mechanical specimen he wished analyzed in Soviet laboratories. "It will be routine," Ochek said, reassuringly.

And so it was. The diplomatic pass to go through Mexican Immigration to the aircraft was handed to him, on examination of his identification tags. Inside the C-47 transport Carrera turned to the compartment where the pouches of the various embassies were regularly placed, and exchanged an amenity with the orderly, identifying himself.

The orderly asked if Carrera needed help. No, Carrera had said, the package was light. The Mexican pouch was, understandably, on top of the heap. Carrera broke the seal, inserted his package, and resealed it with the hand press he carried in his pocket, which he had also shown to the orderly.

He left the plane then and headed toward the little group of embassy officials off at the windowed enclosure on the other side of Immigration. They were expected to show up whenever the ambassador flew away, or when he arrived from abroad. Carrera surrendered the temporary pass, entered the room with his fellow officials and waited.

Not for long. The ambassador and his wife emerged from the diplomatic door of the Immigration room and strode out to the aircraft, waving at the good-bye party in the

enclosure. Carrera noted ruefully that three staff members were accompanying Oumansky.

And then his heart stopped.

For a moment it was as though he had been blinded by snow. Everything was white except for barely discernible movements of photonegative skeletons climbing up a companionway. The last person to climb into the aircraft before the door shut was Mariya Pleshkoff. Mariya Carrera.

Carrera gave out a shout and threw himself against his startled companions in a race for the Immigration corridor. The propellers were now revving up and it was hard over their noise to hear exactly what he was saying, something on the order of his having to get to the airplane. An Immigration supervisor grabbed the little man by his lapel but Carrera felled him with a karate chop. With that a half-dozen Mexican officials dived at him and held him down on the floor and he heard the airplane engine's noise, as the plane taxied out to the runway, recede. He struggled with all his might, shouting to be released.

And then, abruptly, he was quiet. The rudimentary human engine that speaks of survival had choked off his voice. *You cannot stop the plane. If you shout out that there is a bomb in it you will be liquidated by the KGB. And it will not stop the plane.* He lay there, face down, two Mexicans holding down one arm, two Mexicans the other, three more on his legs. Several minutes went by as they waited for the police. He asked in a quiet voice if he might rise, and was cautiously permitted to do so.

"I am sorry," he said. The official he had floored was still brushing himself off, and his subordinates looked to him for instructions. Should they hold him until the police arrived?

"Forgive me, sir," Carrera addressed him. "I was in great

distress, and wished to wave to my wife who is on that airplane."

It was then that their attention was caught by the surrounding cries. The word reached them in moments. The Russian diplomatic plane! Exploded! Right over *there!* Just to the left of Popo. Could see it plain as day! A burst of flame! *¡Jesús, María y José, qué barbaridad!*

His chest heaving with pain, Carrera managed in the confusion to rush out to his car and drive to the office. There was already a crowd on the street. A dozen reporters, trying to get in to interview the deputy, or anybody; cameramen were arriving. Carrera fought his way through the crowd and was admitted by the guard into the building. He walked to his office and spotted, right away, on his typewriter a sealed envelope with his name written in her hand. He tore it open. "My darling. This is indiscreet, but I had to risk it. Believe it or not exactly half an hour ago Colonel Ochek told me I was to accompany the ambassador back to Moscow in case I could be of any service to him. No time even to go home and pack. But don't worry. He said he would make certain that I wasn't detained but would return with the ambassador within one week. It will be unbearable without you. Oh my darling, how much I love you. M."

Mechanically, Raúl Carrera put the letter in his pocket. He opened the door to his office a mere crack. By just standing there and looking through the slit he could see officials coming and going into the office of Colonel Ochek down the hall, opposite. This went on at a hectic pace for two hours, slowly lessening until, at about seven, Carrera reasoned that Ochek was alone, or very nearly alone.

He walked across the hall and opened the door. Ochek's secretary, Anna, was in the outer office, bent over her type-

writer. She looked up, muttered "What a day!" and went back to her furious typing. Raúl Carrera walked over to the door of the private office, opened it, and closed it behind him. Ochek was seated at his desk, telephone in hand. When he saw Carrera he hesitated, then dived for a drawer.

Too late. Carrera thrust two stiff fingers into Ochek's eyes. His scream was short-lived because the chop at the neck brought him prostrate. And then, summoning all the power in his 120-pound body, Carrera kicked Ochek in the temple; and knew, as he turned to walk out, that he was walking away from a dead man. Anna sat frozen at her typewriter.

"What is going on?" she asked hoarsely.

Carrera looked at her, said nothing, and walked out, using the back exit.

He never did return to his apartment, reasoning that it would be many days, weeks maybe, before Mexican security gave up waiting for him. He couldn't even remember exactly how it was that he made his way to San Antonio, or why, or how long the trip took. Arriving there and adopting the name Cecilio Velasco, he put his services as a clerk-translator to immediate use in huge Fort Sam Houston, groaning with Mexican-American recruits who did not know English, in a city greatly in need of white-collar workers to replace those who had been drafted.

He worked quietly in San Antonio, living in a one-room apartment, seeing no one but grieving and following the foreign news.

The war ended, he found that he had qualified for U.S. citizenship which he proceeded to take out, paying more than routine attention to his pledge (hand raised) to defend

the Constitution of the United States. When Czech Radio reported that Jan Masaryk had killed himself in Prague—thrown himself out the window of the foreign office, just like that, pity. Before the day was over, the press, and indeed the entire world, were on to what quickly was called the "Czechoslovakian coup."

Cecilio Velasco stared down at the *San Antonio Express*'s front-page picture of Jan Masaryk. He cut the picture and accompanying story out of the paper and folded them into his pocket.

He drove then to Fort Sam, but not to the War Department Personnel Center where he worked, but to the main administration building opposite the huge parade ground, named several years before in honor of General Arthur MacArthur. He walked into the building and asked the receptionist for the office number of General McIver, head of the Intelligence Division of the 4th Army.

He went to the office and there told the receptionist he needed to see the general, identifying himself with his Fort Sam badge, on a personal matter. A half-hour later he was in the office of the general, who looked up at the slim, taut man in his late forties, and then said, "What can I do for you?"

"My name is Cecilio Velasco," he said. "And I wish to work for the United States Government. I was formerly a major in the KGB."

The general told Velasco to sit down.

Alistair Fleetwood

WHEN ON AUGUST 23, 1939, the news came, Alistair Fleetwood was for an instant unbelieving. But there it was, and later editions of the papers even featured a ceremonial picture: a smiling Nazi Foreign Minister von Ribbentrop signing the accord with Soviet Foreign Minister Molotov. Fleetwood could not know directly the reaction of the communists in Cambridge, or even in London, because by design Alistair Fleetwood had become estranged from them. His very first instructions, on returning to college after the summer tour with Alice Goodyear Corbett five years earlier, had been to dissociate himself emphatically from the communists he had once associated with, and, gradually, even from the socialists: indeed, from the political left. So that by now it had been more than an entire college generation since he had mingled with the hard left community, either students or faculty; over four years since he had mingled with the little clots of fellow travelers among the students and his colleagues (he was on the faculty). Even the Russian he had learned, he was encouraged to let lie fallow. He greatly missed those fervent evenings with the select few, the brainy idealists who recognized that the Soviet revolution was the twentieth century's way of saying no to more world wars, to

imperialism, to the class system. But he was ecstatically engaged in that experience in his underworld life, even if apparently withdrawn; no longer the exuberant first-year socialist who had gone up to Cambridge in 1933.

On August 23 the whole of the British press descended on Harry Pollitt, the General Secretary of the British Communist Party. But he had declined to make any comment at all: and left-leaning apologists for Stalin in Parliament, most notably Denis Pritt and Harold Laski, were not physically present when the House met in an uproar over the news. Winston Churchill observed that perhaps Joseph Stalin had suddenly discovered that Adolf Hitler's party was called the National Socialist German Workers' Party and had discerned the bond between the two ideologies. The Moscow-leaning members of the Socialist Party were in deep distress. The Communist Party was torn.

Not so Alistair Fleetwood. After the initial shock, his mind went to work. It was, by character and training, a mind that could juggle relationships, reducing them to abstractions as required, so that what emerged was on the order of correlations of interest, rather than wrenched static relationships. And by the time his young dinner guest, Bert Heath, came by, Fleetwood was thoroughly at peace with his own analysis.

Obviously Hitler's fascism was a strategic menace to the international communist movement. Clearly Stalin had acted out of prudence. This was hardly inconsistent with Marxist-Leninist theory or practice. Lenin, during the New Economic Plan period, had gone so far as to encourage isolated pockets of capitalism, among other things to attract to the Soviet Union Western scientists who would depart leaving their skills behind.

Bertram Heath, to whom now Professor Fleetwood

handed a glass of whisky, arrived in white heat. Heath swallowed his whisky with a single gulp, and Fleetwood knew it would be a long, long evening. No matter. He would prevail. In the first place he was used to prevailing over problems. In the second place, he could, with all due respect to Bert Heath, persuade him, though he was only a single year his junior, of, well—Fleetwood faced it—anything. Not a reflection on Heath's malleability, rather a reflection on Fleetwood's strength of mind and on his singular capacity to satellize. And then too Heath found Fleetwood engrossing. He was, with Fleetwood, in the company of a man he could not bully and had no desire to bully. Fleetwood's intellectual achievement was too outstanding to be thought competitive. His subtle understanding of the great and noble reasons to hate England, Great Britain, the Empire, the West, the whole imperialist-bourgeois world, was a flame they had in common. Heath would have killed for Fleetwood. To be sure, he'd have killed for a lot of people. But for Fleetwood, he would take pleasure in killing.

Via radio, Fleetwood had been in regular communication with Alice Goodyear Corbett. Her father, two years earlier, had retired from journalism and, with what looked like a world war on its way, returned with his wife to Virginia. Their daughter elected to stay on in Moscow "to continue her scholarly researches," as she put it to them and, indeed, to her friends. In fact she had become a full-time KGB operative, and Fleetwood was one of her charges in Great Britain. It had greatly surprised her that he had never evidenced any impatience, or even restiveness, under her supervision. Whatever her orders, Alistair Fleetwood followed them with near-jubilant docility.

Fleetwood's career had continued on its spectacular course, and by the time he was in his twenties he was widely regarded as among the most inventive and productive scholars in the general field of electricity and electronics in the world, in constant demand at convocations of scholars pressing the frontiers of the relatively young science of electronics.

He affected only detached interest in the worsening situation in Europe, the Sudetenland crisis, the Munich Conference, the obvious preparations Hitler was making for war. He posed as only a bystander of sorts. During this period, he had been made aware by Alice that a clandestine group of Cambridge students was "in very close touch with us." It amused him that one of these—"The Apostles," they styled themselves—might actually approach him, thinking to energize him ideologically, perhaps with the view to interesting him in the common proletarian struggle. For that reason he allowed a kind of dull glaze to come over his eyes when political discussion was entered into. And, soon, though a very young man, he was treated as something of a scholarly fuddy-duddy, and more or less left out of any spirited political discussions.

No one had ever condescended to Alistair Fleetwood, to be sure. He had long ago begun to publish, and showed an originality, a comprehensiveness of knowledge, an interest in the productively esoteric that attracted not only national and international attention but inevitably the presumptive respect of associates even much older. "When Alistair's mind is engaged," a colleague had said of him, in the refectory of Trinity one day, "which is most of the time, he would not notice an explosion in the corner of the room. But he would notice a political discussion, and when that

happens, before your very eyes he simply dematerializes." Fleetwood rather enjoyed the drama of his great imposture, because during the whole of that period he spent many hours doing his chores for his Alice: silly things, he often thought as he compiled clippings revealing the political attitudes of people he had been told to monitor—politicians, professors, newspaper reporters. Indeed sometimes he reflected that special pleasure was to be got from the relative tedium of his work for the Party. "A kind of mortification of the intellect," he once dared say to Alice, who once went so far as to reveal to him, which was not to abide by the protocols of the profession, that more often than not it was not she who dictated what Agent Caruso, as his code name had it, was supposed to do. "Never mind. One day one of your services will perhaps even transform the struggle!"

"Take your time, my dear Alice. I am not hurrying you," he answered.

Fleetwood had made it a point to cultivate scholarly connections in Stockholm. And there he would frequently go, as would Alice Goodyear Corbett, her superiors in the KGB acquiescing in the arrangement on the grounds that Fleetwood would certainly prove extremely useful to them and was evidently disposed to continue to act through the young Soviet-American. In Stockholm the two would pass each other in the lobby of the Grand Hotel as strangers. They would meet in his suite, usually beginning with dinner; or if his formal commitments made that impossible, then later. And there they released their passion. One night he told her that he thought he would turn his mind to a formula that would express with electrical symbols the energy consumed by the average act of love. "In our case, I

would multiply that by a factor of ten." She smiled as she lay by him, stroking his hair, telling him how happy she was, except for the long periods they needed to spend apart. Their shared idealism was a form of communion.

Alistair Fleetwood replied that he believed war lay ahead of them and that the single privation he could not stand was the thought of a prolonged separation. "What will you do if there is war?"

"Whatever I am asked to do," she replied. "Perhaps they will want me in America. Perhaps they will want me to stay where I am. That will depend."

"You must never let them come between us." She agreed, and every time they were together they renewed their pledges to each other.

His first nonclerical commission had been the recruitment of Bertram Heath. Actually, the initiative had been his. Fleetwood had been attracted to the tall, rangy Wykehamist who devoted himself equally to physics, soccer, and politics: the quiet, determined young man with the even-featured straight face and the steady brown eyes that signaled what was coming before the laconic twenty-year-old got out what was on his mind.

It had been well after Fleetwood himself had retreated from overt left-wing activity that he noticed, from reading the daily *Union Reporter,* the Cambridge student newspaper, Bertram Heath's name cropping up in the sports section as a rising star in soccer, and in the Cambridge Union as a fiery socialist speaker. During Heath's second year, he qualified to participate in a seminar guided by Fleetwood prompting, in a matter of weeks, a fascination with the strikingly gifted young scholar by the only slightly

younger student which begged for social intimacy. This came first with Heath staying after class to pursue answers to one or two questions that especially vexed him. This became, a fortnight later, an invitation to take tea at a local café. Fleetwood reciprocated with an invitation to drinks on Tuesday night at the Fellows' Lounge. A month later they were sharing an evening meal at least once every week.

Heath, Fleetwood learned, was highly mobilized on all the requisite issues: the problems of the working class, the threat of Hitler, the hold of the New York bankers on commercial life, the insensitivity of the government of Neville Chamberlain, the class structure that was so especially evident in the public schools, including the renowned school from which Heath had graduated. Fleetwood permitted himself certain hospitable resonances when the young man spoke, and very gradually permitted him to know that he was, however silently, in sympathy with his basic positions, but had been too preoccupied with his professional researches to devote the time necessary to master the whole problem of international politics, and now he was encouraging Heath in effect to instruct Heath's brilliant mentor, an imposture he was sure would not be resented if the decision was finally taken to engage in recruitment.

He did notice about his young friend that he was less than charitable in his attitude toward those who disagreed with him, or indeed toward those who got in his way in any matter, whether it was a student competing with him for the higher grade in a physics paper or a soccer player on the other team or a Cambridge Union orator who disagreed with him, particularly if the form of that disagreement was patronizing. Timothy Bethell, defending the policies of the British government, had remarked a few weeks earlier that

such criticisms as were being made of "the speaker" (it was Bertram Heath) would "lighten the political burden of the nation, especially if, as a consequence, he were to devote himself exclusively to soccer, in which activity he is said to excel, perhaps to the point of failing to recognize that he is in this chamber supposed to treat arguments other than as footballs. They really are different things, Mr. Heath." There was great jubilation in the chamber, most of it at Bertram Heath's expense.

The following night, returning from a convivial supper with friends, Timothy Bethell, rounding the corner of Trumpington Street to approach his college, was accosted by a large man wearing a mask who proceeded to administer a beating so severe as to result in Bethell's hospitalization with a fractured jaw. There was great commotion at the college, and suspicion instantly fell on Thomas Brady, the boxing champion of Clare College, whose steady girlfriend of several months had only the week before been annexed by Timothy Bethell. Brady was asked informally by common friends to account for his whereabouts at the time of the assault, and although he pleaded most vigorously his innocence, in fact he had no way of proving that he was on a bus returning from London where he had done nothing more mischievous than go to the cinema. Some believed Brady, some did not. Alistair Fleetwood did.

The time had come, Fleetwood decided late that spring, and he dutifully consulted Alice Goodyear Corbett, asking her permission to proceed.

It had been a revelation to Bertram to learn that in addition to everything else the man he admired most in all this world was also in fact a clandestine revolutionary, wholly

mobilized behind the cause of the working classes. He joyfully accepted a commission as a revolutionary colleague. They spoke for hours on end about the excitement of their common purpose. It disappointed Heath only to learn that he would need to submit to the same discipline Fleetwood had submitted to, namely to recede from his firebrand mode as socialist and fellow traveler. But he was willing to do everything necessary to qualify fully.

So that by the time he was in his final year, Bert Heath had crossed the aisle to the Liberal party in the Cambridge Union, and his high BTU former colleagues thought him a spent case in whom the fires of idealism had burned out. Though they conceded that nothing else in Heath had burned out: he had become the captain of the soccer team, and was regarded as certain to win a first in physics.

Bert Heath was in Cambridge that summer doing a research project under the supervision of Fleetwood, and they dined together twice, sometimes three times a week in the suite Fleetwood had already begun to aggrandize with a cook-butler who served tolerable food, and a young but discriminating wine cellar. They ate now in the airy dining room, the windows on the side open to let in the summer air. Bert had been heatedly denouncing the pact, Fleetwood patiently counseling him to wait wait wait, that the wisdom of it would one day transpire. He acknowledged that communists would now be on the defensive everywhere, but that what mattered was not such setbacks as these, but progress in major, historical terms. That, he reminded his impatient and severe young friend, "can't be measured by today's headlines." And then, of course, the headlines a week later brought news that Hitler had invaded Poland. And forty-eight hours after that, the government of His

Britannic Majesty George VI declared war, for the second time in a generation, against Germany.

The Army Recruiting Office ruled that certain categories of scholars should not be drafted into the army: they would be more valuable performing special services. Fleetwood fell instantly into such a category, Heath marginally. Fleetwood was asked to report to Bletchley Park where he learned that he was to help with the whole cryptographic enterprise. He had his misgivings, which he confessed to Alice by radio. He was not disposed to help an imperialist power in a fight against Adolf Hitler so long as Hitler was an ally of the Soviet Union. She counseled him to protect his cover by agreeing to serve. And while there at Bletchley Park he could keep Moscow informed of all technological developments that might prove useful, meanwhile being as sluggish as he thought he could get away with in contributing to the war effort against the Soviet Union's ally.

Fleetwood spoke with Heath about coming along into the Government Code and Cipher School. Bert Heath on the one hand longed for more active work, but could not envision himself fighting on air, land, or sea against an ally of the Soviet Union. So he permitted Fleetwood to exercise his considerable influence to bring him into the bustling operation at Bletchley.

At Bletchley, Fleetwood learned what he could from his fellow scientists, but mostly he absorbed himself in a series of experiments about which he spoke little, even to Bert Heath, who throughout the long period that lay ahead of them was manifestly demoralized. Heath was frequently late in coming to work. He was seen at the local bars with different women who, after a few days, were given the op-

tion of sleeping with Bert Heath or being dropped by him like a stone. He calculated one night, as he left the hotel room he had hired for two hours, ahead of the American WAC lieutenant who would leave a decorous few moments later, that his rate of scoring came to about fifty-fifty, and those were reasonable odds. He cared nothing for any of the women he spent time with. His mind was occasionally stimulated at Bletchley, and he became a skilled radio operator, bringing his considerable knowledge of physics to his aid in helping to solve special problems.

Thus it went for two abysmal years, past the fall of France, through the Battle of Britain, through the bombings and blackouts, the shortages and rationing, and the general dreariness. His superiors no longer thought of him as a brilliant young scientist capable of creative work. It could be said that they lost interest in him. But all that changed on June 22, 1941, when Adolf Hitler's armies invaded the Soviet Union.

A week later, Fleetwood was working feverishly on projects directly related to the war effort. And one week later, Bertram Heath was receiving basic training at a camp for commandos in the south of England.

When, at age eighteen, on completing his first year at Trinity, Alistair Fleetwood was given the Duhem Prize for outstanding academic work, which prize customarily went to a graduating student or, every now and then, to a singular second-year student, his parents felt that they would have to yield to his entreaty, resisted during the previous two summers, to travel in the Soviet Union. "He has, quite simply, earned it," the senior Mr. Fleetwood, the librarian in Salisbury, had said after reading his son's letter. Mrs. Fleetwood

agreed, though she didn't like what they had all been reading about the Soviet Union under Stalin, about the show trials and the executions. And so, that night, father and mother went over their accounts and calculated how they might assemble the eighty-nine pounds necessary to give Alistair the month in Russia as a member of the tour sponsored now for the third year by the Cambridge Socialist Society.

The eight students and their guide. Alice Goodyear Corbett, traveled by Soviet steamship, leaving Southampton early in an afternoon of mid-June, arriving nine days later in Leningrad having, at about midpassage, ambled lazily through the long cool green of the Kiel Canal, as it had been called ever since Kaiser Wilhelm lost a world war and with it the right to continue to attach his name to the canal that joins the North Sea to the Baltic, saving five hundred miles of circumnavigation.

The students were very serious about their month in Russia, and the 12,000-ton *Pushkin* was well equipped with appropriate reading for inquisitive young scholars visiting the Soviet Union for the first time.

Alistair's roommate, Brian Scargill, was a third-year student, the president of the Socialist Society. He took his duties as, in effect, the student group leader, very seriously. In consultation with Miss Corbett it was decided that there would be two seminars every day at sea, each lasting two hours. During the first of these Miss Corbett would give general lectures on Soviet life and the history of the Soviet Union. In the afternoon she would teach elementary Russian.

The first day out, in the Channel, they ran into something of a gale. Attendance at the first seminar was accordingly sparse. But Miss Corbett made it without apparent diffi-

culty, as did Fleetwood and two others, not including Scargill who, when late that afternoon he emerged from his stateroom, was volubly mortified that an ordinary storm would stand in the way of his instruction in the great socialist experiment being conducted in the Soviet Union.

Alice Goodyear Corbett was a lithe, pretty, full-breasted, nimble-minded young woman, twenty-four years old. Her father was an American journalist who had been posted to Moscow just four months after the October Revolution, and now was recognized by the community of journalists there as the senior Western journalist in residence. Alice Goodyear Corbett (the convention had always been to use her full name, dating back to when, at age five, asked by a visiting Russian what her name was, she had answered, "*Moye imya* Alice Goodyear Corbett") had attended schools in Moscow from kindergarten and, at first with her father and in due course with others, had traveled everywhere foreigners were permitted to go.

Her early life was confused by the commotions that so absorbed her father professionally and affected her personally. There were the years in the early twenties when she was in grade school and was treated erratically by her teachers, who had not yet been instructed on the proper attitude to exhibit to a young daughter of a representative of the imperialist press. The children, before they reached ideological puberty, accepted her—as a foreigner to be sure, but also as someone apparently as familiar as they were with the ways of Moscow. Alice Goodyear Corbett knew all about their holidays and their history, their museums and their toys. She went regularly to play with other girls, daughters of other Americans and of English and German journalists, but she found, after reaching her teens, that her relations with them

perfectly trained Soviet protégée. Some indication of this reached her father (her mother had never managed to learn a word of Russian and simply ignored her daughter's activities except as they involved domestic arrangements). Her father passed it off as the kind of thing precocious children tended to do—involve themselves in their own culture—and paid little attention to it. Besides, he was himself sympathetic with what the Soviet state was trying to do and not entirely decided whether, when time came to retire, he would go back to Virginia. Perhaps he might just stay on in Moscow.

While a second-year student at the University of Moscow, Alice Goodyear Corbett had been called surreptitiously to the inner sanctum of the Party, located in the Student Union Building, and proudly informed that close observation by her teachers and others had persuaded officials to pay her the supreme honor of extending to her an invitation to join the Communist Party which, if she accepted, would mean that she shared an honor with only three percent of the Soviet population. The principal condition attached to her membership was that on no account was she to divulge this development to anyone, especially not to her father or to her mother, because although they were known to be friendly to the great revolution, if it became known that their only child had become a member of the Party this would embarrass him with his employer, the United Press, perhaps even bringing about his recall to the United States and depriving the Soviet Union of a useful commentator.

Alice accepted the honor with great enthusiasm. During her two trips home to Virginia in the preceding five years she had become practiced in defending Soviet policies. Much of what was alleged about Stalin's Russia was, quite simply, a lie—for instance the charge that the defendants in

the great purge trials were any less than flatly guilty, as charged, of treason. She was happy to think of herself as a consolidated member of an international movement, the great purposes of which would be to remove war and the causes of war and social and class antagonisms from the earth forever.

Alice wrote poetry, and her poetry included paeans to the Soviet state and its leaders, though she had had on more than one occasion to face the metrical choice either of substituting the name of a new leader in place of the name that figured in her original lines but was now exposed as having been treasonable or, if she couldn't find another leader with the requisite number of syllables to his name and ending with the same sound as the deposed leader (she was not able to find someone to substitute for Zinoviev), she would have to toss the poem away. But she had now the equivalent of a little book of poems, dedicated to Soviet leaders, to Soviet cities and villages, to Soviet schools, and to some of her Soviet teachers. One day, she dreamed, when her father's professional interests would no longer be jeopardized, she would publish these poems. What pleased her most was that she had been able to compose them both in Russian and in English, taking here and there the necessary linguistic liberties.

While doing postgraduate work in Russian history, she had been approached by her cell leader and told that Comrade Pleshkov of Intourist desired to see her. The meeting took place late that afternoon in what had been the groom's cottage of a czarist prince, on Herzen Street.

It was wildly exciting. The idea of it was that every summer until further notice she would escort a half-dozen or as many as a dozen British students, bringing them

from England for a month's tour of the Soviet Union. Mrs. Pleshkov explained that Soviet policy was to encourage a true knowledge of the country by intelligent young people from abroad, particularly those who had shown interest in communism. On top of her regular duties—to lecture to the students, to expedite their travel arrangements, to coordinate their programs—she was to keep a sharp eye out for any student who inclined sufficiently toward the great communist experiment, of which Russia was the matrix, to qualify for possible recruitment.

"Do you mean—actually to invite them to join the Party?"

"Yes," Mrs. Pleshkov said in her husky voice, taking a deep draft from her cigarette. "Yes—of course, you will in each case check first with me so that we can conduct appropriate investigations. But I have that authority, to extend membership. And we can hope that some of the young people will in due course show themselves willing to go further."

"What do you mean, Comrade?"

"The imperialist world—as you know, Comrade Corbett—is always poised to do damage to the socialist revolution. We need help from within Great Britain from young people who are loyal to humanity, not to decadent imperialist regimes."

"You mean, spies?"—Alice Goodyear Corbett's calm, matter-of-fact request for elucidation showed that she was not in the least troubled by the nature of her proposed commission, let alone shocked by the idea.

"You might call them that, yes. 'Friends of the Soviet Union,' I would prefer to call them: foreign friends of international socialism. These young men and women will, when they graduate, branch out and take positions in the armed forces, in the foreign service, in the academies: it

would be good to know that our fraternity is always growing, that everywhere—everywhere in the world—there are friends of the Soviet Union."

Alice Goodyear Corbett said the prospect pleased her in every way. Among other things it appealed to the poet in her, the notion that, using her own informed intuition, she might discern which students especially to approach, which other students to let alone.

The first of the Intourist Tours for the Cambridge University Socialist Society had yielded a harvest of two students whose fidelity, tested now for two years, had been established. Granted, there had been a slight problem with young Greenspan who had exuberantly volunteered to assassinate King George. But in Moscow it was judged, however tentatively, a satisfactory enterprise, and it was now established procedure that on their return to Cambridge, those students deemed worth cultivating would be put in touch with, and thereafter serve under the direction of, unit leaders. Both of them, after the first summer, had commended the recruiting instincts of Alice Goodyear Corbett; the second year, three of eleven student tourists accepted her discreetly proffered invitation.

The experience, moreover, had done wonders for Alice Goodyear Corbett, whose self-confidence had blossomed and whose very appearance took on a special, arresting aspect: a handsome, passionate young woman, alight with enthusiasm, confident of her ability, shrewd in her insights.

Alice Goodyear Corbett decided the very first night, when the *Pushkin* was rolling wildly in the cranky seas of the Channel and most of the ships' passengers stayed in their staterooms in varied forms of queasiness and outright dis-

tress, that the young man from Trinity who had completed only his first year at Cambridge was the most attractive prospect for the Party of all the students she had mixed with. Before the evening was over they engaged in sprightly conversation. She discovered that in his subtle, almost childish way (he was, after all, only just eighteen), the slim young man with no trace of a beard on his face, a light sprinkle of faded freckles reaching from his nose to his hair, so quick to grasp nuance, to expand and improvise on subjects only tangentially touched upon, so phenomenally knowledgeable on the subject—the communist enterprise—in which Alice Goodyear Corbett was an acknowledged expert, that notwithstanding his almost exaggerated youth, Alistair Fleetwood was really the senior presence in the group. She was at once perplexed, intrigued, and excited. It was almost midnight, and the bar was all but empty. She asked him if he would care for a nightcap, or would that overstrain his stomach? He answered that his stomach was perfectly fine, and ordered an orangeade. She touched her glass of vodka to his orangeade and said, "You will have a wonderful adventure during the next month, I promise you, Alistair."

"Oh, I am quite certain that is the case, Miss Corbett. You know, that is, after all, why I came. That, combined with the intelligent disgust anyone has, or should have, who knows England as I know England. But we need not go into that: the class system, the public school snobberies, the grinding poverty of the working poor. It is possible that I could teach you something about my country that you don't know. But I am so pleased to be here under your guidance! I look forward especially to learning Russian from you."

They said good night, and even walked out on deck for brief exposure to the howling wind. Alistair Fleetwood

insisted on escorting her to her cabin, on reaching which he bowed his head slightly, smiled, and said he would see her tomorrow at the seminar. "Or maybe even before that, if you are at breakfast." Alice Goodyear Corbett smiled, and on sliding into her bed was mildly astonished to find that that young man—that child! she insisted on putting it that way, in self-reproach—had actually . . . aroused her.

One month later they were again aboard the *Pushkin*, having traveled two thousand miles within the Soviet Union. Mostly, of course, they had been in Moscow and Leningrad. The reactions of the young Cantabrigians, Alice Goodyear Corbett reflected, were not very different from the reactions of the first and second groups, the one last year and the one the summer before. Two or three were traveling, really, only for the sake of the adventure, their curiosity limited to what Alice Goodyear Corbett quickly grew to recognize as the "exciting" historical sites: Lenin's Tomb, the Kremlin, the house in Leningrad where Rasputin had been killed, the prison where Lenin's brother had been held before he was hanged—that kind of thing. The embalmed Lenin was to be expected: it came first with foreign visitors, even as with Soviet pilgrims. But beyond these obvious historical sites, "they are more interested in the guillotine that cut off Marie Antoinette's head than in the French Revolution," as she said, compressing her criticism in one report to her supervisor. These students were visibly bored during the hours and hours and hours spent in factories and agricultural collectives where, by contrast, the ideologically motivated students took copious notes, cluck-clucking over what they were assured was the relative backwardness of comparable British and American enterprises.

Jack Lively, a vigorous young man of twenty who played rugger at Cambridge, was a socialist, Alice Goodyear Corbett suspected, largely because his father was a prominent leader of the National Union of Mineworkers. Jack Lively made it clear from the moment he landed in Leningrad that he expected a little romantic diversion. Alice Goodyear Corbett told him that that kind of thing did not go on under socialism; to which Lively, who was reading anthropology at Trinity, said to Miss Corbett, a) that she couldn't really be right about that, that what she called "that kind of thing" happens everywhere on earth; and b) if in fact socialism has come up with a system in which "that kind of thing doesn't happen," why, said Jack Lively, he would need to reconsider his commitment to socialism.

Most of the group—the conversation took place in the little bus on the ride to Nagorsk, so that they might witness with their own eyes the freedom of religion given by Stalin's government to those "quaint old monks," as Alice Goodyear Corbett put it—sided with their guide. But later, in their hotel room, Brian Scargill confessed to Alistair Fleetwood that though he had sided with Miss Corbett, in fact he thought that probably Jack Lively was correct.

What brought on the concrete problem was when, a few minutes late for breakfast the following morning Jack Lively, sitting down between Scargill and Fleetwood, smiled lasciviously as he dug into his ham and cheese and said, "You know that blather old Corbett was giving us yesterday about how in Stalin's Russia there are no you-know-whats?

"Well," he smiled, "she was wrong. And this one"—his eyes closed sweetly to suggest satiety and then opened again, the eyes now of the accountant—"was hardly dear,

unless you want to call one package of Dunhills and one quid expensive. Say, do you think old Corbett would go along with the idea if I persuaded Tania—yes, 'Tania'—to join us for the rest of the tour? I'm sure she'd be glad to. Besides," Jack Lively was enjoying himself hugely, "there is great advantage to be got from my suggestion, because as in the Soviet Union all things are owned in common, Tania would, I am certain, be happy to oblige the rest of you. Though—" he stopped dramatically, "perhaps not you, Fleetwood. She would probably take one look at you and figure you wouldn't know what to do in bed, and she is not a licensed teacher."

Alistair Fleetwood, though he gave no signs of it, was heavily challenged by this dose of raillery and condescension from Jack Lively. On the one hand he was totally loyal to Alice Goodyear Corbett and felt honor-bound to believe everything she said about life under socialism. On the other hand, his scientific intelligence taught him that facts, among them those that had to do with (ineradicable? Was this defective loyalty to Marx-Lenin?) human appetites cannot be denied by ideological asseverations, and evidently Jack Lively had had a night out with a professional. He was, also, secretly amused and titillated by the fantasy of a traveling tart with the Cambridge Socialist Society Intourist trip through the Soviet Union. If such perquisites were advertised, he was sure there would be more volunteers for the next tour. But above all he was sensitive to the implication that he was not really old enough to be experienced, perhaps even too naïve to be conversant with basic biological formulae.

But meanwhile he had to say *something* to Lively. So he shot back, "Oh really, Jack. So you found someone who

breaks the rules. Whoever said there are any societies any-where where some people don't break the rules?"

Lively was not going to leave it at that. "There are cer-tainly a lot of people who break the rules in Russia, you can say that again. At the rate at which they are executing traitors, Fleetwood, breaking the rule must be a very popu-lar thing to do."

On this point Alistair became truly defensive. "Do you have the figures, Lively, on the number of Roundheads executed by Cavaliers? Or the number of heretics killed during the religious wars of the seventeenth century? When you get around to doing that research, come see me about the Moscow trials."

He recounted, later, the whole conversation to their guide, who told him he had handled the challenge perfectly. "You will be hearing a great deal of that kind of thing. It is not unanticipated. *Stalin is trying to change human nature!* Such a challenge, such audacity, calls for great strength of will."

Alice Goodyear Corbett was by now, though speaking slowly, addressing Alistair in Russian. He had directed his mind to the problem of learning the language with the same intensity with which he had directed that formidable appa-ratus to scientific inquiry. Scargill and one or two others had learned a few phrases, and could order a meal or a taxi—or, in the case of Jack Lively, a woman of pleasure, however unlicensed. By the time they had completed the tour, back in Leningrad, Alistair Fleetwood was speaking regularly in Russian not only with Miss Corbett but with guides, drivers, and waiters. When the tour came to an end, she had made her selection of the three students she would press. First and foremost, of course, Fleetwood. Second, Brian Scargill. And also (she permitted herself an invisible

sigh) Harold Abramowitz, that tall, ungainly, dull young man with the clipped black hair and the mustache struggling to flower but still straggly even after almost thirty days of studied neglect. But Harold Abramowitz's devotion to communism was positively fanatical, and Alice Goodyear Corbett felt she could count on success with him.

They would have seven days on the *Pushkin*, the morning and afternoon seminars continuing, as on the trip out. Even so there were myriad opportunities for two people to sit down in a corner of the dining room, or in the library, or in one of the three sitting rooms, or on deck. She would approach them one at a time, of course. Everyone she approached always thought himself uniquely singled out, so the demands of security were fortified by vanity.

Curiously, it was Alistair Fleetwood about whom she was most apprehensive. This was so, she forced herself to admit, because she was a little bit in awe of him. The speed with which he was learning Russian was merely one example. His natural air of authority extended to all matters. Normally, when recruiting someone into the Party, the seniority of the recruiter is utterly plainspoken. Her authority rested in her established status as a Party member; as a graduate of the University of Moscow; as a linguist; as a longtime resident of the Soviet Union, and yet . . . she felt that perhaps he would be difficult for her to manage. There was that impalpable sense that he knew more than she.

The first night out of Leningrad was festive. A century earlier a French nobleman had written that there is always the inner urge to celebrate on the day you leave the Russian frontier. There was no way, Alice Goodyear Corbett comforted herself, to blame *that* on the communists. But the phenomenon had certainly not changed with the advent of

communism. That first night the passengers aboard the *Pushkin* were given Russian champagne, and vodka, and caviar, and zakuski, including a wider variety of meats and cheeses than they had tasted during the whole of their stay in Russia. During dessert, Alice Goodyear Corbett said to Alistair that she would like to have a few moments of private conversation with him, and what about after dinner?

"Of course, Alice." The students had been asked so to refer to her, after the formal end of the Russian part of the tour. "Where?"

"Well, we could take two deck chairs—it is quite warm. Or perhaps find a corner in the lounge where there isn't too much noise."

"It's going to be noisy everywhere," Alistair said. And then he looked up directly at her, his eyes wide open, and said, "Why not in your stateroom?"

Alice Goodyear Corbett paused, but did not avoid his young, searching eyes. She felt instantly exactly what she had felt when Grigori had asked her, in her final year at the University of Moscow, to come to his room after the birthday party: the impulses she felt racing through her blood were unmistakably the same. Grigori, dear Grisha, gone now to the army . . . But this *child!* Yet such an extraordinary young man. She hesitated, and said, her voice now entirely feminine, so different from the lightly stentorian voice of Alice Goodyear Corbett, tour leader, "If you like."

"Fine." Alistair, rising from the table, was not apparently surprised. "I know the room number, and I will meet you there in a half hour. Maybe I will bring a surprise. No, not maybe: I will bring a surprise. A present for everything you have done for us."

How very much thought he had given to this present.

Quite simply, the most he had to give. And Alistair Fleetwood had been aware for many years that what he had to
give was more, much more, than what others of any age, let
alone his young age, had to give. He felt positively ennobled
by the proposed act of generosity, but also tender in the
knowledge of whom he stood now to patronize with his
largesse: Alice Goodyear Corbett was a very special teacher,
a very special specimen of the new revolutionary. And a
very beguiling . . . woman.

She debated exactly how she would be dressed. She
compromised by simply removing her jacket, leaving herself with skirt and blouse. And by using a quarter of her
precious supply of French perfume, and brushing back her
hair. The cabin, slightly larger than the ordinary cabin, was
large enough for a desk on which she could do her paperwork. There was a flat couch on the porthole side, running
the width of the cabin. And, opposite, the single bed with
the protruding struts, so that it could be made into a double
bed when there was double occupancy. She adjusted the
reading light over her desk, and the light over the couch,
and the single chair next to it, on which she was sitting
when he rapped on the door.

Alistair Fleetwood entered carrying a tray with a bottle
of champagne, two glasses, and a small package wrapped in
red ribbon. He was dressed as at dinner, in white duck
trousers, white shirt, and double-breasted navy blue jacket.
He looked sixteen.

His eyes were bright as he opened the champagne, but
told her she would need to wait before opening the package. It didn't occur to Alice Goodyear Corbett that she had
any voice in the matter, and when she looked at him, glass in
hand, she saw that his expression was at once excited and

entirely composed. She drank down half her glass, and then told him what was on her mind. She was beginning to go on—her packaged recruitment line was extensive, about opportunities to serve the people, humankind, peace: she had never known it to consume less than a full hour. But after a few moments he interrupted her.

"Of course, Alice. I want to help and I will help, and I will help in every way I can. You do not need to press on me the idealistic nature of what you are talking about. I knew this early on, and I *felt* it in Russia."

She smiled, a smile lit with pleasure, surprise, and awe.

"Now," he said, "you can open the package."

Alice Goodyear Corbett said, rather flirtatiously, "I am glad it is wrapped in red. That is an appropriate color today."

Alistair Fleetwood said nothing.

She opened the package, and bared: a condom. She looked up at first startled, but in moments flushed, submissive. She knew now that her young charge was every bit in charge of her.

"Driving to Nagornski one day, Jack Lively told me that if I were to find myself in bed with a woman, I wouldn't know what to do. Well, I have an idea what I would do, but I do need instruction. And I would like to have that instruction from someone I like and admire as much as I do you, Miss—you, Alice. And I am also aware—I am widely read in extra-scientific literature, you know, Alice. I am widely aware that the most precious present a human being can give is her—his—virginity. You shall have mine," he said, in a voice that cultivated gallantry.

Alice Goodyear Corbett rose, turned off the study light, and sat down next to Alistair Fleetwood.

María Arguilla

WHEN FIDEL CASTRO strode into Havana on January 8, 1959, as conquering hero, he took the first of many occasions to give a speech. He spoke, more or less endlessly, for the next three months. Castro announced the dreams Cuba would realize under his leadership, but warned there was much work to be done—many "administrative" and "regulatory" actions to be taken, and yes, some disciplinary action too. In January, one of the activities against which the revolutionary regime would wage relentless war was announced: prostitution and pimping.

After the closing of Santos Trafficante's nightclub, María Raja lived with a succession of lovers in some comfort, in a spacious apartment on Calle Reina. But when word reached her that, the week before, four pimps had been executed (she did not herself use one) and six prostitutes arrested and sent out to a rehabilitation camp, she decided it was time to change not only her profession but her living quarters and to reclaim her name, María Arguilla. There would be too many former luminaries of the Batista period who would have her telephone number, and perhaps even her address written down in little notebooks that would be perused now with avidity by Fidel's newly constituted vice squad.

Among other assets, María Raja had a second passport. Her mother, a refugee from Hitler's Hungary, was above all things fastidious about security arrangements. It was only because she had had the cunning even as a teenager to make contingent arrangements that María so much as existed. As a girl, her mother had become friendly with a patrolman on the Drava River in southwestern Hungary. When the anti-Semitic williwaw of the mid-thirties suddenly threatened to grow to typhonic force, young Astra, age seventeen, led her widowed mother to meet her river friend, the elderly policeman with a fondness for the children who played along the river's verdant banks during the summer. He had befriended Astra when, at age seven, she was first taken there to play, and every summer that friendship was renewed.

He quietly—asking no questions—rowed Astra and her mother, with two laundry bags of clothes and toiletries, in the darkness across the border, letting them out in Yugoslavia. It was two years before they landed in Cuba, where Astra had a bachelor uncle who spared no pains to move them, as it were by remote control, what seemed inch by inch, from Yugoslavia and then to Egypt and finally aboard a freighter to Havana, where they arrived in 1941. Astra, a girl of striking beauty, then married a dashing young Cuban in disgrace with his aristocratic family, whose conventions he regularly dishonored, not least, now, by marrying a Jewish refugee from Hungary whose uncle was a jeweler in the commercial district.

But the young couple lived happily during the first two years of the world war and Astra bore María. It all ended on that gruesome day in which the dashing, stupid young Cuban insisted on responding to a challenge to a duel and was dead five seconds after his adversary drew his pistol. In

return for a very satisfactory settlement, María's paternal grandparents persuaded the widow to adopt her uncle's name of Arguilla, and to bring up her little baby without giving her any knowledge of who her father had been, leaving no clues as to how she might trace her grandparents, if ever curiosity seized her.

Astra had been true to her promise, and María did not know her grandparents. But everything else she did know: that her father had been killed in a duel, and that arrangements had been made with his parents to guard their anonymity. She learned from her mother the need always to give personal security a high priority.

When Astra died (she was run down by a drunken truck driver) María was only fifteen, and she lived then for two years with her uncle, who died leaving María a jewelry store heavily in debt from years of casual credit practices. Her uncle's accountant urged María simply to make her own arrangements with whatever money she had left over from her mother's little bank account, which was less than a thousand pesos. Looking for theatrical opportunities (she had inherited her mother's beauty), María wandered over to the entertainment district and was not entirely surprised— María, like her mother, was born worldly—to find herself talking with a raffish man, Señor Trafficante, who in his plushly upholstered office looked at her carefully, asked her matter-of-factly to disrobe, examined her again, focused lights on her from various angles, and agreed to employ her.

At first it was a fairly conventional skin show, but as the competition increased and María's allure won discreet renown, Trafficante found himself going further and further, and always there were rich tourists, predominantly American, willing to patronize his post-midnight, high-dollar act, and

the further the act went, the better they liked it. He evolved, finally, the program that was eventually closed down, though not before young Fidel Castro, seeking relaxation only a few nights before he left to attack, on July 26, the Moncada Barracks, had stopped in and marveled at what he saw.

María had distributed her substantial savings with some diligence in various banks, and when she moved from the apartment, she selected and paid for in cash a small house in the middle-class neighborhood of Santos Suárez, and, at age twenty-six, gave her profession to her neighbors as a drama teacher who until recently had taught in a private school. (She had, of course, a "letter" from the Mother Superior of that private school, regretting that budget problems made it necessary to let María go.) She was looking for another position, and meanwhile was happy to be able to live comfortably on a modest inheritance from her mother.

She was befriended by her neighbors, most warmly by Señora Leonarda Sori-Marín, the proud but widowed and lonely mother of Humberto Sori-Marín, one of the closest comrades-in-arms of Fidel Castro. Her son Humberto had written the Agrarian Reform Law, promulgated by Castro as one of his most profound social achievements, and there was great excitement in the neighborhood one Sunday morning. The rumor was that he was coming again. And, soon after one, María saw the little motorcade drive up and stop next door. Out of it stepped Fidel Castro, Humberto Sori-Marín, and two or three companions, to have Sunday lunch with Humberto's mother.

It was on the next such visit—Castro & Co. were comfortable there—that Leonarda Sori-Marín told her son and his friends that her new neighbor, María Arguilla, was

among the most beautiful young women she had ever laid eyes on and that in the three months they had known each other, Doña Leonarda had come to look upon María as her own daughter, and then, turning to her honored guest, asked might she, dear Comandante, invite her over to meet the great leader of the Cuban people? Fidel, in animated conversation with his friends, nodded his head vaguely between puffs of his cigar. Delighted, Señora Sori-Marín went to the telephone, rang her neighbor, and told her to come quickly to meet Comandante Castro, Primer Ministro de la República de Cuba. María answered that she would need a few minutes to make herself presentable, and Doña Leonarda said to hurry, hurry, and then went to the front door to tell the guards that she had permission to bring over for a visit the young lady next door.

María arrived and was presented. She bowed in the courtly Spanish manner. Fidel Castro looked at her, pleasantly at first, and then inquisitively. He engaged in routine chatter, with just that touch of *gallant* that he used in the company of beautiful young women, and, for that matter, in the company of old hags whom he desired, back when his word was less than law, to attract to his movement. An hour later Fidel left, bowing in turn to Señora Sori-Marín and to her neighbor, María Arguilla.

At ten that evening, an officer drove up to María's door and knocked.

María, dressed casually in a skirt and blouse—she had been watching television—opened the door, leaving the door chain in place.

"Yes?" she said. "Who is it?"

"I am Captain Gustavo Durango, *a sus órdenes.* I am from the personal guard of Prime Minister Castro. He desires to

visit with you." He squeezed his identification card through the crack in the door.

María looked at the card with the photograph of the bearded young captain, and then looked him full in the face; she was experienced in these matters. She withdrew the chain and opened the door.

"I am honored. For when is the Comandante's invitation?"

"For tonight, señorita."

She thought quickly. There was little point in declining to go. She said, "I shall have to prepare myself." She motioned to a chair. "Can I bring you something while I am getting dressed?"

"A beer," said Captain Durango, "would be just fine. It is warm tonight."

In her room, María made herself up with professional skill. She dressed smartly, in soft-colored silk with pastel shades, and the discreetly applied perfume.

The captain insisted that she ride in the backseat of the 1958 Buick sedan. Their conversation was mostly about the weather, though Captain Durango twice remarked the mounting hostility of President Kennedy, notwithstanding his humiliation early that year with the attempted invasion at the Bay of Pigs, and dwelt on the eternal hostility of the imperialists to the Comandante. They reached a house on a street María could not, passing the street sign at night, make out. A sturdy three-story house surrounded by a picturesque brick wall. The captain marched past a detachment of six guards and knocked on the door. Fidel Castro opened it and bowed to María, his right arm extended. He wiggled his index finger at Captain Durango, who, withdrawing, reacted dutifully: "I shall be on watch, Comandante."

How pleased he was to see her, he said, taking her by the

hand up the stairs to the central living room, and indicating a couch. "I shall have a rum and pineapple myself. Will you join me?"

She nodded. Castro, the two drinks in hand, sat down beside her. He smiled, and there was glitter and a leer in his eyes. "María, my dear, you know that I have seen you before."

"Of course," she said, sipping. "At Humberto's mother's house. Today."

Castro chuckled. "I mean, *before.* I have seen you before today. Indeed, I have seen all of you. Indeed, a month has not passed since that day almost eight years ago, in July—at La Gallinera—when I fail to experience jealousy. A jealousy I felt in those days only for the authority of the Batista impostor government."

María permitted her hand to be drawn by his to his crotch. "If that night my fairy godmother had said, What would you most like to be this minute? I'd have said, the liberator of Cuba. If she had said, What is your second choice? I'd have said—" Castro stretched out his hand and pointed, his head turned up as if at a stage, "that man there—the man, María, who was making love to you on the stage."

María was accustomed to sexual overtures of a great variety, and in any event saw no purpose in being demure with a man who had seen her publicly perform her act when she was only eighteen.

She said, soothingly and ardently, "And I, Fidel, wish that I might satisfy the greatest man to be born in this hemisphere in this century."

Fidel took the two glasses with them into the bedroom.

A few months later, walking from the bus stop to her house, María came on Doña Leonarda rushing out of her

house toward a waiting taxi. María, by now virtually a member of the household, hailed her. "Where are you going, Leonarda?"

She turned and shouted out, "I will come to your house as soon as I get back. Before dinner, for sure." Her eyes were wet. She had obviously been weeping.

Without knocking, just before seven Doña Leonarda came into María's house and collapsed on the couch, exhausted and breathing deeply. María went wordlessly to the cupboard, poured a glass of sherry, and turned on the stove to heat some tea. She walked over to her slender neighbor, whose lined face suggested an age greater than the sixty-one she acknowledged when making one of her frequent references to the precocity of her important son. She was dressed in black and wore a mantilla. She took the glass of sherry, but set it down on the coffee table.

"I have been to see Fidel," she said, her voice trembling. "He admitted me. I had to wait only a half hour, maybe less. I pleaded with him, on my knees—"

"Leonarda, Leonarda, pleaded for *what?* What is the matter?"

"Humberto. Yesterday he was arrested and charged with complicity in treasonable activity. Of course it is not true, not one word of it. It is the action of an anonymous informant, someone who wants his job. But the charge carries the death penalty, and he is to be tried this very afternoon."

She stopped for a moment, unable to go on.

"Before I went in to see Fidel, I knew I could not go too far, I could not beg him to withdraw the charges against Humberto completely. That will come later. All I could safely do," she began to sob, but there was a triumphant smile through the sobbing, "all I could safely do was to ask

him to commute the sentence of death if it is meted out by the court."

She sat back in the chair, and her pose now was regal. "And, María, my pleading prevailed. He took his big hand and stroked my head, over the mantilla. And he said, 'Don't worry. Nothing will happen to Humberto. I promise you, Doña Leonarda.'" Her smile was beatific, and now she took the glass of sherry, but before she had finished it, her eyes closed. María took it from her hand, and Doña Leonarda slept.

Much later, after giving her some soup, María walked Doña Leonarda back to her own house. The following morning María flicked on the radio to hear the news. There was more of the same about the disposition of the survivors of the attempted invasion at the Bay of Pigs. The next item was that Humberto Sori-Marín, having been found guilty of treasonable complicity against the regime, had been executed by firing squad the night before at La Cabaña prison.

María later realized that she reached maturity only that day, at that moment: she felt a concern entirely extrinsic to her own interests. She had not yet learned to love, but she had learned to hate, and, in doing so, felt ready for love.

Two weeks later, Doña Leonarda having been sent off to live with her sister in Sagua La Grande, María's plans were completed. They were drawn from the deep archives of contingency she had taken care to prepare. For this one, she had secured the cooperation of her old employer, Santos Trafficante, based now in Miami. Trafficante, six months before, had agreed, via one of the several agents who remained in Havana, to help her in the event María wished to leave. The plan was this: her grandfather, who fled Cuba when Castro arrived, had died, and in his will had repentantly specified a

considerable bequest to his granddaughter, whose identity and whereabouts the grandfather did not know at the time he made out the document. He did not even know the name under which she went. But the estate's executor, using the old family lawyer in Havana (also Trafficante's), had developed leads that suggested that María Arguilla was indeed the heiress. She would need to satisfy an American probate court of her identity, and this would require that she go to Miami and be prepared to stay there for as long as six months, permitting the court independently to verify her representations. Worth the effort, however, since the bequest would amount to "at least one hundred thousand dollars."

María wrote Trafficante, and one week later received from a lawyer in Miami a letter detailing the fictitious situation and requesting that she travel to Miami.

She had been seeing Fidel every week, though at irregular intervals. Always it was Captain Durango who would drive up. Sometimes his knocking at the door would wake her at midnight, and even later: Fidel worked, and fornicated, into the early hours of the day. When Captain Durango summoned her next, she brought with her the letter from Miami.

She had pondered whether to make her request before or after he led her into the bedroom. She was experienced in male moods, and decided that Castro was better approached before than after, when his ardor was dissipated and instinctive suspicion coursed through his brain.

It hadn't, in fact, been difficult. Fidel was in an expansive mood. But he told her that he did not want her away from him for six months.

In that event, she said, she would endeavor to schedule her meetings with the court over convenient intervals. There was the logistical problem. She could only go to

Miami via Mexico, commercial traffic of course having long since been terminated between Cuba and the United States. No matter: Money, Fidel replied, was not an obstacle. She could go, stay a week or two, and come back via Mexico—he reached into a drawer and handed her a packet of bills, one thousand pesos. "That will do for several trips, Havana-Mexico-Miami-Mexico-Havana." There would be no problem in getting a Mexican visa (he took out his notepad and scratched out a reminder on which he would act the following morning). She was to write him, telling him what progress she was making. He pulled a sheet of paper from his notepad, scribbled on it, and gave it to her. "That is a private post office number and an assumed name. Use them when you write to me."

"And now," he said, smiling, "there is one condition."

"Yes?" she smiled, as he fondled her.

"The movie. The movie you told me about. The movie Trafficante made of you at La Gallinera. I must have it. I wish to see again what I remember so vividly that evening before Moncada. We will watch it together, and then re-enact the scene. You must find Trafficante. That will not be difficult. He is with the Mafia in Miami, and I am sure he will welcome revisiting his great star of yesterday. My star of today!" he added amorously.

She promised to make every effort to secure the film. "If it exists, Fidel."

"It exists," he said confidently. "People like Trafficante never destroy things like that. They are little capitalists, little hoarders. You will see." He led her into the bedroom.

Three days later, María had landed in Miami. Three days after that, she accepted the job as manager of La Bruja Vieja.

Rolando Cubela

ROLANDO CUBELA was a medical intern in Havana at the time of the accident in Mexico. He had become accustomed to the sight of blood, following his father about, mostly around the bullrings of Mexico, before returning to their little farm in Placetas in Las Villas. His father was a farmer in the sense that he had inherited a couple of hectares. By trade he was a bullfighter—more particularly a picador, whose job, every Sunday in the arena, was to thrust his heavy, armored frame onto the wooden pole with the steel point at the end into the fighting bull, piercing the animal's tossing muscle, into which eventually the matador would thrust his lethal blade. The idea was to lower the bull's carriage of head, and hence his horns; and simultaneously to correct faults in the carriage of his head when the bull charged.

Rolando, from the age of six, excitedly accompanied his father around Mexico while his mother tended the little farm. Hand in hand they would go together to the bustling dressing room and from there to the *callejón,* the circular wooden partition that surrounds the bullrings, shielding the bullfighters. If there was an empty ringside seat—a *barrera* seat—above, Rolando was permitted to occupy it.

Otherwise he would stand by the *ruedo,* peering out over it into the ring. He needed elevation—the *ruedo* is very high. Even so, some acrobatic bulls succeed in leaping over it when chasing their antagonists or when, in a seizure of cowardice, they charge forward to escape the torture, bounding over the *ruedo* into the *callejón,* quickly dispersing the bullfighters there into their reserve sanctuaries.

One such bull had knocked Rolando from his *contadero* perch right into the ring, causing a great uproar in the crowd and a much greater uproar at home.

Either from his makeshift seat or hoisted by an idle and friendly peon, he had seen—he could count them—116 fights before he was nine, and this means a great deal of butchery, including two dead *novilleros,* and a dozen horses impaled by the bull, never mind their mattress-thick carapaces. And there was blood at the farm where the Cubela family lived: it was Rolando who would kill the chicken when his mother decided to serve her *pollos fritos.* As a young student at the parochial school, Rolando was recognized by his classmates as a martial type: he boxed and he wrestled and often he picked fights, and there were often bloody noses.

But by age fifteen Rolando had decided he wished to go into an entirely different kind of life—bloody yes, but bloody-salutary, not bloody-destructive. He wished to become a doctor. If he was going to make it into the medical school, and be content as a doctor, he would need to make a major commitment, namely to protect life rather than mutilate it. He came to this decision rather solemnly, and during the week he let pass several schoolboy provocations which, a fortnight earlier, he'd have thought *casus belli.* That weekend when his mother told him to go out to the barnyard and

kill a chicken, he announced to his stupefied parents that to do so was really a violation of the Hippocratic oath. They had never heard of this oath, but Rolando gave them an earnest reading of it, emphasizing what it permitted, what it did not, to medical doctors—which, he shrugged his shoulders, he would one day be. The father suppressed a smile and told Rolando's sister Elena to go kill the chicken, and Rolando to shut up about that doctor's oath, to remember that he was not yet a doctor and would never be one unless he maintained very high grades in school, and even then only if his father, forswearing the Hippocratic oath, could help kill enough bulls to pay Rolando's fees at medical school.

Rolando pursued his studies and, ten years later, after surviving the financial crisis brought on by his father's accident, was a devoted student of medicine, and a devoted revolutionary. His hot blood aligned him, as a first-year medical student, with the young men who were actively in opposition to the reigning Cuban dictator, Fulgencio Batista. Ernesto Sánchez, his roommate, was deeply read in Marxist literature and talked incessantly of the need to organize "at every level." Rolando managed to learn (as much as he wanted to learn) about the theory of class struggle while walking to Dr. Alvaro Nueces's class on hematology; Ernesto talked and thought more, even at the baseball games. As Rolando's indignation against President Batista, who had taken power by military coup four years earlier, heightened, his enthusiasm mounted to help overthrow him. Ernesto introduced him to members of the loose fraternity of young professionals—students of law, engineering, architecture, medicine—who felt the revolutionary bond. Their undisputed leader was Fidel Castro, at

times wonderfully conspicuous, orating to captive audiences, at times furtive, exhorting carefully concealed little knots of fellow revolutionaries. And then one day Castro stormed into a radio station, seized the microphone and inveighed against Batista and praised freedom and democracy and social justice and anti-imperialism for a full ten minutes while his companions kept watch for the police.

Again, at times Fidel was mysteriously gone—but never impalpable: he was "somewhere," fighting the noble fight. Mexico, maybe; Colombia; at the other end of the island; in the mountains. And of course there was the nineteen-month period when Castro was in prison, after the Moncada Barracks attack in Santiago de Cuba. But whatever Fidel Castro was doing, he was always a presence and Rolando, though temperamentally skeptical of authority and temperamentally assertive about his own rights, was greatly humbled at the thought of that singular presence in Cuba—in the Caribbean. Indeed, in the world—Rolando tended, after a great deal of Marx and Lenin, to think in planetary terms.

Rolando Cubela was assigned, on graduating, to Hospital Calixto García at Vedado in Havana, and was kept busy binding wounds in the Emergency Room and helping the doctors in surgery while studying their techniques. Every week he reported to Dr. Alvaro Nueces who, in addition to teaching, supervised the work of the interns at Calixto García. One night in August, after a very long day in surgery, Rolando arrived back in his quarters, shared still with Ernesto, and was given in breathless tones by Ernesto the message: Fidel Castro wished to confer with him. Rolando's brown eyes widened. Slowly, he let himself down on his cot.

"When? Where?"

With some exasperation Ernesto, the professional revolutionary theorist, said to him, "I did not *write down* where you were to go. One doesn't *do* that. I memorized it."

"Tell me, tell me," Rolando said, his whole face under his tousled hair pleading.

Ernesto lowered his voice. "Your instructions are to knock on the door of Calle O number 198 at exactly twelve minutes past midnight. Someone will open the door. You are to say, *'I am looking for my sister Ernestina. Is she here?'* You will then be led to Fidel."

Rolando Cubela gave thought to exactly how to dress appropriately. Fidel was of course hirsute, while Rolando had only the trace of a shadow. He wondered whether to shave, as he would do if he were going to a social engagement, or to leave his chin as it was. There was no way to accelerate the growth of his beard between nine o'clock at night and midnight, though as a doctor he knew enough about cosmetic techniques to darken his general appearance . . . No—that would be, well, foolish.

He decided he would go neatly dressed, but without a tie (just a hint of the proletarian disposition). He would wear a jacket, but his shirt sleeves would be rolled up, in the event Fidel should ask him to take off his coat. Would Fidel quiz him on any particular matter? Certainly he would not be asked the kind of theoretical-philosophical questions that Ernesto would be so much better qualified to handle . . . No—there was simply no guessing what it was Fidel wanted with him, Rolando Cubela, a medical intern.

The interval before he set out went slowly. But, relishing the coolness of the tropical evening and the balm it brought from the awful heat of August, he walked toward the meet-

ing place, a matter of two kilometers or so. He had set his watch by the radio, and at exactly the designated time he crossed the street and knocked on the inconspicuous door, in a block crowded with two-story houses cheek to cheek.

When the door swung open, Rolando Cubela saw a stooped, skinny old man wearing a leather apron. Rolando spoke his lines metallically. The old man stared him in the face and asked to see Rolando's identification. Rolando handed over his intern's card, with his photograph. The old man, after an interval, said simply, "He is waiting for you. Number 257."

Flustered, Rolando asked, "On this same street?"

The old man nodded, and shut the door.

Number 257 was only two blocks away. The building was obviously an aging private house, probably built during the twenties: wooden, shuttered, the paint a flaky pastel blue, a hint of grass on the slender private land between the street and the slightly recessed entrance. Again he knocked.

He was greatly surprised. "Good evening, Rolando," said Alvaro Nueces, opening the door and quickly shutting it.

"Good evening, Doctor," Rolando replied, trying to suppress his surprise on learning that his famous teacher-scientist was a fellow revolutionary.

"You are to refer to me, when not in the hospital, only as 'Varo.'"

"Yes, Doctor. Yes—Varo." The doctor signaled to Rolando to follow him. They climbed one flight of stairs and, without knocking, Varo opened the rear door into a warmly lit room, comfortably large, the walls lined with books, window shades tightly drawn, an upright piano in one corner, a desk opposite, and, in the center, four uphol-

stered chairs, two of them facing the other two, a knee-high table in between. Fidel Castro sat on the mammoth chair on the right, smoking a cigar.

Castro rose and Alvaro Nueces performed the introductions. The other two men in the room, one of them young and fair and wearing a sports shirt and slacks, the second middle-aged, dressed as a businessman might dress going out to dinner, were introduced simply as "Luis" and "Paco." Rolando had not got used to the brevity of revolutionary nomenclature and found it difficult to say "*Buenas noches, Paco*" to a man twice his age, and so said, with a little bow of his head, only "*Buenas noches.*"

Castro asked his young guest if he would like a drink, and Rolando stammered out "Coca-Cola" before recognizing his error. He was wordlessly brought an Orange Crush, a sparkling orangeade bottled in Havana and paying no royalties to U.S. capitalists.

Castro motioned him down onto the vacant chair—Paco, after shaking hands and informally saluting Castro, had walked out of the room, leaving the young man and Alvaro Nueces. Castro began to talk, and soon Rolando felt the hypnotic rush. As a medical student he had written a paper about that famous sensation for his anesthesia class. This must be like what the drug-taker feels, he thought: what I feel now, in the company of this giant, who will surely have a historic future.

Castro spoke at great length and with much passion about the need to liberate Cuba. A full hour went by before he shifted into the interrogatory mode: Was Rolando familiar with weapons? Oh yes, said Rolando eagerly. His father was—had been—a bullfighter, and as a young boy he had been trained to use all the weapons of the bullfighter. He

even knew how to sharpen steel, had known how to do so before seeing his first scalpel; Rolando felt an impulse to boast about *something* to help accord in some way, in any way, for the distinction he was being paid.

Castro said he was not talking about "cutlery," but about firearms. Rolando said that he had been brought up in Placetas in Las Villas, in the open country his father farmed when not at the ring in Mexico. He had used his father's rifle from the age of twelve and had become an expert marksman, shooting rabbits regularly and even—Rolando became a little expressive—"a young deer, on one trek into Camagüey and also a wild pig—two pigs," he said self-effacingly. Though, he thought it fair to add, "I haven't used the rifle since I was fifteen." He added, lest he give the wrong impression, "Too busy becoming a doctor."

"Have you ever used a pistol?"

Yes, his father had a collection of which he was very proud, three pistols, one of them dating back to the Spanish-American War. "The imperialist war," he explained.

Castro came to the point. Varo—he motioned toward the senior doctor—had told him that Rolando had singular qualifications, and that he was eager to participate in the great struggle that lay ahead against the tyrant. Castro had in mind for Rolando a position of some responsibility. But he would need to be tested first.

Rolando nodded his head obsequiously. "Anything you direct me to do, señor."

"You are to carry out the orders of my revolutionary council. An execution."

Rolando could not entirely control his breathing. He could only think to ask, "Who, señor?"

Castro laughed. He laughed uproariously. Such a laugh

as demands of subordinates sycophantic acquiescence. Luís joined in the laughter. Dr. Nueces joined in the laughter. Eventually Rolando found himself laughing. He reasoned quickly that he had asked a naïve question.

Suddenly Castro was silent. He rose. Luís and Alvaro instantly rose also, and Rolando.

"You will be told who at the proper time."

Castro extended his hand. To Alvaro, "Take our young friend to the door." And, to Rolando, "You will receive your instructions." There was no laughter left over; no levity in the room.

There would be—Rolando was given to reconstructing the events of that first night—the difficulty of coping with his roommate's fascinated questions (Ernesto had never met Castro). Walking as in a dream past Calle O, 198, up Avenida Infanta, and through the Eloy Alfaro park, back to his quarters, he prepared his answers.

He concocted a story: Castro had recruited Rolando's cousin "at Oriente"—the far eastern end of Cuba he knew Ernesto had never visited and probably never would. That cousin had become close to Castro and had requested that, when back in Havana, Castro meet with Rolando Cubela, who had starred in his graduating class at medical school and whose sympathies were known to be revolutionary. Rolando (he would tell Ernesto) had spent an hour with the great man and was deeply impressed by his desire to liberate Cuba from the domestic tyrant and from foreign imperialism. Castro clearly had a towering perspective of what Cuba needed and, besides, was wonderfully informed on all matters—he had spoken "intimately" of the principal figures in Batista's entourage, his so-called Cabinet, and the

fake assembly that Batista affected to consult about public policy. That, Rolando thought, ought to do it. He would improvise on details. Ernesto would ask whether Castro had made any mention of any further meetings, or of enrolling Rolando in any particular organization. Rolando would need to be vague.

It went plausibly, and the two young doctors had been up most of the night, talking animatedly of Castro and the future of Cuba.

Two days later, in the mailbox where Rolando generally found nothing more than his weekly paycheck, the schedule for the following week's activities at the hospital, and—occasionally—a brief note from his mother, he received the promised contact. A letter.

The following Saturday, at noon—the interns had off every other Saturday afternoon and Sunday; Rolando would need to arrange a substitute because, on the specified Saturday, he was on duty—he was to be at the Parque de la Fraternidad in Calle Prado, seated on a bench on the west side, reading a copy of *Hoy*, at 12:45. The letter was signed simply, *Luís*.

What followed that meeting, Rolando Cubela in later years had difficulty recalling in specific detail. Luís met him in the park and drove him to a remote farmhouse where a young couple took him in hand, Héctor and Amanda. He spent much of the afternoon in target practice with a 9-millimeter Luger. Ten years of inactivity with guns were quickly made up, given Rolando's training as a boy and his natural aptitude as a marksman. Within an hour he was hitting the bull's-eye at ten meters. "You will be much closer than ten meters to your target." Héctor smiled. "We hope."

The evening, he remembered through the mists that, so soon and for so long, descended on those surrealistic hours, had been greatly convivial. Neither Héctor nor Amanda, who tended their farm informally (that much was obvious to Rolando), knew very much about farming, but he was careful not to ask what it was that they otherwise did. Manifestly, they were college graduates, conversant with literature, philosophy, and, above all, politics. He was careful not even to ask when the—incident—would take place.

The next day, he remembered when taxing himself, as on occasion he did, to re-create the weekend, Amanda went into the city, and at that point Héctor, in the didactic manner of the schoolteacher, paced up and down the room, addressing Rolando but speaking as though a soliloquy.

Rolando's "target" always—"almost always—if he isn't there that particular day, why, we just postpone the operation"—attended the eight o'clock Mass at La Catedral de La Habana in La Habana Vieja. Most often he was alone—his wife and three older children regularly went to Mass at eleven.

Héctor pulled open a drawer and took from it four photographs, the first showing the entrance to the church, the second a picture of the building opposite, and pictures taken of the area from one side of the church, and from the other. Rolando was to sit in the front seat of a car with Héctor. They would park opposite the church, arriving at 8:35—"Mass usually ends between eight-forty and eight-fifty." Sometimes there were two or three cars parked opposite, cars belonging to "rich capitalists," but it would be easy to adjust to the situation. "Our car will be parked so that we can make a fast getaway."

The execution was to take place the following Sunday unless Luís got word to Rolando before then that for whatever reason the operation was postponed. When the congregation began to come out from the church, Héctor would point to the target. Rolando, wearing a ranchero's broad-brimmed hat and dark glasses, would wait until Héctor identified the target. He would then step out of the car, approach the target, fire the pistol at his face—"shoot three times at least, we do not want a wounded target"—return to the car—"don't run, there will be no need, and remember that the man who is calm, even if he is the assassin, is the man in psychological control of the crowd"—open the door, and Héctor would drive him away.

The following week, Rolando remembered, always in that haze, had been odd, both endless and stampede-speed fast. It required intense effort to concentrate on the work at hand, much of it delicate as he himself began to engage in the surgery for which he was being trained; but then, suddenly, he would find himself performing feats of extraordinary intricacy with the fluency of a Paganini going through a concerto, never mind that he had never practiced it. It was especially hard in the evening, when he had to chatter with Ernesto as though unpreoccupied. When, in their tiny little quarters—one room, two beds, two desks, a single window, a washbasin, the wheezy secondhand refrigerator his mother had given him as a graduation present stocked now with fruit and soft drinks and beer and bread and cheese— the overhead light was turned off, by common agreement at midnight, conversation would cease. Rolando lay fitfully on his bed, breathing the hot summer air. He thought of his Hippocratic oath, now not a child's affectation but a formal vow. He agonized, yet he did not waver in his determination

to do what he had told Fidel he would do: Anything you direct me to do, señor.

It went flawlessly. They were strategically parked at 8:35 when, a minute later, a car drove up and parked in front of them, close enough to make a forward departure impossible without first having to maneuver. Héctor had reacted quickly, backed up his car, edged it out of the space he had occupied, and slowly reversed, double-parking alongside the car behind. "Nobody will complain," he whispered. "Sunday. We are obviously waiting to drive somebody home from church."

It was at that moment that, for the first time, Héctor showed him a picture of his target. He took it from a shirt pocket. A 3×5 photograph of a man in a colonel's uniform, glass in hand, trees in the background. A man in his late thirties, perhaps early forties; relaxed, smiling. Smiling warmly. A candid shot, taken presumably at a social function. He wore a trim mustache and had a full head of hair. Rolando discerned a small cross just below the neck, visible because the shirt was open, in the style of the Cuban military on all but the most official occasions.

Just before 8:45—Rolando had looked down at his watch, his heart pounding—the doors to the church opened and the worshippers began to file out. Héctor had trained a small set of binoculars on the entrance. A minute later he whispered hoarsely, "There! *There he is!* Quick! Quick!" His mouth dry, Rolando opened the door, his hand gripping the pistol in his pocket. Rolando walked a few paces in broad sunlight toward the chatting parishioners. He spotted the colonel without difficulty. He came out of the church his right hand holding his wife's, his left on the shoulder of a boy in his early teens; his family had accom-

panied him after all, Rolando thought in the blur. Rolando approached the colonel with a slight feint, turning him slightly to one side, as though he were bent on entering the emptying church. Ten paces away he stopped, pulled out the pistol, took aim, and fired three times.

He thought he heard the wail of a chorus of wailers—it sounded, in his memory, as if they had been trained to wail—and then the screams. Then he was back by the car. He opened the door, and Héctor sped off.

Clearly Héctor had rehearsed the escape route. They drove at an unprovocative speed, turning every few blocks in this direction and that. The license plate in the rear of the car had been smudged with mud. No one would be able to say more than that it was a Ford sedan; and yes, they might correctly guess that it was a 1953 model car; and yes, they would know it was dark blue, though no one would readily guess that the blue had been applied that morning from a bucket filled with watercolor. In an hour, back at the farm, the Ford's original old metallic gray would be easily restored.

Back at the farm. What had happened? Rolando could not remember, beyond the laundering of the car. He remembered only that at some point, later in the day, Luís had come by and driven Rolando off to within walking distance of his quarters, dropping him on Calle San Lázaro, near the hospital. He did not remember getting out of the car, did not remember where he went, remembered only returning to his room well after nightfall to find Ernesto jabbering. Jabbering about the assassination that morning of Colonel Blanco Rico.

On hearing that name Rolando asked Ernesto to repeat it. Then he lurched toward the washstand and vomited.

Blanco Rico! Blanco Rico! he repeated to himself.

Ernesto laughed, and asked whether Rolando had been out drinking. "It's not like you to throw up."

Then Ernesto had decided to be solicitous, asking Rolando whether he wished a thermometer. "Maybe you ate something. Where were you tonight?"

Rolando washed his face, and said he must indeed have eaten something.

He longed for privacy, and the thought crossed his mind to go out and spend the night at a hotel. But he had only a few pesos. And then he thought of his medical kit. He walked over to the corner and opened it.

"What are you taking?" Ernesto asked, inquisitive.

"Fifteen milligrams of Compazine." His back was turned to Ernesto when Rolando discreetly opened the little red bottle and took out two Seconals, which he threw into his mouth, running the washbasin faucet, cupping his hands, and swallowing a handful of water. Without taking off his clothes, he went to his cot.

He dimly remembered in the course of the night Ernesto massaging his chest with Vicks, and that he had forced on him a sweater and socks.

"You are having one hell of a chill, Rolandito. If you're not better tomorrow, you'll be a patient at the hospital, not an intern."

The next day, during surgery, Dr. Nueces came by, doing his rounds. Rolando looked up from the open abdomen with the inflamed appendix. "I need to speak with you, Doctor," he said, in a voice as controlled as he could manage.

"Come to my office after the operation."

An hour later, the office door shut behind him, Rolando

stood in front of the doctor who was leaning back at his desk, tense but prepared.

Rolando spit it out. *"Blanco Rico! Are you—are we—all mad?* Blanco Rico, the *one true, humane, patriotic* gentleman in Batista's entourage! He has performed more generously as head of military intelligence than anyone in memory! He is personally responsible for releasing over a hundred political prisoners. He is beloved even by people who hate Batista!"

"Yes," Dr. Nueces had said. "Yes. You are quite right about Colonel Blanco Rico."

"Then . . . ?"

"That is the point. Fidel doesn't want *anyone* around Batista whom the public admires. It's that simple. And Fidel is not our leader for nothing."

Rolando Cubela stared at the famous doctor, his teacher. He attempted to speak, but his mouth could not open, and three times he gagged. He turned, opened the door, arrested himself in the act of slamming it shut, closed it quietly, and walked down the hospital corridor, down the steps, the three blocks to his room. Ernesto would not return until well after dinnertime, and it was not yet noon. He lay on his bed, and wept.

Tucker Montana

December 9, 1941—Austin, Texas

ON TUESDAY, two days after the attack on Pearl Harbor, the line outside the army recruiting station at the corner of 7th Street and East Avenue went almost around the entire block. The next day the *Austin American,* in its story on the rush to enlist in the armed forces, remarked that it was the longest line seen in Austin since the opening night of *Gone With the Wind* two years earlier. The difference in the composition of the two lines was obvious enough: today's line was composed of very young men, though there was a scattering of thirty-five- and thirty-six-year-olds, the paper reported. The recruiting station had broadcast repeatedly that thirty-six was the oldest eligible age—the youngest, of course, being seventeen, but to enlist at that early age required the acquiescence of the applicant's father or, if dead, his mother.

Tucker Montana's father was dead. He had been run over by a taxi while hailing a bus in a rainstorm to make a delivery of an electric fan he had repaired for a parishioner who operated a souvenir factory near the Alamo. Tucker was six and his father had struggled to feed wife and son, doing odd jobs at St. Eustace Church during the day. Fara-

226

day Montana, who traced his background to General Sam Houston and one of his Indian concubines, conceived during the year the general left Tennessee en route to Texas, was proud that he could offer his services as an electrician, as a carpenter, as a plumber, as a mason, or for that matter as a janitor: there wasn't anything, really, he could not do with his hands. Fr. Enrique would almost always find something in the large church that needed fixing, and on good weeks, when Fr. Enrique would give a particularly galvanizing sermon at all six masses, he would manage to count out enough nickels and dimes to pay Faraday fifteen, every now and again twenty dollars. Although the elderly priest and the twenty-eight-year-old jack-of-all-trades got on wonderfully well, Fr. Enrique knew that Faraday was looking about, always, for more lucrative work. Far from resenting this, Fr. Enrique kept his own eyes open and it was he who had told Faraday about the opening at the Alamo.

Fr. Enrique had stopped by the little factory-shop on a summer day to chat with his parishioner, Al Espinoso. Sweating profusely in his Roman collar, the priest had looked wistfully at the idle electric fan behind the counter. Why wasn't it turned on, on so hot a day? Al Espinoso said it was broken and he hadn't found anybody who could fix it. Moreover, the only one of his workers who knew anything about electricity had left the factory the week before to join a brother in Houston.

Fr. Enrique pounced. He would have the fan fixed by a young man of extraordinary talents as a craftsman if Al would agree to interview him for the opening. It was agreed, and the exciting news was given to Faraday that if he landed the job, he would be paid thirty dollars every week. Whereupon Faraday (Fr. Enrique would tell and retell this to young

Tucker in the months and years ahead) "took that old fan, it was in pieces in about"—he snapped his fingers—"maybe four minutes, then said, the trouble is in the armature, and in about eighteen more minutes the copper was stretching right from there"—Fr. Enrique pointed to the door into the sacristy—"to the main altar. But five minutes after *that,* he had it all rewound. Then what really impressed me about your father happened. He said he was ready to take the fan to Señor Espinoso, and I said to him, 'Faraday, what you *mean* you ready to take the fan to Señor Espinoso—you don't even know if it *works!*' And he said to me, he said, 'Father, of course it works. I just fixed it.' So I said, I said, 'Now look here, Faraday Montana, you plug that fan into that socket right now and we'll just *see* if you fixed it.' Well, he did that—and the fan began to turn, and in a couple of seconds it was shooting out a fountain of air.

"You know what your father made me feel like? He made me feel like St. Thomas! You know about Doubting Thomas, yes, Tucker?"

When he first heard the story at age six Tucker hadn't read about Thomas, who had doubted the resurrection of Jesus until Jesus asked him to probe His wounds, and then Thomas knew. Because Tucker didn't know, that first time, about Doubting Thomas, and because he didn't want to lie to Fr. Enrique or confess his ignorance, he managed to change the subject. As soon as he got home he asked his mother, who told him that when he wanted an answer to a question like that he should consult their little library, in which there were two—not one—copies of the Bible. Tucker, with his mother's help, found the reference, and afterward it seemed as though a month didn't go by without Fr. Enrique talking about Faraday's tragic last afternoon on

earth, and about how, just before the end, he had made a Doubting Thomas out of Fr. Enrique.

His mother took a job as a receptionist-bookkeeper-telephone operator at a small hotel, coming back to the little apartment late at night but always with a fresh book for him from the library. She would stop there on her way to work—the library wouldn't let children under twelve take books home. When Tucker ran out of reading matter, often on Sunday afternoons, he would leave the apartment and go to the drugstore, which was never closed, and read through one magazine after another. Mr. Eggleston let him do this, but only on the understanding that he would wash his hands at the sink in the back of the drugstore first, so as not to leave any marks on a magazine that might be sold to a customer. Tucker liked especially *Life* magazine, whose pictures he would stare at with hungry curiosity, and *Popular Mechanics,* and *National Geographic.* There was only one copy of the *National Geographic,* to which the store subscribed, and it was earmarked for a professor at St. Mary's University, but the professor never got around to picking it up until after a week or so, giving Tucker time to come in, even during weekdays, to make sure he hadn't missed anything.

Tucker attended the parochial school at St. Eustace's and during the afternoons stayed on after classes to help Fr. Enrique. By the time he was thirteen, Fr. Enrique would discreetly confide to anyone conceivably interested in the point, Tucker Montana could perform any job his father had been able to perform. "I don't know where he picked up the knowledge," he told Tucker's mother one Sunday after Mass on Tucker's eleventh birthday, "but he did." He pointed to the cathedral-shaped wooden Victor radio. "That stopped working on Friday. I thought it needed a new tube and I told

Tucker to take it to a radio shop. He said he would have a look. He took it apart. I mean, all apart. In a half hour he had it working. Wasn't a tube, your boy said. Some kind of short circuit. He is some kind of a kid!"

By the time Tucker was fourteen, Fr. Enrique knew that he had to do something about him. So one afternoon, after making an appointment over the phone, he went over to St. Mary's, the Marianist men's university at San Antonio, and was told where he could find Mr. Galen, the professor of physics. He explained the problem and Mr. Galen agreed to see the boy, and the following afternoon, at the designated hour, Tucker arrived in Mr. Galen's study, which was also his classroom.

Tucker was tall for his age. His hair was cropped close but not mercilessly short. A "bean shave" meant fewer quarters spent at the barber. (Tucker had begun, at age seven, restricting himself to four haircuts every year, explaining to his mother that hair grew at the rate of a half inch per month, and that if cropped close enough, once every three months was all he really needed to spend at the barber's—exactly one dollar per year.) He had lately taken to asking Antonio if there was anything in the barber shop that needed to be fixed—one day he said, to his own and the barber's astonishment, was anything "malfunctioning"—and as often as not there was: a chipped mirror, dull shaving blade, whatever. Tucker would fix it, sharpen it, clean it, paint it, and Antonio would remit the price of the haircut. Antonio took to cutting Tucker's hair less drastically than directed because Antonio didn't want to go a full three months without seeing him. So that although Tucker, entering the physics professor's domain, had had his hair cut the day before, he didn't look as spare as he would have a year earlier.

He was tall, but somehow not ungainly. His arms and legs

seemed fully developed, and Mr. Galen found himself wondering whether the boy was full-grown at fourteen. At five feet six or seven inches his body seemed mature, though his face was that of a prepubescent boy. His brown eyes were oddly adult, penetrating but not obtrusive, and his ears lifted slightly when he was spoken to (though perhaps this would not have been noticeable if his hair had been a little longer). Tucker's chin was slightly pointed, and since he did not smile, one saw only a trace of his white, regular teeth. He was beardless of course but there was the peach fuzz, lighter in color than the light-brown hair on his head. His manner was direct—polite, obliging, but not in the least intimidated or obsequious.

Mr. Galen told him to sit down. He turned then and pointed to the blackboard. He asked Tucker whether what was written there meant anything to him. Tucker looked up and said Yes, of course, those were the basic propositions of calculus. Mr. Galen then asked him if he knew anything about the subject of physics, and Tucker said only what he had read in a textbook.

Which textbook?

Tucker pointed to the book by Hatteras and Guy sitting on top of one of the desks in the classroom. Mr. Galen, who used that book for his introductory physics course, asked if Tucker had experienced any difficulty with the subjects covered in that book, and Tucker looked up at him with quite evident dismay.

"Difficulty? What do you mean, sir?"

"What do I mean? I mean just that. Some students have a problem with spatial mechanics, some with the introduction to electricity, some with theories of motion—did you have any problem with these?"

Tucker still found it difficult to answer. He was obviously thinking about the social consequences of the fix he found himself in. He did not wish to appear boastful.

He found the solution. He said brightly, "Sometimes I have a problem with Latin. For instance: I can never absolutely remember whether *pre, in,* and *post* take the ablative or the accusative case. I just forget."

Mr. Galen said nothing. Then he stood up and went to the bookcase behind his desk and reached for a large volume bound in maroon-colored cloth. He pulled it out and brought it to the boy, who obediently looked at its title and pronounced the title out loud: "*Theories in Advanced Physics.* By"—he looked up at Mr. Galen. "Did you want me to read the names of all the authors? There must be ten, fifteen maybe."

"Those authors," said Mr. Galen, "twelve men and one woman, are at the frontiers of the study of physics. Do you want to have a look at the book?"

"Oh, yes. Yes, sir. I promise to take very good care of it."

Mr. Galen, who stood six feet one inch tall, looked down at the fourteen-year-old boy. "Take it. And come back here next Tuesday, same time. We'll see how you get on with it."

Tucker said thank you, extended his hand, and left the room, his heart pounding with excitement at the treasure carried under his arm. He remembered, on the way down the staircase, to recite a quick Hail Mary of gratitude in thanks for his good luck.

The recruiting sergeant scanned the application.

"This your mother's signature?"

"Yes, sir."

"You might as well begin your training. I am not a 'sir.' I am a sergeant."

"Yes, Sergeant."

"And this is your birth certificate?"

"Yes . . . Sergeant."

Sergeant Brisco looked at it. He then looked up at Tucker. "You were seventeen day before yesterday. On Pearl Harbor Day?"

"Yes, Sergeant."

Sergeant Brisco looked at him. "And you entered the University of Texas as a freshman last September?"

"Yes, Sergeant."

"That means you were only sixteen when you came to Austin."

"Yes, Sergeant."

At this point Brisco took the heavy lead ashtray on his desk, raised it and with all his strength struck it down over Tucker's application form. "You know something, kid," he said, his lips parting into something between a smile and a snarl. "I don't think you are seventeen. I don't think that '1924' on your birth certificate was written by the registrar of public records in San Antonio. And I flatly doubt that your mother signed this piece of paper.

"Now I'll tell you where we go from here. One possibility is we go to the police, and they call the registrar in San Antonio and verify your birth certificate. Then we call your mother and ask if she signed this certificate. Then we take you to the juvenile court and suggest thirty days in the juvenile lockup for forgery. That's one alternative."

Tucker stood, almost as if at attention.

"You want to hear the other alternative?"

"Yes, Sergeant," he whispered.

"Get your baby ass out of this office before I light my next cigarette"—he reached for a pack of Luckies—"and go

back to your freshman class and let us big boys fight the war." He searched theatrically for his matches. When he looked up, Tucker was gone.

One year later Tucker *was* seventeen, and he knew that if he really worked on her, he could get his mother to sign the application form listing his true date of birth, December 7, 1925. But he had been told informally by the major in charge of the V-12 program on the campus that on the recommendation of the chairman of the department of physics, no application of Tucker Montana for early enlistment in the Army would be accepted. Moreover, said the major—he had come to Tucker's little room at the Zeta fraternity house, a most flattering gesture—he had already written, at the request of the dean, to the local draft board, flagging Montana's name and registration number. "You're not going to be seeing any trenches in this war, Tucker, as far as I can figure out. They'll probably scoop you up and put you in an Army lab." He smiled. "There you can design radios or bombsights, to help us win the war more quickly."

Tucker didn't reply. He didn't smile either. On the other hand he didn't want to appear rude, so finally he said, "Okay, Major. We'll see how it goes."

The major smiled and started out the door. Suddenly he turned around. "Listen, Montana. If you want so badly to serve your country, don't be so fucking stupid about how you can do that best. Every now and then—not often, just every now and then—the Army does the smart thing, and the smart thing is to keep you in physics. If you don't like that idea, go over and join the Japs or the Nazis, because you might as well be on their side as to refuse to use what you've got for us." He looked Tucker directly in the face, and then shut the door quietly.

Two years later, Tucker was working under very strict Army supervision at an installation called Los Alamos in New Mexico. He was helping Professor Seth Neddermeyer with the infernal problem of developing a trigger mechanism that would detonate what they referred to as an atomic bomb.

Fifteen months later, Division C, as Professor Neddermeyer's department was called, was confident the thing would work. There was no such thing as a fully reliable laboratory test. Tucker Montana thought briefly of Fr. Enrique recounting the story of his father, so confident he had fixed the electric fan that he didn't think it necessary even to plug it in. Well, this was very different. Those frontiers of knowledge about which he had first heard from Mr. Galen had been pushed a long mile forward, if that was the right word for it. And no one doubted that he, nineteen-year-old Tucker Montana, had done some heavy rowing against that current of physical stasis that kept saying No, you can't get there from here, nature won't permit it. Day after day, month after month, he had worked out the implications of this and the other tiny alteration in the known sequence. And when Professor Neddermeyer had seen that last schedule of Tucker's he had gone right to Dr. Oppenheimer who one hour later said, "We'll build this one."

And then those fateful decisions, in two stages.

He was to join the professional Los Alamos crew who would first disassemble Little Boy, as the bomb was called, for shipment to San Francisco where it would board the *Indianapolis* for Tinian, in the Marianas. Tucker would fly to Tinian with the other Los Alamos scientists to reassemble Little Boy and prepare it for its mission. At Tinian the technical crew would check, check, check, every hour, to

record any electronic movement, impulse, vagary. No human patient, Tucker thought one night after making the routine tests with his meters and noting the results, had ever been subjected to more intense stethoscopic scrutiny.

And then the time came, D-1. He was present at the briefing of the airplane crew as they were told for the first time about the special aspects of the bomb they were to drop the following day over the city of Hiroshima, Japan.

And then, the next morning, he was called in by the deputy mission commander, General Groves's representative, and told that he was to be the twelfth member of the large crew—for the purpose of applying, four times an hour during the five-hour-thirty-minute flight, his instruments to the nerve ends of the bomb, carefully recording every registration. "We want a log on Little Boy just like the kind we've kept since we left New Mexico right up to when she leaves the bomb bay. You're one of the six people on this island who know what to do, and the other five are old enough to be your father. So I've decided it will be you."

Tucker was glad, as he was being fitted up with a pilot's suit, that he hadn't been told the night before. The large crew was led to the runway for pictures. It hadn't yet been decided in Washington when or whether to release the pictures (much would depend on reaction to the bomb). It occurred fleetingly to Tucker as the photographer adjusted a bandana around Tucker's neck to give him a little of the fly-boy look that, not inconceivably, he might have been selected to go on this mission instead of one of the older men because of his youth, yes, but also because of his poster-boy-innocent good looks—a young Gregory Peck— not easily linked to an apocalyptic episode. And it was true:

Tucker, at six feet one inch, his hair—longer than Antonio used to leave it—framing a thoughtful and animated face, permitted himself these days a more frequent smile, associated with the tension—relief needed by scientists who work in close quarters almost around the clock.

Sleep would not have been possible. He could not believe his good fortune. With his own eyes he would see it—happen. The fruit of many men of genius, but the fruit, also, of his own efforts and imagination. He had heard it said at Los Alamos that if this thing worked the Japanese would sue for surrender. Surrender! That could mean saving half a million American lives. Half a million American lives! Among them maybe—Harry Evans. Joe Savage. Helicio Espinoso. Stowie Cleaver. Johnny Galliher. They marched through his imagination one at a time, his fraternity brothers at Zeta Psi; his fellow students in the physics classes and in the history and Spanish classes. The barber's son. Mr. Galen's son. They had all gone off to war and, he hoped, most of them were still alive. Now, if this—thing—worked, they would stay alive, instead of dying on Japanese beaches. And he would actually see the breakthrough happen.

Since the test explosion at Los Alamos, no communication of any sort had been permitted, even to friends or relatives, except routine messages done through the official clerk reporting nothing more than that the writer was in good health. But he felt he *had* to write a letter. He would leave the letter in a sealed envelope, and mail it after the embargo was declared ended, at the finish of the mission. There was the possibility they would not return, in which case at some point the adjutant would see the letter, accompanied by the note asking that it be mailed, posthumously. He wrote:

Dearest Mother:

One hour from now I will be flying very high over the Pacific Ocean. I will be in direct charge of an instrument that may mean the end of the war. I have been with that instrument *pre partum, in partu, post partum* (ask Fr. Enrique what that means). If it works for the best, we have God to thank for letting us come up with a response to people who set out to advance themselves by visiting Pearl Harbor early on a Sunday morning with dive bombers. If I do not live through it, know that you were in my thoughts at the last moment when I was free to think about those I love, instead of those I must help to kill.

Your devoted,
Tucker.

They wanted him to stay on at Los Alamos. Professor Neddermeyer told him that he possessed singular theoretical talents and that he must continue to put them to the use of his country, and also of science. Tucker wished above all not to intimate that what was troubling him was a moral question that simply hadn't afflicted his colleagues, so far as he could see. He would say only that his mother was ailing and he absolutely needed to be with her as soon as possible, that perhaps the next season, the next year. . . .

By January of 1946 he had accumulated enough points of service to qualify for discharge. One final effort was made to persuade him to stay on at least until the atomic tests of that summer at Eniwetok. He smiled and said that if there was a turn in his mother's health, in one direction or the other, he would be in touch.

There was the final dinner, only six or seven people, but Tucker felt that he knew them as well as he would ever

know anyone, given the close intellectual and emotional company he had kept with them for over two years. (There was no talk of what it was that had held these men together during these frantically busy months: Tucker had noticed that. They never spoke of the bomb, except in the laboratory.) A soft-spoken toast was given by the commander of Division C, and it was clear that these men, four of them scientists, two of them professional Army, would miss the energetic, focused, and brilliant mind of their young associate, missing also that conduit to the innocent world which he uniquely provided to two men who had commanded battalions and the four others who for years had been separated from students who once upon a time had been the center of their professional lives. Tucker responded to the toast only by saying that he would never forget their joint experience, which was a safe thing to say, and true.

Two months later, after visiting with his mother, whose health was robust as ever, and spending four weeks at St. Luke's, where the attempt was made to diagnose his depression, he took a taxi from Providence, Rhode Island, to Portsmouth to the rendezvous he had arranged, after the long exchange of letters, with the Benedictine abbot at Portsmouth Priory. Arriving just before five in the afternoon, he was taken from the office of the abbot a few minutes later by a novitiate to the small spare cubicle with the bed, the modest hanging locker, the table-desk, the straight-backed chair, and the empty bookcase. The novitiate told him there would be vespers at 5:30 in the chapel, followed by supper in the refectory. The monks would be silent at supper, while they listened to a reading from St. Benedict, but directly after supper the Benedictine habit was to gather

in the adjacent reading room with their coffee, where general conversation was engaged in for thirty minutes. After that, conversation was rare, save for those monks whose job it was to supervise the activity of the boys. A preparatory school was an administrative function of the monastery. The other monks and the novitiates maintained silence throughout a day spent in prayer, in reading, and in physical work on the 150-acre farm. Every novitiate had a sponsor, a monk with whom he could converse at any time during the two-year period, after which vows were taken and you were then a Benedictine monk, from that moment until you died.

He would from now on be Brother Leo. And his sponsor was Brother Hildred, the elderly monk to whom the abbot had communicated, at the urging of Fr. Enrique, everything he knew about Tucker's background. On the afternoon of the following day the older monk invited the novitiate to walk with him. "We'll go past the orchard, then alongside the Sound. You will enjoy the view of Narragansett Bay." A half hour into the walk, Brother Hildred, who taught physics, asked "Leo"—the monks called themselves by their sacerdotal first names—if he would like to visit the school's physics laboratory that afternoon. Tucker replied that he would not like to visit it this afternoon, tomorrow, next month, or next year. But quickly he recoiled from his apparent asperity, and said simply that he did not wish to revisit any aspect of his past professional life. He went on to say that at Austin he had studied history and Spanish as well as physics, and that there was much reading he wished to catch up on in history, so he would not be idle. Brother Hildred understood, and changed the subject quickly.

Fr. Enrique had sent Tucker's troubled letters, written from Los Alamos, to Brother Martin. What Tucker had

written to his old patron was not formally confessional in character, so that Fr. Enrique felt free to send the anguished letters to Brother Martin for his own appraisal. Fr. Martin had gone on to select Brother Hildred as an appropriate sponsor for young Tucker because he was, in a way, the St. Augustine of the Benedictine community. He had lived, up until just after his fortieth year, a robust sensual life, in America and in Europe, using up most of the toothsome legacy he had been left by his parents. When he decided to enter the monastery, he gave the remainder to the Benedictines and decided, as a novitiate, to impose upon himself the intellectual mortification of learning physics, which he had never studied during his school days, and to which he had never been attracted. Five years later, only a year or so after taking his final vows, he exchanged his dissertation for a doctorate in physics from Harvard. Brother Hildred's perspectives were cosmopolitan and at times earthy, and at one point, a week or so after their first walk, he counseled Brother Leo in gentle but grave tones. "Don't try to excrete it all at once, as if it were one large spiritual bowel movement. It doesn't work that way. It takes time."

And it did. But nine months later, Tucker was a well-integrated novitiate in the Benedictine community. He had decided to study Spanish intensively, and did well enough over time to undertake with confidence to teach the introductory course in Spanish to the eighteen students who signed up for it at the beginning of the fall semester. The abbot, who prided himself on his own fluency, achieved during his missionary work in Mexico, enjoyed their conversations in Spanish. Indeed it was on that account that Brother Leo was given another assignment. He was designated as the appropriate monk to drive to Newport to visit

with Doña Alicia, the ailing widow whose wealthy husband, sometime ambassador from Spain to the United States, had made a critical contribution to the monastery. Indeed, the ambassador's money was much of the fund raised to construct the impressive modern chapel in which the monks worshipped, as well as the 180 schoolboys (or in any event, they pretended to do so). When Don Luis Alargo knew that he was in his final days he asked the abbot to keep an eye on Doña Alicia, so helpless in her resolute ignorance of English. The abbot had made the promise, and frequently called upon her himself. But now that it was clear that she would need regular attention and instruction, he thought it appropriate to introduce her to the newest brother.

When Leo rang the bell at the mansion, he came face to face with Josefina, Doña Alicia's beloved niece. She had, it turned out, lost both parents during the Spanish Civil War. Luis Alargo had paid the cost of Josefina's schooling while she lived with a maiden sister near Barcelona. Now the closely knit Spanish family thought it right that Josefina should repay her debt to the Alargo family by being with her aunt during her illness.

Josefina had arrived in New York on the *Queen Mary,* traveling in tourist class. Traveling in first class was the ravishing Ava Gardner, returning from making a movie in Europe in order (that, at any rate, was the rumor) to pursue her romance with Frank Sinatra. When Josefina, dressed in a bright red cloth coat, descended the tourist gangway, a paparazzo, one of many guarding the first-class gangway, spotted her. So! *Ava Gardner was attempting a hidden exit down the tourist gangway, dressed in a simple cloth coat!* He rushed toward her, his large camera in hand, and began to flash bulbs at the startled Josefina. Other reporters and photogra-

phers quickly joined him and there was a large commotion until suddenly it settled on the press corps that the young lady who was saying in sentences that she was not Ava Gardner, acting out her lines in fractured English as she might have done for a Hollywood director, really was *not* Ava Gardner. She was someone called Josefina Delafuente.

A month later Brother Leo in his monastic cell consulted the diary he kept of his activities, and counted nine visits to the Alargo mansion. He stood up and pulled at his hair by the roots with both hands until he felt genuine physical pain. He went, then, to the chapel, and on his knees prayed most earnestly. He tried to distract himself. He forced his mind back on those five hours and thirty minutes from Tinian to Hiroshima and back; forced himself to re-create in his mind the memory of the huge mushroom cloud that rose behind the *Enola Gay* as she flew back to the sanctuary of the island; he thought of his father, run over by a taxi on his way to a bus with a big electric fan in his hand; thought back to his humiliation at the hands of the recruiting sergeant in Austin.

But the daemon would not detumesce, so that when, during the social hour immediately after the monks' dinner, he was called to the telephone, as he knew that he would be by prearrangement with Josefina, he took the call in the office of the abbot, said the prearranged words, and went back to the sitting room where he whispered in Spanish to the abbot that Doña Alicia had taken a turn for the worse and had asked her niece to bring Brother Leo to console her. The abbot nodded. *"Por supuesto. Véte, cuídale bien"*— Of course. Get on with it. Take good care of her.

Josefina was there in the car, radiant, the smell of her intoxicating. It was raining. She didn't speak, nor did he. She drove toward Newport while Tucker reached over to

the backseat, opened the suitcase, and pulled out the gray flannel pants, the shirt and tie, and the blue blazer. He slid into his pants without difficulty, as he had been wearing a monk's surplice. This he pulled over his head, putting on the shirt and then the tie. And, finally, the jacket.

Josefina now spoke, attempting a gaiety of spirit as she stared in concentration through the windshield, making her way in the driving rain. "Too bad," she said, "taking so much trouble getting dressed. It is so much faster getting undressed." She reached for his hand and slid it through the cleavage of her silk blouse under her breast. Tucker nestled her and then moved his hand to her other breast as she made the sharp right turn to the motel with the bright red light flashing VACANCY, under the incandescent NEW-PORT ARMS MOTEL. She parked the car. *"Vamos corriendo. No olvides la petaca"*—Let's make a dash for it. Don't forget the suitcase. They ran and in a few seconds were protected by the portico. In the lobby, he signed the register for himself and his wife. The receptionist asked for the twenty dollars and suddenly Tucker was dumb. He had no money. But Josefina spoke: "Dahrling, you leaves your wallet in my *bolsa*, don't you remember? Here," she pulled out a twenty-dollar bill and handed it to the clerk.

"Do you need any help with your baggage, Mr. Engaño?"

"No no, thank you. We have just this . . . one bag."

They were shown the direction in which to go, and he fumbled with the key to Room 219. He closed the door behind her. She opened the suitcase and brought out a bottle of chilled wine, the cork unstopped. Then she turned off the overhead light. "I get glasses from the bathroom." She emerged three minutes later, with two bathroom glasses filled with wine. She was nude.

Nikolai Trimov

August, 1968

NIKOLAI TRIMOV was raised by an aunt whose job it was to cook eighteen meals every week for the Kolkhoz Collective Farm in Brovary, a half day's journey from Kiev on bicycle, over mostly flat farm country, lumpy only here and there with groups of glistening birch trees. His aunt was responsible for feeding 112 farmers, and they breakfasted at 6:45. This meant that she had leisure time with Nikolai only on her day off, which was Wednesday; but Nikolai was at school for most of Wednesday, so that it was only late in the afternoon and early in the evening that Nikolai really had time with his aunt.

He looked forward eagerly to those Wednesday afternoons, when Titka would read to him and talk to him and play chess. She owned only a dozen books, so she went regularly to the library. Nikolai couldn't remember ever being without reading material. Titka would always ask, when she was still reading out loud to him—he took to reading for himself when he reached six—"What would you like me to read to you about?" His answer was always the same, and Titka loved to hear it from him. "Anything." That meant, for a year or two, stories about animals or knights or high adventures on sea and on land.

But one day Titka thought to play a little trick on him. She had brought home from the farmers' refectory a discarded copy of *Pravda,* which she privately considered the most boring text in the Soviet Union, in particular the editor's page.

"Anything?" she asked teasingly.

"Yes, Titka. Anything."

So Titka opened the paper to the editorial for the day before, August 28, 1968. She read in her usual monotone, but moving along at a good clip, and the words were clearly enunciated. "'The developments in Chicago yesterday at the Democratic National Convention resulted in a clear collision between the progressives, who were represented by Senator George McGovern, and the warmongering forces represented by Vice President Hubert Humphrey. Mr. Humphrey emphasized the need to bring more armed pressure to bear against the revolutionaries in Vietnam in order to frustrate them from achieving socialist liberty. President Lyndon Johnson, who remained in Washington because he is clearly afraid to expose himself even to his own Party, has thrown his considerable weight in favor of Mr. Humphrey as presidential candidate, in arrant opposition to the popular will. The fascist police of Chicago, who are creatures at the disposal of the Mayor, one Daley, whose public career has consisted in imprisoning and torturing any progressive voice in Chicago, in particular among the oppressed Negro people . . .'"

Titka stopped. She had expected to be interrupted after the second or third sentence. She turned to Nikolai, who sat on the floor next to her, his bare knees crossed, his coarse shirt open at the collar—it was warm in August in the Ukraine—and said, "Are you . . . enjoying this, Nikolai?"

"Yes," he had replied. "I do hope that the progressives in Chicago will prevail."

Titka blinked. She laid the paper down on her lap. "What do you know about the progressives in Chicago?"

"Only what you just said, Titka. They are being opposed by the fascist police of one Daley."

Titka was flustered, but continued to read through the one-thousand-word-long editorial, right to the end. Then she picked up the volume of Grimm's Fairy Tales and read to Nikolai the tale about "Iron John." His expression did not change.

But the following Wednesday, on his return from school and after doing his chores in the little patch of vegetable garden, when they sat down he said to her, "Did they win? The progressives in Chicago?"

Titka said that she did not have that day's edition of the newspaper but she had scanned it at the collective and in fact they had not won; Mr. Humphrey had been nominated and would pursue his warlike course in Vietnam. Nikolai said that that was truly a pity, and he hoped someday Mr. Humphrey would come to Kiev, and maybe even to Brovary, so that he could see how progressives can live peaceful and orderly and productive lives. Titka turned her head away, her heart pounding, so he would not see the flush she knew betrayed her feelings. She thought fleetingly that perhaps now was the time to tell Nikolai about his grandparents in the winter of 1933, or about his parents, one month after he was born. No, she stopped herself. Not yet.

Titka was prudent, because she had been under regular surveillance by the local KGB ever since . . . Grigori and The Episode, as the farmers in the village continued to refer to it.

It had all begun when Nikolai's father had taken the lead in organizing a protest. With twenty dirt farmers grouped about him, he approached the Chief of Section to request

slightly higher hourly pay and shorter hours—a work week of sixty hours instead of sixty-six. The Chief of Section said he would refer the request to a higher authority. At the end of the day, four uniformed officials came to the small cabin—the same cabin in which Titka and Nikolai now lived—and informed Grigori that he was under arrest. He was taken off to spend the night at the collective's little detention center. The following day, after a half-hour trial before the Chief of Section and two magistrates brought in from the neighboring collective, Grigori was sentenced. He was taken off to ten years of hard labor for counterrevolutionary activity, under Article 70 of the Criminal Code.

The following day, Lidya went with her month-old baby to her sister Titka at the collective center and asked her to look after him.

"I will be back before the end of the day," were her last words as she bent over and lingeringly kissed her baby.

Lidya then went to the detention center, her husband's army rifle in her arms, cocked. She walked to the desk, pointed the gun at the startled sergeant, and demanded the release of her husband. The sergeant, wide-eyed, rose and told Lidya to follow him to the cell. While pretending to cope with the key to open the cell, he brushed his holster, pulled out a pistol and shot Lidya, whose finger closed simultaneously on the trigger of the rifle, firing a shot that killed her husband.

There was wide resentment over the treatment of Grigori and much grief over the fate of Lidya and her husband. The Chief of Section felt a near-mutinous resentment and made a public gesture designed to appease: Instead of sending Nikolai off to an orphanage, he turned the little family cabin over to Titka and the baby. But even now, eight years later,

purposes, including the tool shed from which, every day, her father brought out his equipment to wrestle with the planting which, when it yielded crops, yielded them to the Soviet monitor pacing alongside. He would seize them—barley, corn, vegetables—roughly and stack them in the truck nearby. She and Lidya shared a single piece of bread in the morning, on which a kind of gruel was poured, something boiled from what seemed like weeds stripped off a neighboring tree. Her mother ate nothing, waiting until the afternoon for hot water and tea leaves, and the dried corn soaked in water on which she and their father gnawed at sundown.

It was the day when her mother could not lift her head even to take the cup of tea that her father had acted. It was the habit of orderlies from the Soviet detachment in the officers' recreation room across the road to bring out the leftovers from the midday meal and pour them into a barrel right by the barbed wire that protected the enclosure from the surrounding farmers' cottages. From their little window, Titka's father Fyodor could see poured into the barrel in a single deposit, as garbage, enough food to keep his family healthy for a month. He looked back at his wife, lying motionless on the cot. He grabbed the pitchfork in the corner, opened the door, and moved with determination toward the barbed wire. He asked the orderlies please to pass him the refuse they were throwing into the barrel. They answered with laughter and taunts. Using his pitchfork as a kind of rough shield, Fyodor threw himself against the barbed wire, seeking to reach a hand into the barrel.

The rifle sound came from back at the officers' quarters. A single shot fired by a lieutenant sitting on a bench outside. He had been fondling the rifle, and found now something quite unexpected, something practical to do with it.

He was a good marksman. Fyodor was dead, straddling the barbed wire. His widow did not have the strength to rise to help pull him away—she did not leave the cot until she was placed in the rude coffin. Titka and Lidya did their best, finally recapturing their dead father with the help of a neighbor who labored with the corpse at half strength because he was weak from starvation.

. . . Titka would not be the one to tell Nikolai about the death of his grandparents, though someone in the community of course eventually would. Everyone knew about those terrible days and months in 1933. The grandparents of a half-dozen boys and girls in Nikolai's class had been victims of the great kulak purge.

All in good time, Titka reflected, looking over at young Nikolai, buried, as ever, in his books. What, after all, was the hurry?

Nikolai advanced quickly in school, so much so that when he was fifteen the director reported to her superiors in Kiev that the boy was two, perhaps three years advanced beyond his fellow students and that she had nothing more to teach him. Either, at age fifteen, he would join the farm work force, or else he would go to Kiev and attend the university.

He was summoned to an interview. The rector, peering below his eyeglasses, studied him carefully. The boy sat respectfully on the bench at the far end of the office while the rector attended to random paperwork. Nikolai Trimov, like so many Ukrainians, was blond, but his features were not those of the typical peasant. The fine nose and chin were more Mediterranean. His lips were thin, his expression sober. He looked more nearly seventeen or eighteen than fifteen, the rector thought as he lowered his eyes and

turned his attention to the folder supplied by the Chief of Section at Brovary.

It told the story of Nikolai's parents, of the dramatic events of September 11, 1962. But there had been no adverse notation on the boy's own record. Nikolai had been elected president of his class, he was skilled in chess, in fact he no longer had a challenger of any age in the village, and the physical education director had written that Nikolai would certainly qualify for special training, should Kiev wish to aim for Olympic qualification in figure skating.

The rector summoned the boy to approach, pointed to a chair at the side of his desk, and told him to sit down. Wool cap in hand, Nikolai did so, furtively tightening his tie, though his Adam's apple protruded through a shirt clearly too small for a boy already grown to five feet ten inches. The rector was an academician by training, not a bureaucrat. While administering the affairs of the 15,000 students on his campus he also taught one course in the philosophy department. It was called the Philosophy of the Working Class, taught to the top-rated one hundred students, who were summoned to take that course in their senior year.

The rector faced a problem he had faced only once before—a fifteen-year-old academically qualified for university training. The time before, it had been a disaster, because the girl could not adjust to the company of young men and women three, four, five years older than she. He had sent her away after two months, back to her village. It would not be easy to predict whether young Nikolai would get along with the older students. The rector decided to begin by probing the boy's mind and his capacity to handle himself.

"Is it so, Nikolai, that you have read all the books in the library at Brovary?"

"I think so, Comrade Rector. At least I cannot find any book I have not read. Of course, I haven't read every word in the Soviet Encyclopaedia, although I consult it often."

The rector reflected that a student bent on reading any edition of the entire Soviet Encyclopaedia would have to rush to do so before a revised Soviet Encyclopaedia came in, according as this revisionist in Moscow prevailed over that one. "Have you read Marx?"

"Oh yes, Comrade Rector. Although I cannot say that I fully understand him. But of course that must be the reason why Marx is taught all the way up"—Nikolai gestured with his hand pointing to the ceiling—"through graduate school."

"Do you have any difficulty in understanding the central thrust of Marx-Lenin historical imperatives?" Perhaps that would slow the boy down, the rector thought.

"Oh no, Comrade Rector. None at all. Marx and Lenin divined the secrets of history, and we need now only to wait until historical evolution validates, as it must, their thought."

The rector eyed Nikolai Trimov. The rector was on guard. Nikolai's responses might have been written for a student prepared to be exhibited to visiting ideologues. But there was no trace in Nikolai's face of disingenuousness, let alone cynicism.

"You realize that the Soviet state is being asked to bear the very considerable burden of sending you to a university where all your expenses are paid, and where you are provided with free room and board?"

"Yes, Comrade Rector."

"What is it you wish most to study?"

"Anything, Comrade Rector. I am interested in every subject, and will be glad to specialize in any field you recommend."

This boy is . . . the rector was inclined to smile, but he was accustomed to suppressing such temptations. There was clearly no point in questioning Nikolai Trimov's capacity to mix with older students. If anything, he would find them childish.

He dispatched him home to Brovary. Three weeks later, Nikolai was back in Kiev, moved into a dormitory with twenty other students, each with his own cubicle. He had his own desk and a small locker, a bed and a lamp, and this room he occupied for five years. At first he was the object of much raillery from lusty eighteen-year-olds who thought him a quaint biological anomaly, a fifteen-year-old with the manners of a confident but self-effacing young man. He accepted their taunts, but his behavior was altogether conventional. In two respects he dissimulated. When he played chess, he would often contrive to lose to his competitors. And when, at the end of the first semester, the time came for posting grades, Nikolai requested an audience with the rector. His plea was straightforward, and modestly put. Might it be contrived to reduce his grades by one or two levels? The rector's astonishment Nikolai had anticipated. He gave his reasoning before being asked to do so. He said that at his age it was difficult as it was to be in competition with young men and women who were older. If his grades were dramatically in the first rank, this would make social adjustments even more difficult. The rector smiled inwardly—he almost never smiled on the outside.

He said quite simply that he would confer with the relevant faculty and see what could be done. This meant, when spoken by the rector, that what would be done was what the rector ordained would be done. When the grades were posted, Nikolai Trimov got straight B's. In fact he led his

classmates in every subject. In his third year, the rector summoned Trimov and told him that as a practical matter, he needed to decide in which subject he would acquire professional accreditation. Nikolai replied that he would do as counseled: In which field of studies did the rector think he might be most useful to the Soviet state that was treating him so generously? The rector responded that students should never forget the apothegm so firmly grounded in Soviet legend, Lenin's doctrine that communism was Soviet power plus the electrification of the whole country.

It followed that Nikolai should become, by training, an electrical engineer. He would not be discouraged from developing his other affinities, most especially the study of foreign languages, in which he was singularly gifted.

The years went by, and Nikolai was not only accepted by his classmates but became a favorite. He was nominated for president of his class when he was a junior but declined, pleading that he did not feel that at his age he was equipped to assume any position of leadership in dealing with his elders. His withdrawal from candidacy as president was accepted as another token of the young man's modesty. But when time came to begin the military training in which all the students participated, he was not able to shrink from the responsibilities that attached to someone of his standing: He was required to accept officers' training. He did his work as an officer's candidate with characteristic calm and proficiency.

What seemed a mere season went by quickly: five years, at the end of which he received two certificates on the same day. He was now an electrical engineer and a second lieutenant. He could not know when he would be put to work as a professional, but it was instantly clear that no time would be lost in dispatching him to duty as a soldier. The need for

platoon leaders on the Afghanistan front was acute. After a two-week leave spent with Titka in Brovary, he reported for duty. He found himself, with the soldiers assigned to him, on a troop train headed for Kabul.

It had been a tortuous journey of very nearly 4,200 kilometers, even though the distance as the crow flies was only 3,500 kilometers. London, Nikolai calculated, was closer to Kiev than to Kabul.

The trip had begun on March 2. On March 11, 1985, Lieutenant Nikolai Trimov and his relief company of infantrymen reported for duty, and Mikhail Gorbachev, a junior official in the Kremlin, was named General Secretary of the Communist Party.

March, 1985

Nikolai had read reports about Soviet wounded in Afghanistan in the great military offensive under the leadership of Leonid Brezhnev that dismayed those who believed Soviet expansionism had finally ended with the consolidation of its hold over Eastern Europe. But the reports that reached Soviet citizens were oblique and muted. At Kiev, Nikolai had seen at first hand a dozen disabled veterans. One he saw struggling across the cobbled pavement of Lenkomsomal Square, trying to get used to artificial legs. Another, a startlingly young-looking boy, blind, being led by a young woman through the market while he maneuvered his long, slender white cane feeling out, tentatively, the contours of the ground.

And there had been all those whispers at the university. He had enrolled in January of 1980, only one month after Brezhnev began the military operation, after solemnly announcing that the Afghan government had petitioned for

help against fascist elements. It was everywhere assumed that the war would quickly be over, given the preponderance of Soviet arms. But by the third year, at the end of which Andropov succeeded Brezhnev, fighting was still going on and triumphant reports in the Soviet press about front-line activity were increasingly rare, supplanted more and more by rumors of extraordinary Afghan resistance. The students drew the obvious inferences.

In Nikolai's fifth year at college, Andropov died and the doddering Chernenko became the head of the government. The dominant rumors were to the effect that the old man would find a means to acknowledge that the Afghan venture was no longer, well, required, even under the Brezhnev Doctrine that held that any land once governed by Soviet socialism would forever be socialist. But there was no sign of decreased military activity or of official irresolution, and the war went on and on, and relief units like the unit Nikolai was now attached to were sent down regularly to the front.

As the capital city of Kabul came finally into view after the long journey from Kiev, Nikolai sensed that he might come upon discouraging sights. Carrying his full field pack, leading his platoon toward the assigned barracks, he found himself marching parallel to the hospital unit. He had been prepared for the wounded, but he now got a sensation of the scale of the suffering. The army "hospital" was one barracks building after another, converted from their use as shelters for able-bodied soldiers into shelters for soldiers who were casualties. Nikolai counted thirty-two such buildings in a row, and at that, he could not tell whether the parallel lines of barracks were also being used for the wounded. His platoon followed him, in loose formation. As they walked along the length of the area, Lieutenant Trimov

attempted to mute the sounds they heard from within the hospital by gradually widening the distance between his unit and the hospital complex. But he had to follow the jeep with the guide from headquarters, which was showing him the way to his platoon's quarters. He could hardly ask the driver and warrant officer kindly to move out of earshot of the moaning and screaming they now heard even through the husky wooden barracks walls, designed to shield soldiers from the fabled Kabul winter.

They arrived at last. After seeing that his platoon was housed and that arrangements were made to feed his men, Nikolai walked to the bachelor officers' quarters, into the room he had been assigned. He opened the door and saw a very large figure entirely naked, straining, before a small mirror pinned on the wall, to trim his mustache. The man turned his head slightly, seeming to keep one eye on the mirror, and said, "You Trimov?"

"Yes," Trimov said, tossing his heavy pack on the unoccupied bed.

"They told me I'd be sharing a room. If you don't mind my saying so, Trimov, I rather wish you were a girl." He laughed as he snipped the final hair on his mustache and put down his scissors. "Belinkov. First Lieutenant Andrei Belinkov, when I have my uniform on." He extended his hand, and Nikolai took it.

"I suppose," Belinkov continued while dressing, "that at some point we can become acquainted. But my suggestion is that we go now to the field club and have a vodka before supper. It is quite necessary, Trimov—your first name?"

"Nikolai."

"It is quite necessary, Nikolai, to have some vodka before you eat. Otherwise you will not ingest, to say nothing of

digest, the food they serve here. In fact, it would be quite useful if you brought a blindfold into the mess hall. The food tastes better if you do not view it."

Nikolai said he would be glad to accompany Belinkov. "But I shan't join you with the vodka. I have never taken vodka."

Belinkov, struggling to put on his trousers, stopped in mid-motion, unbelieving. *"You have never taken vodka? Eighteen weeks of basic training and no vodka?"* He paused. "What did you do before basic?"

Nikolai explained that he was a university student, that his monthly allowance had been barely sufficient to buy him an occasional foreign book—

"You know a foreign language?"

Nikolai said that in fact yes, he had studied foreign languages.

"Foreign *languages?* What languages have you studied?"

Nikolai had once or twice before run into this problem. Either he would tell the truth or, for fear of being thought a braggart, he would dissimulate. The fatiguing experiences of the three hours since getting off the transport bus at Kabul impelled him to recklessness. "I have studied English and German. Also French and Italian."

Belinkov completed pulling up his pants, reached for a shirt and, finally, spoke softly. *"Can you understand English when it is spoken?"*

"Yes. Provided it is not too rapid." The hell with it, Nikolai thought. He would tell the whole truth. "But even if it *is* rapid, I can understand quite well."

Belinkov leaned over to his locker, dug his large hand deep within it, and came up with what was discernibly a portable radio. "The Russian-language channels from En-

gland and America are blocked. But at ten-thirty at night and six-thirty in the morning there is a news broadcast in English. It will tell us what is going on. Or at least, that is what old Foxov told me he heard from one of the doctors who was English; the poor dumb bastard, why didn't he stay English?"

"Who, Foxov?"

"No!" Belinkov exploded with frustration over such a gross misunderstanding. "The *doctor* who heard the broadcasts told Foxov—*he* was raised in England. Foxov is dead. Maybe the doctor is dead also. But the English broadcasts continue, they are not dead. Every now and then I tune in, just to check that they are still there." Belinkov was dressed now, and while he talked, Nikolai had prepared himself—he threw off his bulky jacket and put on a lighter parka—to go to the club and the mess hall.

At the club they occupied a small corner of the crowded room. Belinkov had a half pint of vodka, Nikolai a bottle of ginger beer. Andrei Belinkov was beginning his second year of duty, he revealed, and would serve as company commander of the unit, one platoon of which would be led by Nikolai. "I will not tell you about conditions out in the field, because what you are drinking is not enough to anesthetize you to what I would describe. You will of course get the regular indoctrination from General Zaitsev—you will be interested to know that officers who have been in combat not only aren't invited to be present at indoctrinations of the new officers, they are not permitted. Such . . . *manure* as they will give you. Much good it does, since it will be only a matter of weeks—who knows, maybe days—before they move us all out; and then you will see for yourself." He stared into his glass. "But sometimes I wish to scream

because the same human beings, flesh and blood, who fill those festooned uniforms know exactly what is going on and what use is it for them to think they can hide it from such as you, when you will see it yourself, taste it yourself, in no time at all? What did you study at the university? I mean, besides Dutch, Urdu, and Romansch?"

Nikolai laughed, and told Andrei he was now a licensed electrical engineer, and that he had done twenty-two hours of history.

"Russian history? Or Soviet history?"

Nikolai replied cautiously. "Both."

"I should have known. They do run into each other a bit, ho ho, but let's get off that. Me, I did not go to college, I went right to the army. I was commissioned an officer in the field three months after I got here. Promoted in January. I could use the extra pay. Ah!"—Andrei wavered: Should he order another tumbler of vodka?—"*Money,* it is so very important! If I did not have a little money, including"—his eyes widened, his hand slipped under his trousers, moving quickly from one side of his stomach to another, a zipper unzipped—"including *this!* One, two, three, four, five, six, seven, eight, nine, ten, eleven, twelve! Twelve U.S. dollar bills, oh my, what they will get for you! While you lie down in the room and dream of it, I will be"—he got up, closing his eyes in rapture—"experiencing it. She costs ten—ten!— rubles, or one—*one*—American dollar, my little dark- skinned beautiful slut, my Akta! Come along, or the mess will close down and the horse manure they serve us will poison the pigs."

Nikolai Trimov followed Andrei out into the dark, into the cold, past yet two more barracks-type quarters to the squat compound that served as the officers' mess hall.

Nikolai knew that his grandfather would have killed to have whatever they would be given to eat at the mess hall.

For the thousandth time in the ten years since in his teens he had pieced together his family history he felt those pulsations of fury against the system for which he was now being asked to fight, if necessary to the death.

March, 1985

Colonel Stepan Dombrovsky addressed the assembly of regimental, battalion, and company commanders. Dombrovsky had taught at the War College. He was too young to have seen action in the Great Patriotic War against Hitler, so that when he arrived at the front he was received with some skepticism by the veteran soldiers. That skepticism went quickly, after he was observed in command of the front regiments, which he directed with bravery, assurance, and sophistication. He was promoted now to operations officer. He was entirely comfortable back at a lectern, as in the old days at the War College in Leningrad.

The plan, he disclosed, was to drive the mujahedin re-sisters up to the high peak of Mountain "A"—the Colonel pointed to the enlarged section of the map. "Behind it is the high range, this side of the Pakistani border. We will"—he described a semicircle with his baton—"use small arms, artillery, and mortar right along this line. The rebels will need to seek shelter in the mountain crevices. From there they have no alternative, as we keep up the fire, than to head for the range, along this line"—again he used his baton.

"Beginning on the third day, the whole regiment is bound to seek relief, and it is the toughest of the resistance units, seven to ten thousand men. But they are armed only with rifles. *Then,*" said Colonel Dombrovsky, who spoke

with something of a lisp because two teeth were missing, as also a section of the adjacent lip, "when they begin to go for the range, our fighter planes will go to work and our bombers will drop big payloads. They will be bottled up"—he pointed to the map—"in this ravine here. There is no way to avoid traversing it when seeking the shelter of the range. With luck"—the Colonel tapped his baton playfully on the head of Battalion Commander Major Lapin—"we will put the Zeta mujahedin regiment completely out of business before the end of the week."

Were there any questions?

There were. But it was only the question asked by Lieutenant Andrei Belinkov that rattled the Colonel. "Will there be Stingers?" Andrei asked.

"How in Hades would *I* know, Lieutenant Belinkov, if there will be any Stingers? In the engagement last Thursday there were no Stingers and our fighters managed to do plenty of damage to the enemy, would you not agree, Lieutenant Belinkov?"

Belinkov said yes, he certainly agreed that there had been plenty of damage done to the enemy on Thursday. He had no problem recalling the events of the day. Soviet fighter planes had ripped into a column of mujahedin, killing and wounding over sixty rebels. The survivors of the Afghan unit, surrounded, had dropped their rifles. You could hear the clatter of steel barrels landing on the rocky soil. The cold mountain air, working on the warm exhalations, gave the impression that the rebels were all smoking cigarettes. They were led, their hands behind their necks, to the edge of the neighboring forest. At a signal from Major Lapin, a Soviet machine gunner stationed just inside the forest that gave him camouflage began firing. He mowed them all

down, investing at least five bullets in each of the resisters. The major had then walked nonchalantly along the row of scattered bodies, firing his pistol into the heads of the half-dozen soldiers that showed any sign of life.

"The Stingers are the responsibility of the air force," the Colonel explained, "with which of course our own operation is completely coordinated."

There being no other questions, the company commanders were told to give the appropriate instructions for the next day's operation to their platoon leaders.

Inside the combat zone, ten days later, Andrei Belinkov, along with Nikolai, faced the problem of the evening meal. It was necessary to eat early—in the daylight hours cooking fires didn't attract sniper fire. Andrei took his ration of beans and rice and that evening's fishy gruel, wrapped himself in his great overcoat and sat, his back against the side of a tank, alongside Nikolai, who had not fully mastered the technique of handling his army fork while wearing the heavy gloves without which his hands would freeze in the bitter cold at 7,500 feet.

"Great sport, eh, Nikolai?" Andrei began. "It will not be so easy tomorrow, you will see. Well, but then tomorrow will not be so difficult, because our artillery is very heavy, and there will not be much counterfire. We will drive them up to shelters in the mountain, yes, and probably, yes, Muhammad Ezi will seek the greater refuge of the range, perhaps even the shelter of Pakistan. But the success of the operation will depend entirely on the air offensive, the fighters especially. We will not be able to use our artillery effectively into the ravine—"

"Why not?"

"Why not? My dear Nikolai . . . because the same artillery we will be using to assault Mountain 'A' will require four, five hours, maybe more, to transport around the mountain to get within firing range of the ravine. We rifle soldiers will be able to ascend and take our positions and begin firing into the ravine quickly, in less than an hour. So the heavy barrage will need to be from the airplanes. Without American-made interference—You have seen the American Stingers? . . . Of course not. We have been in the field only ten days and on Thursday there were no Stingers, I do not know why." The pitch of Andrei's voice was interrogatory: "It is very surprising.

"Oh my God what I would do for some vodka, it is two days since I ran out. Do you know, Nikolai, I have absolutely *no* idea what you think of this madness we are engaged in. You are *the most reserved man* I have ever associated with! As a matter of fact, Nikolai, I do not really know why I continue to seek your company. We have slept in the same two-man shelter now for ten days. You listen to me, and sometimes you laugh, and you answer my questions. But I do not know what is on your mind, and surely you are the only officer in the army who does not complain of Moscow policy in this accursed war."

Andrei put down his aluminum plate. He spoke now gruffly. "*Say something*, for the love of God, Nikolai, *say something!* You may not be able to say something two days from now, because *you may be dead!*" Andrei stared into the eyes of Nikolai and, grabbing his collar with one hand, shook him hard, though suddenly his voice modulated, as it traveled from exhortation to entreaty. Andrei Belinkov wanted desperately to hear Nikolai condemn the mad vicious bloody venture in which the Soviet Union was en-

gaged *"for no purpose except a meaningless enlargement of empire and the sweet smell of nearby Iranian oil.* That's the *only* purpose of it," he half muttered. His hand loosened its grip on Nikolai's collar and a tear came to his eye. He dropped his hand. "It is a quite dreadful way to die, is it not, Nikolai?"

Nikolai spoke now. His voice had acquired a new timbre, one Belinkov had not heard before.

"It is a terrible way to die, yes, Andrei. The death of the mujahedin who surrendered to us on Thursday, that too was a terrible way to die."

Belinkov turned away. "What are we *supposed* to do with the prisoners?"

Nikolai did not answer.

Belinkov relented. "You are right, it was a terrible way to die. I have not got used to it."

Operation Bottleneck worked according to schedule for the first two days. Early on the third day, a Soviet surveillance plane flying at 50,000 feet reported that the mujahedin appeared to be consolidating on the southern base of Mountain "A" preparatory to crossing the ravine to the safety of the high range, two miles across. Colonel Dombrovsky was elated and ordered two battalions of light infantry to begin the forced march to the east side of the mountain, proceed to deploy, and fire at the enemy. Orders went out to the artillery to begin their arduous trek to both sides of the mountain. The radio from the surveillance plane alerted the Soviet fighter-bombers on standby seventy-five kilometers to the north.

One hour later, several hundred mujahedin began to cross the ravine. At 8:35, the Soviet air force could be

spotted on the western horizon—as heavy a concentration of SU-17s and SU-25s, thought Nikolai, as one might expect to see flying over Moscow on May Day! He continued to lead his men, at quick-time, to the western side of the mountain, where they would squat down and contribute their own firepower to the slaughter. The bombers, he guessed, would come in at about 5,000 feet, the fighter planes at 1,000 feet. And now the explosive sounds of falling bombs began, synchronizing with the deadly rat-tat-tat of the fighters' machine guns.

And then—Nikolai stared in disbelief. Six fighter planes, almost as if exercising a joint maneuver, abruptly left their offensive configuration. Three exploded before hitting the ground. The ten surviving planes in the squadron, executing the Soviet plan, consummated their 180-degree turn at the east end of the ten-mile-long ravine and whizzed back to strafe again the mujahedin, whose numbers, designed to swell as Muhammad Ezi's regiment pursued them to the range, were however rapidly diminishing. Suddenly, four of the fighters were struck, three going down directly in flames; one, with a smoky contrail as if gasping for air, lost its altitude slowly, crashing, finally, an eternal twenty seconds later, into the north face of the range. The surviving six fighters abandoned the cauldron and suddenly the bombing fleet dematerialized into the horizon.

It was then that the rebels' rifle fire concentrated on the Soviet battalion that had been poised to fire into the ravine, by now almost empty of targets as the mujahedin completed their ambush. Nikolai shouted at his men to take cover. It seemed only seconds before Nikolai heard a bullet's thud a few yards ahead of him. And it was only minutes later that he discerned that the heavy rifle fire was coming not only

from ahead of him, from the southern flank of the mountain, but from behind. The mujahedin had descended from their mountain crevices, taking positions to the rear of the Soviet regiment, which now was taking concentrated fire from ahead and behind. Belinkov's voice came in over the radio to Nikolai. *"The bastards are everywhere. Dig in. I am radioing to the artillery to head back and give us cover."*

Soon after midday, Soviet artillery began to pepper the northern flank. The withering fire from the rear gradually decreased and the order came to the Soviet commanders to turn about and make their way back to where they had come from. Nikolai shouted out the order for his platoon to retreat. Platoon B provided cover from the front. At this moment, standing to shout out his commands, Nikolai felt the bullet in his thigh. He dived down and began to crawl. He could no longer run, though he'd have felt no safer doing so.

It was midafternoon before there was anything like a reassembly at the regimental station from which the offensive had begun. Thirty-five men in Nikolai's platoon were checked in, ten of them wounded. Twenty-five were not accounted for. The casualties in the other platoons were comparable.

Colonel Dombrovsky did not appear, and no one came forward to testify to what had happened to him. It was not until nightfall that the military radio from Kandahār brought them the news: a radio intercept of the enemy revealed that Dombrovsky had been taken prisoner.

Andrei Belinkov made it back with a dozen survivors of his own platoon. He went to the field hospital and found Nikolai. Only penlight flashlights were permitted and it was with a penlight trained on his thigh that Nikolai saw the scalpel dig into his flesh to bare the cavity in which the

bullet lay. He did not remember the yank that dislodged it, feeling only the intense pain and hearing the voice of Andrei ("Easy, Nikolai Grigorovich, the worst is almost over . . ."), who held a second flashlight for the pharmacist's mate officiating. He remembered hearing the voice of another officer saying hoarsely to Belinkov, "A bloody ambush. The whole thing. Including Thursday—no Stingers—whole thing—bloody ambush."

Nikolai woke the next day in a truck in which he and a half-dozen—a dozen?—other soldiers lay, some of them moaning, all of them freezing in the cold as they made their bumpy way back to the division headquarters fifty kilometers away. Every day for four days Andrei would come and exchange a few words with him. They spoke about every subject except the war, except the killing. Nikolai spoke of his childhood, ascribing his orphan status to a local plague, and then about his college years. Andrei spent relaxing moments describing the sports he had so much enjoyed, the karate lessons he had mastered, and the friends in boyhood who joined him in attempting to eke some pleasures from their drab lives. Where-were-you-when-Stalin-died did not work for them, since neither had been alive in 1953, but they did recall the great Olympic triumphs of the gymnast Nikolai Andrianov in Montreal in 1976. Neither of them brought up the American boycott of the Moscow Olympics in 1980. That had been a reaction to the Soviet Afghan offensive that had brought them here, an engagement they would not willingly evoke.

On the fourth day, using crutches, Nikolai made his way to the canvas-covered army theater, where movies and documentaries were shown. Three hundred men and officers were assembled there, under regimental orders, to view a

documentary flown in from Moscow. Andrei Sakharov had denounced the Afghanistan war from his exile in Gorky, the announcer reported. The camera then focused on Sergei Chervonopisky, a thirty-two-year-old former major in the Soviet airborne troops who had lost both legs in the war. He was one of 120 Afghan war veterans in the Congress. Chervonopisky lashed out at Sakharov for telling the reporter from the Canadian newspaper *Ottawa Citizen* that Soviet pilots sometimes fired on Soviet soldiers to prevent them from being taken alive by Afghan rebels.

"To the depths of our souls we are indignant over this irresponsible, provocative trick by a well-known scientist," Chervonopisky declared. He accused Sakharov of trying to discredit the Soviet armed forces and attempting "to breach the sacred unity of the army, the Party, and the people." The camera turned then to General Secretary Gorbachev. He was joined by the entire Politburo in a standing ovation for Chervonopisky's censure motion. Chervonopisky had shouted out, *"The three words for which I feel we must all fight are state, motherland, and communism."* Speaker after speaker heaped opprobrium on Sakharov. "Who gave him the right to insult our children?" a middle-aged farm worker had declared indignantly.

Nikolai Trimov closed his eyes and formulated a sacred pledge. Something that had been gestating deep within him since he first absorbed the details of The Episode from the lips of a schoolboy ten years before, and fused them with what he had learned about the death of his grandparents.

Nikolai resolved to assassinate the leader of the Soviet enterprise. That meant, to kill the General Secretary, Mikhail Gorbachev.